Deadly Desire

Lance Figgins 3/14/21

LANCE FIGGINS

PAGE PUBLISHING, INC.
Conneaut Lake, PA

First originally published by Page Publishing 2020

ISBN 978-1-64628-481-8 (pbk)
ISBN 978-1-64628-483-2 (hc)
ISBN 978-1-64628-482-5 (digital)

Printed in the United States of America

Introduction

L ogan sat astride of his beautiful paint stallion on the top of the bluff that overlooked a river valley that ran through the northern part of his seventy-five-thousand acre ranch.

He could see someone or something moving through the trees on the far side of the valley. Nudging CJ (Count Joker) forward, he headed in that direction.

Patting CJ's neck, he said, "One more thing and then we can head for home." The paint stud nickered and nodded his head. Logan smiled and thought, *You know there are times I think you actually understand me.* CJ whinnied and nodded his head again as they came into a small mountain meadow. Logan laughed and said, "Now you can read my mind."

He reached down and slid the Winchester saddle gun from the scabbard, opening the action just enough to ensure it was loaded. Checking the hammer, he made sure it was in the safe position as he slid it back into the boot.

This was the wilds of Montana. His ranch was just north of the Wyoming border. Cattle rustling was something that still happened on a regular basis. It was also grizzly country. Logan did not want to get caught unprepared by either.

He rode in a northerly direction, trying to get ahead of whatever he thought he saw. The trail down the mountain was steep and narrow. He came out of the trees and could see several hundred of his cattle grazing on the rich grass in the valley along the river. A little over an hour later, he got into the general area and found one set of tracks moving deeper into the ranch.

It was getting toward dark; looking around Logan thought, *I don't want to have a battle on my hands. At least not after dark.* Turning CJ back toward the ranch house, he figured that he would come back the next day and follow the tracks.

Logan rode across the valley, looking at the beauty of his ranch. He started thinking about his parents and the ranch history.

Logan smiled as he thought about sitting on his great-grandpa's lap as a child listening as he told stories about the ranch's early days. About Indian attacks and rustlers. Outlaw gangs that hid from the law in their valley. Grizzly bears, mountain lions, and wolves that tried to feed on the beef they raised. About hunting trips into the high country. Snowstorms that held them captive in the valley for months at a time.

His parents where both gone, killed in a plane crash as they headed home from a business meeting. Being the only child at age fifteen, Logan had inherited the ranch.

With the help of some of his parents' friends plus the ranch foreman that stepped in and dedicated himself to Logan and the Rocking L, it grew to where it was today.

He was a fifth generation rancher. His fraternal great-grandparents had come west on a wagon train in the mid-1800s. The wagon train was headed across the Montana territory and had stopped in Billings.

Jim was at the livery stable and overheard a man talking about a valley to the south. Jim had talked with the man a few more times. When the wagon train left, Jim Lathrop, his wife, Kathey, and their two children did not follow. They had hired the man and turned south looking for the valley.

Their guide was a trapper and knew the country. The trail headed south was narrow and steep. From the trail high in the mountains, they had seen the valley. The trail had gotten so narrow and steep they had to abandon the wagon and pack their meager possessions out of the mountains and into the valley. So started the Rocking L.

The first time Logan heard that story, he told his great-grandpa that he wanted to find that wagon and figure out a way to get down to the ranch.

Over the years while hunting and just riding, he finally found it. It took him months to dismantle the wagon and pack it off the mountain. Then finally months later, with the help of his dad and grandpa, they finished restoring it. Now the wagon that carried his ancestors from Illinois to Montana sets on the turnaround in the middle of the ranch yard.

Over the generations the ranch grew and grew. To where it was when as a young man Logan started to put his mark on it.

At the age of eighteen, Logan had purchased two other ranches. The Rocking L had nearly doubled in size.

It was starting to cool off after a warm day for this part of Montana in combination with the elevation of the ranch. About halfway across the valley, he started turning up his collar when he saw someone running a horse across the far end on the valley. *At least they were headed out and looked to be alone,* he thought.

The paint stallion could have been chiseled from black and white marble. He had purchased the horse as a colt three years earlier from the lazy M. CJ had an explosive start. In six or seven strides he was running all out. With the natural strength of the quarter horse plus the build of the mountain mustang, he had gotten the best of both along with being very intelligent. As they headed for the ranch house, Logan could hear the wolves howling in the distance. CJ's ears moved continuously, picking up all the sounds of the evening.

There was only one trail out of the valley they were in, and it had a spot that Logan hated. It twisted around and passed between two rock walls that were narrow and confining. As they entered the narrow passage, Logan reached down, patted the Winchester. Just a reassuring touch.

Just as they came around the last corner, the snarl of a mountain lion shattered the silence. The large cat leaped from the rock wall; CJ, always aware of his surroundings, bolted. Logan, still not used to his explosive starts, slid out the saddle and hit the ground, only feet from the crouching lion.

As Logan scrambled trying to regain his feet, the large mountain lion leaped. Logan dove to the side, trying to get out of the way.

The two collided. Logan was knocked sideways; in the fall his head struck a rock and was knocked unconscious.

As he lay there, totally helpless, the cat slowly started walking toward him. CJ, sensing his friend's imminent danger, spun around and charged the huge cat. It was nature at its savage furry. Hunter and hunted survival of the strongest. CJ has the stallion survival instinct to always protect his herd.

The huge cat leaped at CJ and was met with deadly striking front hooves. CJ came down on the cat. One of CJ's front hooves scraped the cat's front shoulder, raking down its leg, it left a deep, bloody cut. The other scraped down the side of its head. Then spinning around, he kicked out with both rear legs. One connected solid with the cat's ribs, sending it running for safety.

CJ stood over his fallen friend, watching for any more danger that may come their way. After a few minutes, the stallion reached down and bit Logan's jacket collar and started dragging him toward the ranch house and safety.

As they came out of the timber, a couple of the ranch hands stood in amazement and could not believe what they were watching. Looking at each other, they started to run toward the stallion and their boss.

CJ stopped and spun to face them. Ears pinned, he stood to protect his fallen friend. The ranch hands stopped, just out of reach of his deadly front legs.

Speaking softly along with moving very slowly, they were finally able to get a hold of the bridle. Slowly they coaxed CJ away. Getting to Logan, they started helping him just as he started to come around. The two ranch hands told Logan what they had witnessed. They then helped him back on CJ, and together they all headed for the ranch house.

The Rancher's Life

CJ's dam was Queen Joker. A prize-winning quarter horse that belonged to Martha, the owner of the lazy M. The Joker line of cow horses were prized all over Montana. The lazy M was known for its cattle horses. They breed some of the finest cattle horses. The Joker bloodline was included in the best of the best. A cattle-smart horse is natural, they either know it or they don't. It's not something that can be taught.

Logan was there buying cattle, a new breeding stock for his Rocking L ranch. He saw the young colt and asked Martha if he was for sale. Martha said, "Absolutely I have no idea how she got pregnant. I've never had a paint stud on this place."

Logan was pretty sure that he knew what had happened. This was mustang country. There was a large herd of mustangs just on the other side of the mountains in northern Wyoming.

He had seen a beautiful paint stud in the herd and was sure that he was the colts' sire. Martha and Logan looked over the cattle he wanted plus several young bulls. They agreed on a price as they walked over to look at the horses. The young colt ran right up to Logan and stuck his nose under Logan's arm.

That was all it took. Logan bought the colt, and a friendship began that would become a lifelong partnership. They agreed on a price for the colt also. The shaking of hands sealed the deal. A handshake in Montana was the same as a signed contract back east. Logan told Martha that he would back the following week with a trailer and start bringing his stock home.

Martha said, "I'll keep the stock you want in this area so they won't get mixed up again." They talked a few more minutes as they walked toward Logan's pickup.

Logan headed for home. He had work to do. Running a ranch as large as the Rocking L was a full-time plus job. Machinery to fix, fences to mend and cows to watch. Not to mention trying to keep wolves, mountain lions, and bears out and away from his cattle. There was also still cattle rustling going on. A cow and calf could bring $3,000.00 at the sales barn to the east.

Logan got everything ready in the next couple of days. The following Monday morning, he headed to the lazy M to start moving the stock home. The last trip he also picked up the young colt. Getting back with the colt to the Rocking L, he put Count Joker or CJ in his new home.

The next morning CJ came and met Logan at the door. Logan looked at him and started laughing, saying, "You are an escape artist." Logan put him back, and an hour later, CJ was out and following him around. This happened several times over the next few days. Finally Logan just gave up, and CJ was allowed to have the run of the ranch.

The colt was quickly becoming a pain. He was inquisitive and into everything. Constantly getting into trouble. Logan said to one of the ranch hands, "You do this. It's time for that troublemaker to learn some manners. I think it's time to do a little training."

There are two ways to teach a horse. One, you break them. This way is faster but not always the best. Logan did not want to break CJ's spirit. So Logan chose to train CJ himself. Logan worked with CJ every day in the next few months. CJ learned quickly, and the training was going great.

Besides training him to be a riding and hopefully a cow horse, he was also teaching him tricks, like to sidestep, shake or nod his head to answer questions, open some gates, turn on and off the lights. CJ was highly intelligent and was quickly becoming everything that Logan thought and so very much more. With CJ's natural intelligence, the training was going faster than Logan thought. Watching CJ one afternoon, he thought that maybe, just maybe, this would be a good time to introduce CJ to a saddle. Just to get him used to the added weight.

As the ranch hands were working, CJ would walk in and tip something over just to cause someone to yell at him so he could prance off head and tail held high.

"Just showing off," someone would say. "The ranch pest," said another. Although every guy there would love to have him. He was fast becoming the pride of the Rocking L ranch. There were nights when Logan worked with CJ and people from town would come out just to watch.

One afternoon Logan started the saddling part of CJ's training. As Logan started to put the blanket on CJ, he would reach around, grab the blanket in his teeth, and drop it on the ground. When Logan went around to pick it up, CJ would nudge him with his nose, knocking Logan over. This went on for a couple of minutes until Logan started turning to face him as he picked up the blanket. Finally after a few minutes, he got CJ to leave the blanket on.

Next came the saddle. Same thing, Logan would put the saddle on CJ and he would either pull it off or walk forward just as Logan was lowering it down. As Logan worked at getting CJ to allow the saddle to stay in place, everyone on the ranch was watching.

One of the hands said, "Yo twist an ear."

Logan looked at him, saying, "Don't you ever touch this horse, he is totally off limits to everyone."

As the months passed, it wasn't long and Logan was riding CJ. Just over two months from when the training started. CJ was turning out to be even better than Logan had thought possible. As horses go CJ had all the intuition to be one of the best cow pony's Logan had ever seen. He could turn faster than any calf. Outrun the fastest steers. He was by far the fastest horse on the ranch and maybe in the valley, also the smartest.

This is cattle country with free or open range as well as deeded land. You had to prove ownership. Branding was a way of life, and all livestock had to be branded. The brand is a symbol that showed the name of the ranch. Logan's registered brand was a capital L with a half-moon slash under it. In the old west cowboys would say, "I ride for the brand." Which meant that they were loyal to the ranch.

It was spring, that meant branding time. A very busy time was fast approaching. Logan was looking forward to see just how cow smart CJ really was. They started locating and bringing in small herds of cows and calves. CJ figured out what his job was immediately. As a cow and calf bolted for the brush, CJ took after them so fast that Logan found himself sliding over the rear of the saddle, grabbing the saddle horn just before CJ ran right out from under him.

The round up continued; Logan kept looking at the timber line, trying to see if there was anyone watching them. He thought that he had seen movement a few times plus a reflection. His ranch borders were posted although a ranch as large as the Rocking L, it was totally possible that someone could have cross onto it by accident. If there was someone out there, he wanted to know who and why.

All of the hired hands were busy either rounding up and bringing in cows and calves or roping and branding. Logan was overseeing everything the best he could. CJ was absolutely loving his new job and more than once he nearly unseated Logan.

As cow horses go, CJ was amazing; he watched the herd while Logan watched what was going on and the woods. All of a sudden it happened—CJ bolted after a cow, and Logan was not ready and slid off over his rump. CJ immediately stopped and turned around, watching Logan getting up and using his hat to brush himself off. CJ slowly walked over and put his nose under Logan's arm as if to say, "I'm sorry you fell off."

A couple of the ranch hands saw this. They could see the bond between Logan and the "ranch pest" as most of the cowboys where calling him.

It was late in the afternoon, and Logan was sore. It was a long drop off CJ's rear end. Logan said, "Hey, guys, just pen up those unbranded cows and calves and call it a day. We can start again the morning."

As they all rode back toward the ranch headquarters, CJ could tell that his best friend was hurt. The horse walked along very slowly and very carefully, trying not to jar Logan.

Arriving at the ranch, one of the hands said, "Hey, boss, let me take care of CJ. You go on inside and relax."

Logan replied, "Yeah, thanks, Jesse," as he slowly walked to the ranch house. Walking through the door, he noticed that Nancy, the ranch cook and housekeeper, had just finished setting the table.

As she walked passed, she called out, "Get cleaned up, supper will be ready soon." Stopping she turned and asked, "What happened to you?"

Logan replied, "Nothing, I just have to learn to ride again." Chuckling and rubbing his lower back, he added, "CJ is more horse than I've ever had before." Slowly he climbed the stairs to the private part of the ranch. No one was allowed upstairs; this was the only part of the Rocking L that Logan actually called his.

After supper everybody was sitting around talking about the day's activities when Alex said, "I thought I saw someone or something moving in the woods." Looking around he asked Logan, "Is anyone on the ranch?"

Logan replied, "Yeah, I thought I saw something or someone also. In the morning maybe a couple of us should go have a look around." Then Logan excused himself, saying, "I'm going to check on CJ." Everyone could tell that the young stallion was fast becoming Logan's best friend.

The morning dawned cool and clear. Logan had saddled CJ and was riding out the ranch yard at first light. He was still a little stiff and sore. CJ sensed this as they headed out of the ranch yard at a very easygoing lope.

Logan was headed for the area where he thought he had seen someone the day before. He rode and climbed toward a bluff where he would have a great view of the area.

Montana or Bust

Rene sat and looked over the pictures she had taken on her last trip. She had captured the beauty of the canyon lands of Utah. As great as the pictures were, she knew only a few would be good enough to make a magazine.

As she sat there looking over her work, her cell phone lit up. Glancing at the caller ID showed a Montana area code. She almost let it go to voice mail but answered at the last second. "Hello," she said.

The caller replied, "Hi, I'm Tim Anderson. I'm the managing editor for *Montana Western Magazine*." Rene was about half in shock as she listened to what Tim had to say. He continued, "I've seen your work and would like to make you a job offer. You'll work exclusively for us." As she listened, she grabbed a notebook and started taking notes.

They had offered to pay all her expenses to move her to Montana where they had a house with most everything she would need. Plus the salary was nearly twice what she was making now. She couldn't believe what she was hearing. She sat quietly, listening and thinking. Finally Tim asked, "So do you have any questions?"

Rene looked at her notes and asked a few questions. Tim answered yes to all of them. Pausing for a minute, she then asked if she could think about it overnight and call him back in the morning.

Tim replied, "Absolutely, you have my number. I'll be waiting for your call."

Rene sat at the table looking at her notes. She couldn't believe that they had offered this kind of package to her. She knew her work was good. Although this good? This was like a dream come true. She knew she had to say yes. Although she was sure her parents would be upset.

So the first thing the following morning, she called her parents. As she talked about the job offer, her folks could hear the excitement in her voice.

Her parents said, "You have to do this. We don't want to see you move that far away although this is the chance of a lifetime."

Next she had to check with her apartment managers to see about getting out of the lease, explaining about the call from the night before. The manager said, "Thirty-day written notice and you are free to go."

Rene said, "Really? Wow thank you."

She handed him the notice she had already written the night before. Smiling, she turned and headed for her apartment. Sitting down at the table, Rene took a deep breath and called Tim. He answered on the second ring, saying, "*Montana Western Magazine*, this is Tim."

Rene replied, "Hi, Tim, this is Rene. I'm calling you back about the offer we talked about last night."

Tim said, "Yes, yes, although I have something new I have to tell you."

Rene closed her eyes and slowly let out her breath and replied, "Oh okay, what would that be?" Thinking that they filled the spot.

Tim said, "I was told this morning that we have a couple of horses there. Now, please, listen before you say no. You can ride all you want although you have to care for them. We will pay all the expenses although you have to do the work, and like I mentioned before, it's part of your salary."

Rene started smiling, saying, "Really, like you mean feed and water them?"

"Yes," Tim answered, adding, "just turn in all receipts. We pay all expenses, but like I said, the care for the horses is part of your salary."

They talked for a few more minutes. Rene said, "I'll take the job and see you later this month. It will take a few days here to get everything in order." Adding, "I should be headed your way in, say about two or maybe three weeks."

Tim replied, "Fantastic! We will see you in about a month. Keep me posted if anything comes up."

Rene answered, "Oh absolutely." Adding, "Thank you again, and I'll be seeing you soon."

Disconnecting, Rene yelled, "OMG! This is unbelievable."

She started jumping around doing fist pumps. *Twice the pay, a house, and horses. Everything I want or need. Can it get any better?* she thought.

She immediately called her parents, going over everything again, then she told them about the horses. Her mom and dad were nearly as excited as she was.

Her mom said, "This is truly a dream come true for you, isn't it?"

Rene replied, "Oh, Mom, absolutely. To finally make a living doing what I loved to do." Adding, "The pay is unbelievable plus a house and the horses. Wow."

The next morning Rene started calling and writing letters, getting everything ready to start her new job and her new life in Montana. The next week flew by, and she got her pictures sent in, plus turned in her notifications that she would be changing jobs. She put a forward on her mail, cancelled her newspaper, and started packing to leave. After a week of run, run, run, everything was done. She sat at the table going over her checklist. She had two checks next to everything on the list.

Then sitting there, she read it over again, making sure that once she left, there would be no surprises. Suddenly she thought about the one call she had been dreading. Picking up her phone, she found Kay's number and pushed call.

Kay answer on the first ring, saying, "No matter what they are, I want them. I've told you before, I don't want my competition getting a chance to see your work."

Rene replied, "Oh, wow thanks, but you already bought most everything I have."

Kay laughed and said, "Most?"

Rene answered, "Yes, most. There were a few shots not worth buying." Then taking a deep breath, Rene said, "Kay, I got a job offer. I'm moving to Montana."

Kay sat silent for a long minute. Finally she said, "*Montana Western Magazine?*"

Rene said, "Why, yes?" Adding, "How did you know?"

Kay replied, "Tim called me a few weeks ago and asked if I knew you and what I thought of your work. I told him that we were friends and you were the best I knew of. Although I thought he was looking to maybe buy something. I didn't expect him to give you a job offer."

Rene asked, "What do you think of him and the magazine?"

Kay replied, "Tim is a fantastic guy, and the magazine is one of the best in that class." Continuing she said, "I hate to see you leave, but you would be a fool not to take it."

Rene let out a breath that she didn't even realize she was holding. They kept talking about the job and what it would pertain to. Rene said, "I'll stop pass before I leave and say goodbye in person." Talking for a few more minutes, both were in tears as they disconnected.

Early the next morning, the manager knocked on her door. She handed him a cup of coffee as he walk in and started looking around. Turning, he looked at Rene and handed her the check for the damage deposit.

Rene said Thank you as they walked to the office together. Giving him a hug with tears in her eyes, she handed him the keys to her home for the last five years. Then looking at him again, she said, "Thank you again for everything you have done, I really enjoyed living here."

He reached to give her another hug and said, "It's been our pleasure. You have been a fantastic tenant. I wish everyone was like you. It would make my job a breeze."

Rene replied, "Thanks again for everything." She turned, walked out the door, and headed for her car.

Traveling Tears

Looking through the things she was bringing with, making sure that everything would stay where she had put it, Rene just sat there for a minute, thinking about everything. She hit the key, reached down, and slid the Grand Cherokee in gear, looking in the mirror; Rene headed west. Her first stop after leaving Chicago was her parents. The 340-mile drive to her parents' house flew by. In just a little over five hours, she was hugging her mom and being hugged by her dad.

Rene spent two days with her parents knowing that it might be a year or more before she would see them again. The last night that Rene was there, she took her mom and dad out for dinner. They talked about her new job, where she would be, and what it pertained to. Rene took out a map and showed her folks where she would be living.

Her dad said, "Wow, talk about a small town. You know this will be big change from what you are used to."

Rene replied, "Yes, I'm sure it will although I'm never home anyway. So I hope I can adjust quickly."

They talked about her living in Montana and the mountains. Rene told them about the horses and that she could ride all she wanted. They belonged to the magazine, but they were hers to take care of.

The next morning Rene sat and drank coffee with her folks. They talked again about Montana and her new life there. She was anxious to get going although she knew that she would miss them dearly. Finally she kissed and hugged her parents goodbye, and with tears in her eyes, she headed west to Montana and a life she had only have dreamed about.

She was still single, and her old job was too demanding to have any kind of a serious relationship. She spent just way too much time traveling and living in motels. Now she was going to be based out of this town in Montana and only traveling in Montana; maybe, just maybe, she could have a relationship with someone. As she drove she started thinking about what the future held; the possibility of a relationship enticed her.

She had past relationships that always ended because of her job. It seemed that guys just couldn't accept the idea that she had to be gone so much. As she drove west into the setting sun, she started dreaming of meeting a cowboy in Montana, a true cowboy. A fairy-tale-type romance of the old west where he came riding to her defense against a gang of outlaws.

Smiling she thought, *Wow, what a dream.*

Is anything like that even possible? Was that kind of the old west possible or was it gone forever? She knew that there were still cowboys in Montana, and the town looked to be close to the Wyoming border where there were even more. *Dreams,* she thought, *silly childhood dreams.*

As the miles flew by, Montana was getting closer and closer. She could feel her old life passing by and was getting excited to think about what lay ahead. She didn't know what the future held. All she knew was that she was going to make the most if it, making sure first that her work was the best it could be. That would make *Montana Western Magazine* very happy and insure her future. Everything after that would fall into place.

Late morning of the following day, she stopped in front of *Montana Western Magazine.* As she stepped out of her SUV, she looked up at the building. Wondered if she would have an office here also, where it would be, and how often she would have to be here.

A New Life

As she walked into the building, she saw the receptionist. Walking up to the desk, she told her who she was.

The receptionist said, "Hi." Adding, "I know all about you."

With that she called Tim. She was handed a badge and explained how it worked. Then she was told that Tim's office was on the twentieth floor.

She walked to the elevator and placed her badge on the call reader and stepped inside. Looking at the buttons, twentieth floor was all the way to the top. *Wow*, she thought, *this place doesn't mess around when decisions are made and carried through.*

When the elevator opened, Tim was standing there to meet her. They talked as they walked into his office, and he began to explain in more detail what they were looking for.

She started filling out all the paperwork for her new position and was looking through the written explanation of her job. In short it was to travel some, looking for the perfect picture to capture the old west to the new west that *Montana Western Magazine* was trying to keep the old west in junction with the changing times of the new west.

The main business in Montana was ranching and logging. The ranchers were the same for years, slow to accept changes. The tried and true ranching techniques is what they knew. A man and a horse could do the job. Why try to fix what's not broken? They were slow to accept the idea of the ATV or UTV although some places the

UTV was showing its strength. Although most still felt a cowboy on a good horse was still the best way.

As she read the articles in the job description, she knew this was going to be exciting. Working and talking to ranchers. Sharing and talking about old versus new ideas. Taking the pictures that captures the old west with a modern twist. The more she read and thought, the more excited she got. She wanted to start now, right that minute, the head-on collision between the old and the new west. This really was an opportunity of a lifetime.

After getting all the paperwork done, Tim said, "We have a few more things for tomorrow. I'll call and get you a room just down the street. Just sign the slip there." Adding, "It's on our account. There's a restaurant there also, have dinner on us. Bill it to your room, and we will see you in the morning."

As Rene got up to leave, she saw a picture of a beautiful paint stallion running across the prairie. She stopped and looked at the horse and could see the raw power and pride of the magnificent animal.

Turning she asked, "Tim, where was this taken."

Tim replied, "About five miles from where you are going to be living." Continuing he said, "I think it's a mustang that crossed the border from Wyoming although I'm not entirely sure."

Rene took out her phone and took a picture of the picture. This is what she wants and needs to do. This picture was that one in a million.

As she drove to her motel, she thought about the picture and what Tim had said about what her job was. To capture the old and new west side by side. Raw emotions as the cowboy does his job with everything he has today. How the UTV competes with the horse. Was modern technology still losing out to old tried and true ranching techniques.

Rene arrived at the motel after check-in and got settled in her room. She went down to the restaurant for supper. There were a number of men sitting around a large table. She took a booth not far away where she hopefully could hear their conversations and not look like she was eavesdropping.

One old rancher said, "You can't hear a calf bawling on that thing. They are just too damn loud." Continuing he said, "I've heard more calves than I've ever just happen to see. Calves are money that's why we do this. If we lose too many calves, we can't pay our bills. Then we are out of business, a horse is the only way to go." He said, "There are places where an ATV would do the job faster, but it takes a man and a horse to do this type of work."

As she sat there, one of the ranchers said something about the town she was to be living in. That got her attention really fast. They were talking about a ranch there and about the young man that owned it. As she listened they talked about different things that he was doing. Although mostly they talked about an amazing black-and-white paint stallion that he rode.

She opened her pictures and was looking at it as one of the ranchers said, "Someone took a picture of that horse as he ran across the pasture on the ranch. I saw it in *Montana Western Magazine*."

Slowly she ate, trying to catch every word about the Rocking L and the other ranches in the area. She knew that she could ask questions if she wanted to. Although she thought that she could probably learn more by just listening. They kept talking about different ranching jobs.

One rancher said, "I just bought a new UTV. There are times it comes in handy although it scares the cattle and they'd run from it."

Another man said, "A man on a good horse is still the best thing on a ranch." To this they all agreed. The guys slowly started getting up and leaving. Rene thought that she should leave also, not wanting to look like she was just there to eavesdrop on their conversation.

The next morning Rene was up, showered, dressed, and drinking coffee in the restaurant when a few of the ranchers walked in. They sat at the same table as the night before. Rene heard the conversation, it was pretty much the same. However, there was a new topic. The wolves were on the move out of Yellowstone and were moving into the valleys and on to ranches in the area. A calf was simply on the menu.

Okay, thought Rene, *something new, something exciting, a new problem for the ranchers. How would they deal with this and even better, more ideas for pictures.* She got up, paid for her coffee, and headed for the office, her new job. More important than that, this was the first day of the rest of her life.

Tim was already in his office as she walked out of the elevator. Seeing her he got up to meet her.

Rene smiled as she walked toward him, saying, "Good morning."

Tim replied, "Good morning to you also. How was your night? Was the motel room sufficient?"

Rene replied, "My night was great. I sat next to a group of ranchers and overheard their conversation about ATV versus a guy on a horse. Oh, and the room was fantastic."

Tim said, "That's great overhearing their conversation. That's journalism 101. What else did they talk about?"

Rene replied, "Wolves."

Tim stopped, and turning toward her, he said, "Wolves?"

Rene smiled as she replied, "Yes, wolves. It seems the wolves the government reintroduced into Yellowstone are on the move. They have already moved this far east and causing a problem."

Tim stared out the window for a minute then turning, he said, "I just knew hiring you would bring new life to this magazine." They continued to walk, and Tim asked, "Oh, hey, would you like see your new office?"

Rene smiled, saying, "Yes, that would be great." She thought, *Wow, my own office and on the twentieth floor. Wow!*

Opening the door, Tim said, "You probably won't be there very often. Although this is yours when you are."

Rene spent the morning finishing up all the rest of the paperwork. Then she started to set up her office. *Wow,* she thought, *my office and on the twentieth floor. I can't wait to call Mom and Dad.*

She hung a few pictures that she had packed in the jeep. She arranged her desk the way she wanted it. Stopping at Tim's door, she checked to make sure that everything was done.

Finally shortly afternoon she headed for her new home and the exciting career and life that lies ahead.

Beauty of the Wild

Rene had seen the mountains and their natural beauty. Although where she was now was unbelievable.

Driving south toward her new home was exciting, not to mention beautiful. She had to pull over several times as she wound her way through and over the mountains.

The pictures that she took of the valleys below and the snow-covered peaks above were some of the best work she had ever done.

As she looked she thought, *It would be hard not to take a beautiful picture.* She had to write an article about the area she was looking at and describing what she saw. It was simply breathtaking, and those words didn't come close to describing the beauty she saw.

She continued to take pictures as she slowly started down the south side of the pass. Every turn brought something new and if possible even more breathtaking than the last.

As she rounded a corner, a mother grizzly with two cubs walked across the road in front of her. The large female watched the car approach as the last cub crossed the road. Rene knew that she could not get out of the car. So she continued to snap away and took as many pictures as possible before they walked off into the timber.

She continued driving and enjoying the beauty of the area. Several more times she pulled over to take better and longer looks along with better pictures. *This country is absolutely, breathtakingly beautiful*, she thought. *And I now live here.*

Finally by early evening, she arrived at her new home. Rene stepped out of her jeep. Looking at the surrounding, she had tears running down her cheeks. "This is a dream come true," she said out loud. Taking a deep breath, she started bringing in everything that she had with her into her new home. The home was furnished, so she made a list of things that she would need to get over the next couple of weeks.

She heard her phone ring as she walked in with the last of her belongings. Checking her voice mail, it was Tim. The voice message said, "Rene, this is Tim. The mattress and box spring are new, also there are sheets and blankets in the closet." Continuing, "Now, please, if you needed anything, just call."

She looked at the computer and found it had everything she needed to send in the pictures she had already taken. Sitting down, she located the USB cables and started the transfer. *Hopefully*, she thought, *Tim will be excited about the fact that I had already started working on my way to my new home.*

Then taking one picture of the snowcapped peaks, she sent it to Kay along with a quick little note telling her that she was in Montana and would call in a few days, that everything was even better than what she had been told.

First Sighting

After getting about half moved in, she decided to take a walk and just look around before it was too dark. The people in town were very nice. All the ladies said hi and all the men said ma'am, a few even tipped their hats. She smiled as she continued to walk around thinking, *So this is the old west? Or new west? It would have been fun to live during that time.*

As she walked around the corner, she ran into a guy coming the other direction. She was knocked off balance and landed hard on the street. She put down her hand to start getting up and put it directly on something wet and soft.

"Yuck," she said as she wiped her hands on her jeans. She looked up at the clumsy idiot that knocked her over.

He extended his hand to help her up, saying, "You really should watch where you are going."

Rene's temper flared, saying, "If you were paying attention, maybe I would not be sitting in this, this whatever it is." Continued, "Maybe from now on, maybe you should have a warning sign that says 'I don't watch for others.'" Wiping her hands on his coat, she stomped off.

Rene got home and started cleaning off her hands and trying to get the mud and yuck off her jeans. *What a mess, what an ass*, she thought, stripping down, putting her clothes into the washing machine. Then she headed for the bathroom. A nice, long, hot bath would help soak some of her anger off. As she walked out of the bathroom, she could hear people outside.

Quickly she grabbed her robe as she walked toward the door. Two guys were walking toward her, and they were leading two horses. *I wonder if those are the horses Tim told me about*, she thought as they approach.

One of the guys said, "Tim called and said you were here and we could bring these two back."

As they came into the light, she saw that one was the idiot that had knocked her over.

He looked at her and said, "Oh, it's you." He tied the horse to the porch pole and told the other guy to do the same. Rene stood there as they turned and walked away into the darkness.

Rene stared into the dark Montana night. Swearing under her breath, she went inside to put a few more clothes on. Untying the horses, she led them around back and put them into the pasture. She double-checked the gate. The wolves were howling in the distance. She walked rather quickly back into the house.

Turning on the television and sitting down to relax, she thought about the first day here. Lots of really nice people and one jerk. *Oh well*, she thought, *can't judge the entire town by one idiot.*

The morning broke cool and clear. Rene thought that it would be a good time to check out the area. As she walked to the pasture, one of the horses came walking up.

Taking her by the halter, she led her to the tack room. She threw a blanket and saddle on her then slipped on the bridle.

Looking at the surrounding mountains, she was off for a morning ride. Crossing the road, she took a dirt trail that lead to the west. The country was beautiful, and as she rode, she started seeing cattle. She kept going and rode most of the day, checking out as much as she could.

Late in the afternoon she found herself a little turned around getting into an area she wasn't sure of. Remembering that most horses knew their way home, she finally let the horse have its head. Giving her a little kick, they broke out of the woods and headed back in an eastern direction.

Getting home, she unsaddled Star, gave her a quick brushing, and let her back into the pasture. Rene realized that she was hungry, so she walked to the local diner to eat. A few minutes later Logan and a couple other cowboys walked in. They sat at a table not far from Rene. Logan glanced at her then turned and sat down. It took her a bit to realize who he was.

Most of the other guys called him either Logan or boss. She sat there trying to enjoy her dinner and listened to what they were all talking about. It seemed that Logan may have had a run in with a mountain lion. One guy said, "You know it looks like CJ scared it or maybe chased the cat off."

Rene sat there trying to listen yet not be noticed. She heard the name of the ranch and where it was. She thought, *It sounds like where I was today. It could be a great place to take pictures. Especially if I could do it without anyone knowing. That would be true cowboy-type pictures.* Sitting there, she kept listening. *Raw and wild,* she thought. *A true western experience.* The waitress refilled her coffee, and she opened her phone, pretending that she was reading. All the while she kept listening. The spring round up had started, and it was branding time. *Okay,* she thought, *now how can I get on there again without being seen or caught?* Looking at Logan she thought, *He is one big guy! And I'm sure he would be some kind of mad.*

The next morning she packed everything she thought she could or would possibly need. Saddling Star, she headed south before turning west. Taking pretty much the same trail she came out on the evening before. Making sure no one was following or around her, she headed into the timber. Following a game trail, she got above the valley.

The location that she picked was perfect, she could see that was going on. The roping and branding along with the cowboys bringing in more stock.

As she watched, she realized that it was highly organized. Everyone knew exactly what they were doing. The cattle being rounded up were put into one area. The branded calves ran bawling to their mothers and were turned loose. As she walked from tree to tree taking pictures, she noticed Logan looking her way. She froze, staying completely still, and watched. In a few minutes he continued his work. She stood there watching Logan, his horse seemed to be watching the cows while he watched everything else. All of a sudden, a cow made a break for the brush and freedom. His horse reacted so quick that Logan nearly slid off the horse's rump. *Wow*, she thought, *what an amazing animal.*

She kept watching and taking pictures when she noticed Logan riding off to the north. She continued to watch him as he turned toward the timber. Quickly packing her camera and other belongings, she mounted Star and headed south, staying in the timber to the far south end of the valley where she had to ride across and enter the timber on the other side. Once in the timber, there was a trail that she had used a few days earlier. It was a game trail that took her through a small cut in the mountains and came out just south of town.

She road through town. Looking around, she noticed that no one even gave a horse a second glance. It was like an everyday event. Getting home, Rene unsaddled Star, brushed her, then gave both horses some grain and went inside. Looking over her pictures, she decided to send them all in.

Feeling a little hungry, she shut down the computer and walked up town. As she ate dinner, she started writing an article about what she had seen that day. Tried and true ranching techniques.

While she sat there writing, Logan and a few others walked in. They sat just a few tables away. A couple of the guys looked at her. One even tipped his hat. Logan never even glanced her way.

Logan and the guys sat at the table talking about what was left to do. One of the guys asked, "Hey, boss, what were you looking at in the timber all day?"

Logan just sat there thinking, he answered, "I'm not entirely sure. Although I thought I saw movement and a reflection once up in the timber."

Another one guy said, "Yeah, me too." Although I'm not sure what could reflect in that area. I've ridden through there several times."

Logan added, "I rode through there today. There was fresh tracks of just one horse. It looks like someone was watching us." He asked, "Have any of you heard anyone say anything about missing any livestock?" Everyone looked at each other, either shaking their heads or saying no.

Rene sat there watching out the corner of her eye and listening.

Why did it bother her? He wasn't anything special. Tall, well built, dark blond hair. Worn just a little too long for her taste. Although it fit him, gave him that bad boy look. She knew that she was attractive by anyone's standards. She was tall, thin, had a great body, athletic with shoulder-length, brown hair. Why did it bother her? How did he get under her skin? Standing up, she walked past their table. As she passed, she could see her reflection in the mirror.

"Wow," Logan watched her walk away. Smiling, she put just a little more wiggle in her walk, payed her bill, and headed home.

*****

The Montana morning broke cool and clear. Logan and the rest of the cowboys headed back to finish the branding. They still had several hundred to do. Logan had over ten thousand head of cattle plus around seven thousand heads of yearlings that would be rounded up and shipped yet that spring or early summer. While rounding up the cows with calves, they would also cull out the yearlings and put them in a different area so they could have access to them come the time to ship them.

Rene looked at her camera; should she go get more pictures today or work here getting everything ready to send in? What if Logan saw her pictures? Would he be mad? *Have I invaded his life and privacy?* she thought. *Maybe I should go ask. Maybe I should ride out there and try to get permission. Tell him I would like to do an article on him and his ranch. Ranching techniques, old versus new. Where the old west collides with the new west.*

She had a degree in journalism although her true love and passion was photography. She called Tim, explaining what she wanted to do and asked if anyone had ever done anything like this. Tim said, "Oh my god, what a fantastic idea. Although I think you had better talk to him and get his permission."

As they discussed the idea a little more, he agreed that it would be an article that would last throughout the summer. Tim loved it, saying, "Go for it, you've got this run with it."

Sitting there, she thought, *Car or horse?* She got up and headed for the pasture. Saddling Star, she headed for Logan's Rocking L ranch. Hoping beyond hope that he would allow it. As she rode to where the work was being done, she spotted the beautiful paint horse and Logan. Smiling, she rode up to him. Logan looked at her and had a slight smile when she stopped.

She stuck out her hand and said, "Hi, I'm Rene, I work for *Montana Western Magazine.* I would like to do an article on you and your ranch. It's going to be ranching techniques, old versus new."

Logan smiled and said, "I was wondering when you would stop sneaking around and ask me." Continuing he added, "It's fine, but, please, stay out of the way. Take your pictures from a distance. This can be dangerous work. I don't want you or any of my guys getting hurt. Also, if I say move, it's move now and keep moving until you're safe. These cattle are domesticated but just barely. They're range cattle. They would rather stomp on you than run."

Rene agreed and moved out of the way. She continued to take pictures all day as the cowboys worked either roped branded or cut out yearlings. The work looked hard and dangerous.

She watched as a couple of the guys started to separate out the bulls. Some of the bulls were absolutely huge. Logan rode over and said, "Stay away from these bulls. They weighed close to three thousand pounds, and they are always grouchy."

You could tell that they were not used to people and did not want to go where the guys wanted. Several times they would spin and charge toward horses. The horsemanship of these men was absolutely fantastic. They could outmaneuver a mad bull or steer. With ropes and yelling, they got everything to go where they needed to be.

Late in the afternoon, Logan called it a day; everyone was free to do what they wanted. One of the cowboys named Jesse asked if Rene needed anything. She replied, "Nope, all handled." She threw the saddle back on Star.

Logan rode up and said, "We are done for the day and headed to the ranch then into town." Then he asked, "Would you like to join us?"

Rene readily agreed and said, "I'll see you about six at the Clumsy Steer." With that she turned Star toward town and galloped away.

Arriving home, she took care of the horses, grabbed a quick shower, put on new jeans and a nice top that brought out the woman in her. She looked over her shoulder at the mirror as she walked out the door and headed for the restaurant.

Logan and the guys were already there. She took the empty seat next to Jesse, and they all sat there talking about the day's work, about what was left for tomorrow and the rest of the week.

Logan said, "We are short several thousand head. I think there's more cows and calves plus yearlings in that west valley. Tomorrow, I'll take a couple of you and go see. We'll be gone a couple of days. While we are gone, the rest of you continue branding and looking for whatever we missed and go over this side of the mountains again. It looks like we are several thousand head short, and we need to find them."

Then he looked at Rene, saying, "Would you like to ride with us tomorrow? We will be gone a few days and be sleeping out under the stars. There's another valley west of where we are now. I'm thinking there could be a sizeable herd over there." Looking out the window, he continued, "We need to find as many as we can. I need to ship all I can this year. Last year the price was down. So I shipped short, keeping the majority over the winter."

Rene asked, "Wasn't that dangerous to do?"

Logan replied, "Absolutely, winter snow disease or a forest fire could have finished me." Continuing, he said, "I shipped just enough to make ends meet. Hoping for a gentle winter and a better price this year. So far this year I've heard the market is up. A few of the ranches have gotten top dollar for their beef. I've talked to a few of the buyers. They are really dealing this year. I already have a contract although I can overship at the same price. So I'm prepared to ship all I can, and the price is really good."

As they ate, they made the plans for the following morning. It started getting late, so Rene excused herself and said, "I'll see you all in the morning, six thirty, right?"

Logan looked at her smiling and said, "Where we are going is a long ride. Let's make it six."

Rene smiled and said, "Okay, sounds good see you at six." With that she got up; turning, she said good night to everyone, caught Logan's eye, smiled, and headed for home.

As she walked home, she thought, *Wow, 6:00 a.m. at the ranch. I'll be getting up about four. Oh wow, that is just way too early.* She got everything ready for morning and crawled into bed. The 4:00 a.m. alarm was a shock. Rene threw a pillow at the clock as she slowly started crawling out of bed. As she was getting ready and trying to gulp down some coffee, she heard a truck pull up outside. She opened the door to find Logan standing there.

He said, "Good morning. I'm going to haul your horse to the ranch. Saves time, and we are going in another way. It'll be a shorter ride. The trail is steep, very narrow, and dangerous. Although it's a lot faster."

Walking toward the barn, Logan started explaining where they were going and what the trail in would be like. Rene put a lead rope on Star and led her to the trailer, tying her in place. Logan grabbed the saddle while Rene got the rest of what she would need. After everything was loaded, Rene walked around the rear of the trailer and tripped over the ramp in the dark. She cried out as she fell, cutting her leg open. Logan ran back to where she was laying. Helping her up, he then picked her up and carried her to the open door of the pickup. He carefully slid up her pant leg and looked at the cut to see if medical attention was needed. Rene felt the strength in his hands as he slid his hand up her calve.

Logan grabbed the first aid kit and slowly and carefully cleaned the cut, putting on some triple antibiotic cream and wrapped it with gauze and a stretch wrap. Rene could feel the strength yet tenderness of his touch. Even though she was hurting, it was affecting her in a way she that didn't want to feel.

Logan looked up at her, saying, "You won't need stitches, but this might be tender for a day or so." Adding, "Do you still want to go?"

Rene answered, "You're not getting rid of me that easily." Continuing, she added, "I would not miss this for anything."

Logan smiled kissed her knee and said, "Good, I'll close things up. The guys are meeting us there in an hour, so let's get going."

Rene and Logan walked back into the house, grabbing a thermos of coffee and a large cooler. Rene had made lunch for everyone. The coffee though was for her and Logan on the drive there. Everything was packed, her leg hurt like the dickens although they were ready to go. Rene was pouring the coffee as they left town.

Logan explained that the valley they were headed to was part of his ranch though it was hard to reach. The trail over and between the mountains was narrow and steep. The road went around the mountains and was not a whole lot better although it was wider. At 6:00 a.m., it was getting light out. The country was beautiful. Rene started taking a few pictures as Logan drove the narrow, twisting road.

She could see the snowcapped mountains that reached over twelve thousand feet. She looked at Logan and asked, "Have you ever been up there?" She pointed to the tops where she could see the snow.

Logan laughed, saying, "Yes, I've hunted that area a couple of times. It's really rough country. Although there are some huge elk up there plus big horn sheep and mountain goats. You had to camp up there to hunt the area that it takes way too long to go in and back out in one day." Continuing, he said, "That is beautiful yet wild and rough terrain. It's also home to the grizzly, wolves, mountain lions, and wolverines." Adding, he said, "People are not on their usual food source, but they will attack humans. A few weeks ago, I had a run in with a mountain lion. I'm sure if it wasn't for CJ, I wouldn't be here."

Rene asked, "Who is CJ?"

Just as Logan was pulling over to stop, they got out and walked around the truck. Logan opened a side door, and CJ stuck out his head. Logan said, "Rene, this is CJ, CJ, this is Rene." CJ shook his head up and down and whinnied.

Rene started laughing and asked, "Did he just say hi?"

Logan replied, "Yes, I believe he did."

Rene asked, "What does CJ stand for?"

Logan replied, "Count Joker." Adding, "He comes from the Joker bloodline of cow horses on his mother's side. I believe his father is a mustang from a herd just south of here in Wyoming."

They closed the door and walked back to the truck and started out again. About an hour later, they were there. The rest of the guys were still getting things ready to go and checking over the large holding pen. It was decided the night before that if the pen was in good shape, they would bring any cattle they found there out this way. Then either haul or use the horses to drive them down the road rather than try to go over the mountains to the main area of the ranch. This way would take longer though it was far less dangerous. That trail over the mountains was just too treacherous.

Everything was packed, checked, and rechecked. It was time to go. Logan asked, "Are we ready?" He nudged CJ and headed into the mountains.

It was going be a long day. They would spend many hours on steep, narrow mountain trail, but the horses were mountain born and bred. They were used to being in the mountains and were sure footed and calm even in the most dangerous of areas. Rene was riding directly behind Logan; she knotted her reins, dropped them on Star's neck. She let Star follow CJ as she started taking pictures.

Logan looked over his shoulder and noticed that every time the trail got dangerous, he would tell her when to pay attention. There were a few spots where it was straight up and down with the trail, only being a few feet wide. In those areas, they would get off and lead the horses. Just in case one or more would get nervous and start acting up. It's easier to control from the ground and less chance of the rider going over the edge with a scared horse.

As they rounded the last corner, the valley came into sight. Rene gasped at the sight. It is absolutely beautiful. From the elevation, she could see a valley, lush and green with several hundred grazing cattle. Logan scanned the valley, looking at a spot on the far end.

He pointed and asked, "Hey, does anyone have a pair of binoculars?"

Rene said, "Here use this, there is a zoom on my camera."

Logan looked through the camera, focusing slightly. He said, "I think we have trouble. Looks like a large herd of buffalo down there at the south end. Right where that other trail goes out and twists around to the river and our penning area." He added, "I think maybe we can round up the cattle and get them to this end. Then a few of us stay with the cattle, holding them here. While the rest can try and chase the buffalo to the south east and out of that trailhead area. We don't need a cantankerous old buffalo bull causing trouble."

A few of the guys ground hitched the pack horses unloaded the packs. As they prepared to get started.

The cattle were restless and spooked easy. These were range cattle domesticated, yes, but barely. They would rather run or stomp on you that go where you wanted them to. It took several hours to get them rounded up. Determination and hard work finally started to win out, and finally after several hours, the cattle were all together in the northern end of the valley.

It was late, so a camp was made, and everyone started to settle down. There was a river running just out of sight of the camp, and Rene wanted to clean up a little. Grabbing some clean clothes, she told Logan that she was going to take a swim.

Logan said, "Be back here before dark."

Rene answered, "Absolutely." She walked toward the river.

The evening was beautiful, a slight breeze to just stir the leaves. After a cool swim, Rene dried off, got dressed, and walked into camp before dark.

One of the cowboys called out, "Hey, Logan, she's back."

Rene looked over and smiled as she thought, *Aww, he's worried about me.*

They sat around the campfire talking and telling stories of long-ago trips into the mountains chasing cattle or hunting. As Rene listened, she couldn't believe some of the things these backwoods country cowboys had done. Their life was hard. Just like the work they did. As she listened, she thought, *Is this really 2018, or are these guys right out of the late 1870s, the day of Sitting Bull, Crazy Horse, and General Custer?*

The stories of working in and on these wild country ranches along with hunting trips into the high country was fascinating to say the least. She listened about early fall or late spring snowstorms, being caught outdoors, and how they survived gave her a deeper understanding and affection for these men and the life they lived, their knowledge of the outdoors, and the cattle they took care of. How they tried to anticipate what these cows would try next. What was that three-thousand-pound bull thinking. Was he in a fight or flight mood. The knowledge they gain through hours in the saddle was the same now as 150 years ago. Old versus new. New versus old. One in the same, a man on a horse is what these mountain ranches needed and survived on while the ATV and UTV had a job here. When it came to the cattle, man and horse would win out every time.

Rene was getting tired, it was a long day. They would be sleeping under the stars tonight. There were a few tents, and she asked Logan, "Where should I put my sleeping bag?"

Logan said, "You can use that tent. I'll be right here if you need anything." Adding, "If anything goes wrong or if you get scared, wake me up."

With that Rene said, "Good night." Turning, she crawled into her tent, and in a few minutes she was sound asleep.

Morning was cool and clear. Rene woke to the smell of coffee as she crawled out of the tent. A couple of the guys had already left to make sure that the cattle were still in the north end pen.

As they rode back into camp, they said, "Hey, boss. Everything is looking great. The cattle have settled down, and the buffalo are still at the south end of the valley."

Logan replied, "They have to be chased to the south east corner today so we can drive these to that trail to get out of here. There's no way we can take this many over the mountain trail. We will lose way too many." They started making a plan to move the buffalo. Logan called to Rene, saying, "I want you to stay back and use your zoom lens to take pictures of this." Continuing, he added, "These buffalo are dangerous even to us on the horses. They are not scared of people and would more than likely charge and fight rather than run."

They started for the south end of the valley. Rene asked, "Can I cross the valley and take pictures from the top of a small hill by the small group of trees?"

Logan looked across the valley and said, "That's a great idea. I'm sure you'll be safe there."

Rene broke away from the group and headed to the other side of the valley. Logan and the rest watched her go and then headed back toward the herd of grazing buffalo. A cow saw them coming and started to trot away. The rest of the herd followed her. As the guys started to try to get around to the other side of the buffalo, they spooked and started running. Everything went wrong at once.

The leader swung to the north. Rene saw them coming her way. She grabbed Star, trying to get out of the way. Logan saw Star reared up and broke free. Rene started running for the trees although Logan knew that the small trees would not protect Rene from the charging mass of horns and hooves.

Logan swung CJ around and headed for Rene at a dead run. CJ was stretched out and running with all he had. Soon he was even with the charging stampeding leaders. All Logan could think of was hundreds of sharp hooves and horns. As the stampede kept heading for Rene, CJ seemed to sense what Logan wanted. Logan could feel him gather the reserves of strength and gain a little more speed. The huge heart and lungs of the quarter horse and the stamina of the mountain mustang combined with the love CJ had for Logan.

They were cutting across the front of the herd. Logan knew that he had to reach her. If he failed, it was all over. If CJ tripped, all three would certainly die. A painful scary ending for Rene, Logan, and CJ. They raced across the valley; all Logan knew was he had to get to Rene.

Logan was headed straight for Rene. He dropped the knotted reins and looked over his shoulder, he was only yards ahead of the charging mass; he knew it was a one-time shot at picking her up. If he missed, the buffalo wouldn't.

Rene was running for all she could. Logan reached down, with one arm he grabbed the collar of her coat. With the other arm, he reached around Rene, pulling her up and forward at the same time. He also gave CJ total freedom to go where he wanted just to get away from the stampeding mass of horns and hooves.

CJ had slowed slightly as they reached Rene. Gathering his strength again, he raced at an angle away from the buffalo and didn't start to slow down until they were in the timber and out of the path of raging mass.

Rene was crying and nearly hysterical, scared beyond all limits. All she could do was cry and hold onto Logan as he held onto her, gently rocking side to side and telling her she was safe now and everything was over, that he had her and nothing would ever hurt her. As he whispered to her, he also kissed her hair and her forehead. He then kissed her eyes, trying to calm her down.

They slowly leaned away from each other, and with no warning, they came together in a kiss that made both of them weak in the knees. A kiss that ended minutes later, leaving them both wondering what had caused it. A few seconds later, Logan kissed her again.

As she broke away, she also walked away, leaving Logan standing by himself. He stood there and watched as she walked to a large tree several yards away. She leaned against the tree, closed her eyes, and thought, *What had just happened?* Had they just gotten off to a bad start? He had just risked his life to save her. She turned and saw him still standing in the same spot. She looked into his eyes and saw something that surprised her. There was a tear running down his face.

Was he scared or hurt or what? Had he just fallen for her? This huge cowboy and a city girl. Can she live this life? A ranch life with cattle and calves working outdoors all day long? Looking again at Logan, she smiled and ran into his open arms. *Wow,* she thought, *have we just fallen in love? Can it happen this fast? Is this love? I think, no, I know I love him.*

She reached up and kissed him again and again. Logan picked her up and carried her back to where CJ was grazing. He removed his saddlebags, untied his bedroll, and then took off CJ's saddle and turned him loose. Taking Rene by the hand, they walked up a small hill and lay down in the shade of a large tree. The grass was soft and cool to the touch. Logan reached for Rene, kissing her again; he slowly laid her down on the bedroll that he had unrolled in the shade.

Rene felt the gentleness of his touch as he slowly removed her shirt and undid her jeans. His kisses were warm and gentle, his hands moved slowly as he carefully slid away the rest of her clothing. Rene undid his shirt and unsnapped his jeans. They slowly slid away as she kissed and felt her way up his back.

She felt the movement, then it was all about the movement. She felt everything, yet nothing else mattered; all she wanted was Logan right then and now. As they lay together, Logan kissed her lips and neck. Rene again felt the softness of his touch as he continued to make love to her. Rene could not get enough of him. She wanted to stay right there forever. Just keep her on the hilltop in the shade of that tree and love her. She knew she would love this man for the rest of her life. She also knew that he would protect her at all cost. That he was hers and she was his. The world could end tomorrow as long as they had tonight, nothing else mattered.

They lay together in the shade of the huge tree in the middle of a mountain valley. Logan stroked her hair, and Rene rubbed his chest.

Slowly Rene looked into his eyes and said, "You know we have met once before."

Logan looked at her and said, "Really? Wow. When?"

Rene replied, "Kay and Joe's wedding. Remember that beautiful little country church in Illinois?"

Logan asked, "How do you know Joe?"

Rene laughed and said, "I don't, but I do know Kay. I did a lot of work for her. She needed some pictures of a certain area, and I was only a couple hundred miles away."

Logan lay there thinking and said, "Remember when you asked if I had ever been up in those mountains?"

Rene looked up and said, "Oh yes, those ones on the way in."

Logan said, "Yes. I was in town, and a guy asked if he could hunt my ranch. At first I said no, but after taking a second look at him, I could tell he wasn't your normal idiot from back east. We talked for a couple of minutes, and I told him he could. The following morning he was at the ranch and started getting ready to head for the high country. I stood there watching him and could see the kind of man he was." Continuing, Logan said, "We talked a few more minutes, and I asked if I could tag along. Joe looked at me and said, 'Sure I hope you can keep up.'" Logan continued, "'Walk? Oh no, I have horses. Let's repack, and we will be out of here in a couple hours.'"

Rene asked, "What's he like in the woods and while hunting?"

Logan lay there for a minute then slowly started, "He's a cross between a mountain goat and cougar. He can walk all day and is an excellent shot. That trip started a friendship that will last a lifetime."

Rene, snuggling a little closer, said, "Kay is the best friend I've ever had, and of all the people I left behind, she's the one I miss the most. Every time I got back from a photo shoot, I would send all my pictures to her first. She almost always bought something and usually several. She would look for my best and purchase all of them. There were a few times I don't think she needed them although she didn't want the other magazines to get them."

Logan got up and grabbed his saddlebags. He had a small survival kit. Rene walked around and started collecting wood to get a fire started and keep it burning all night. Logan got the fire started, and Rene started making them something to eat out of what they had packed in their saddlebags. Logan kept collecting wood, and soon there was enough.

They were still both nearly naked when they heard horses approaching. They both grabbed for their clothes and were nearly dressed when two of the guys rode in. They had found Star in the northern end of the valley. Fearing the worse, they started looking.

"Seeing smoke from a fire, we hoped it would be both of you," Jessie said.

Rene added more food, and they all sat and enjoyed an evening together. After they ate, Logan said, "You two go back to the cattle and get a camp set up. We are going to stay here tonight and will be over in the morning. Then we can start driving the cattle out the south trail and to the holding pens."

As the guys rode away, Logan heard them say, "I think Logan just got branded."

They both started laughing as the other said, "Yep, and I think it's time someone put a brand on him."

Rene stood there smiling as Logan turned around, asking, "What are you smiling about?"

Rene said, "So I've branded you?" Giggling, she asked, "What would a Rocking R L look like?"

Laughing, Logan said, "I think we've kind of branded each other."

Rene smiled, wrapping her arms around Logan and said, "I love you."

Logan answered her with a kiss, adding, "I love you too." Continuing, "How did this happen?"

Rene replied, "Blame the damn buffalo."

Logan said, "I guess so. That's what caused it to start, after that nature took over."

As the sun started to rise in the east, Logan was up. He whistled for CJ and walk over and lead Star back to camp. He had both horses saddled and ready to go while Rene made some coffee. They sat quietly and enjoyed a cup watching the shadows race across the valley. Rene poured the last of the coffee on the fire, making sure it was out while Logan packed the sleeping rolls and saddlebags. Rene walked over to him, reached down, and took his hand. As they stood there, she reached up and kissed him. Logan pulled her close and held her tight as they stood there.

Rene looked up into his eyes and asked, "What happened yesterday and last night? I don't want to brand you. I want you absolutely and forever but to never own you. You are a free spirit. No one could ever take that away. You are part of this beautiful yet untamed land. Let me into your life. Open up, show me the true you. I'll love you forever although I won't ever try to change you."

Logan pulled her close, kissed her tenderly. As he backed away, Rene pulled in hard and kissed him with enough passion to cause them to stay there for a few more hours. Logan started walking her back into the shade of the tree.

Rene stopped and said, "Oh no, you don't, we have work to do." She stepped around Logan and climbed on to Star. Logan stood there, looking at Rene.

As she spun Star around, Logan said, "We can continue this tonight."

Rene laughed and said, "Only if you beat me to the herd."

Logan whistled for CJ as Rene spurred Star into a run. CJ came at a run, sensing the urgency of Logan's second whistle. As CJ slowed, Logan grabbed the saddle horn, and CJ exploded into a run, trying to catch Rene and Star as they raced across the valley.

Rene had a good lead although CJ was without a doubt the faster of the two horses. He was gaining on Star with every stride. Soon Rene could hear CJ coming up on her. She leaned forward, and Star responded with a little more speed. As they topped a small rise, she could see the cattle. Would she, could she actually win? Was her head start enough to outrun Logan and CJ? She could hear them gaining, his footfalls were getting louder and louder. Just as she thought she had won, she felt Logan's hand touching her shoulder.

She turned to look as CJ slowed down and settled in beside her and Star. Logan was setting up right in the saddle in easygoing position.

She couldn't believe what she saw. Logan and CJ looked like they were just out for a morning ride. As they slowed, Star was breathing hard, and CJ, that damn pest, was barely winded. He was a magnificent animal. Just like Logan, he was part of this hard, wild country and truly belonged here.

Logan called out to the guys, asking, "Hey, are we ready to get started?"

They still had a couple of days before they would get all these cows back to the main part of the ranch. Over some rough country, these mountains were steep and dangerous. If they lost a cow or two, it was too bad. Logan just wanted to get everyone out of there safely. He knew the trail although it was safer than the northern trail, it was still rough country where one misstep was the making for a disaster.

Everything was packed and ready to go. Logan rode around to the end of the herd and got them to start moving. It would be ten or twelve hours before they would be stopping for the night. He knew of a small valley a little over half way. If they could make it there, that valley had plenty of grass to keep the cows happy plus a small river for water. The horses and cattle could get everything they needed. Plus there would be plenty of clean water for cooking and washing the trail dust off. He also knew of a pool and a small waterfall where it came down from the highlands. He told the guys to try and keep the cattle away from that area. It would also make a good camping area.

The day was cool and made for good traveling, everything was going great. One of the guys pointed toward the timber. There was a huge grizzly walking at an angle toward the herd. Logan knew that bear could be trouble. He looked for Rene, she was between the bear and the herd. He spurred CJ into a run and started yelling and pointing. Rene saw him coming fast. She turned to see what he was pointing at. The huge bear was still headed her direction. She spurred Star and rode toward Logan. As soon as she was clear, he turned and headed toward the bear. CJ didn't like being that close although he knew that it needed to be chased off.

As they raced toward the huge bruin, Logan could see a few more guys riding toward the bear. They started spreading out, making a half moon barrier between the bear and the herd of cattle. Finally huge, old grizzly turned and ran for the timber. As the bear half walked half galloped away, they slowed and gathered together to watch as it disappeared into the mountains.

Rene had ridden up and stopped next to Logan. He looked over at her and said, "That was one really big bear. I hope it keeps moving that way. We are going the other direction." They all laughed as Logan slid the Winchester back into the saddle boot. All the guys had Winchester saddle guns in .375 caliber or larger. Lots of power but only short range.

Looking at the guys, he said, "I'm really happy that he didn't want to fight. I would really hate to kill it. It is such a beautiful bear." They turned and headed back toward the herd and got them moving again. Rene rode along, taking pictures of the country and the cowboys doing what they do. She heard a horse coming up behind her. It was Logan riding in an easy gallop. As he closed the distance, CJ started to slow to a walk. They came up beside Rene and Star. Logan handed her a couple of wildflowers. Smiling. he turned and galloped away.

Rene stopped and just looked at the two flowers. They were the most beautiful flowers she had ever seen. She looked up and watched Logan as he rode away. With all the thoughts she had running through her head, she again looked at the flowers in her hand. *Oh, boy*, she thought, *I think I'm in trouble.* Again she looked at the man she had just fallen for. "No," she said out loud, "I know I'm in trouble." Rene looked at Logan as he and CJ made it looked easy. Riding toward him, she asked, "How far to the valley?"

Logan looked around and replied, "At the speed the herd is moving now, I'd say it's still a couple of hours."

They headed out of the valley, and the trail narrowed. They would be following a game trail that cut up around and between the mountains although they would be climbing. As they traveled, everyone was watching for trouble. A couple of hours into the morning, it started going bad. First a cow lost her footing and fell, sliding down a shale slide.

Logan and another guy grabbed their ropes and headed down after her. She was stuck on the edge of a cliff. Logan put a rope around her neck and tied the other one to it. Logan was between the cliff edge and the cow. As he worked to get her tied off, the wrangler headed uphill as another cowboy was coming down. They tied his rope on also then they started pulling using the horses to get her away from the cliff edge. Suddenly the cow started kicking. Logan was still on the edge of the cliff. The cow kicked out, just missing him.

As Logan tried to get clear, he slipped. He grabbed on the cow's kicking legs, trying not to go over the edge and fall to the rocks below. The wrangler that was closest grabbed his hand just as the cow kicked again. Slowly he used the cow as leverage to pull Logan to safety. Logan gained his feet, grabbed the wrangler in a hug. The wrangler fell backward, dragging Logan over the cow and to safety.

After a few minutes, they started pushing, pulling, and dragging her until there was a place where Logan figured she could get up. Far enough away from the cliff so she wouldn't go over the edge. Logan and another cowboy were behind her and kept pushing as the guys up the hill were pulling slowly; they kept her moving up hill.

Rene stood back, taking pictures. She was capturing the true essence of the American cowboy old versus new or new versus old one in the same. A man on a horse. This country was too rugged and wild for anything else. As she watched Logan and the other guys work, she could see the determination to save this one cow. With sweat pouring and muscles bulging, slowly but surely they got her up the side of the mountain.

As they gained the trail, Logan got the ropes off. The cow trotted off joining her calves. Rene slowly walk to Logan; as he turned around, he saw her. Rene lost control and started crying. She put her arms around this wild, untamed cowboy. Logan held her as if he would never see her again.

Slowly Rene got control and asked, "So do things like that happen often?"

Logan just said, "I hope never again." Adding, "That was just a little too close."

They got the herd moving again, and just before dark cleared the mountains, they stopped for the night in a valley that the mountain road they used to get up there cut through. The cows quickly settled down. The guys tended to the horses, feeding and watering them then get them settled down for the night.

Rene decided that she was the camp cook and started making supper. Turning, she asked Logan, "What do you have for meat? I'm going to make supper."

Logan grabbed his rifle and said, "Sure, about nine hundred head. How many do you want?"

Rene laughed and said, "Not that much. I was only going to use some to feed you guys."

Smiling and putting his rifle down, he walked to the pack horses and grabbed a cooler. He walked back to the fire and put it down next to Rene. "There," he said, "I'm sure you'll find enough in there."

With meat sizzling over a campfire and potatoes frying in a pan, the guys started gathering around. Rene looked up and saw them all coming her way. She said, "You, guys, look like a pack of wolves. Get cleaned up and find a place to sit. I'll start bringing you plates all dished up."

Everyone scrambled for a spot. Rene started handing out plates of panfried potatoes and steaks. Logan was the last to receive a plate as Rene sat down next to him. Everyone started teasing him about being last. Logan smiled and said, "We have to feed the help first." Adding, "Rene, honey, I think we need to talk."

That got a laugh out of everyone. After they finished eating, everyone pitched in to clean up. The plates were burned in the fire. All the leftovers were stored away in airtight storage containers.

"This is bear country," Logan said as he hoisted the last cooler high in a tree. He walked back to the fire. "I don't want that big, old grizzly to pay us a visit tonight." Bed roles were rolled out, and most everyone settled down for the night.

Late that night the cattle started mulling around and making all kinds of racket. A few of the cowboys were standing watch. A shot rang out, and everyone woke up with a start.

Logan, grabbing his rifle, threw more wood on the fire and pulled Rene close. Whistling for CJ, he quickly saddled. Mounting, he reached down and pulled Rene up behind him as he headed for the herd.

As they rode out of camp, Jessy headed them off. Logan asked, "Who shot and what's happening?"

Jessy replied, "I think a lion got a calf although I saw a couple of wolves and fired a warning shot to scare them off."

As they sat there talking suddenly, the wolves started howling, another shot rang out.

Rene pulled Logan a little closer together. Logan and Jessy started walking the horses toward the sound. Logan reached down and slid the rifle out of the boot and laid it across his lap as they continued to ride toward the other side of the herd.

Alex saw them as they approached. Turning their way, he said, "I think the lion retreated to the timber, and I took a shot at the wolves as they crossed the valley and disappeared."

Logan look at Alex and asked, "Do you think you hit anything?"

Alex replied, "Nope, it was to scare them off. They were all running when they made the timber. I don't think they'll be back tonight."

Logan looked around and could see that all the ranch hands were out riding around the herd. Whistling loudly, they all gathered around.

Logan said, "I think we had better have a couple of guys watch tonight. I don't want to lose anymore."

Jessy and Alex said, "We will take first watch."

Turning, they headed back toward the cattle as Logan said, "Someone will be out to relieve you two in a few hours."

Morning broke cool and clear. They were about seven thousand feet in elevation, high enough to be cold but no snow. At ten thousand feet, snow was possible all year.

Rene started making breakfast as one of the guys asked, "Hey, is she coming with every time?" Adding, "She's a great cook. Nothing against you, boss, but umm."

Logan just snickered and said, "I guess we will just have to wait and see. Although for that I'll cook your eggs."

Darrel turned and walked away, saying, "Figures." Laughing, he continued "I'll just have coffee" as he went to check the horses.

After breakfast they cleaned up, packed up, and headed down the road toward the pens. Logan figured that they would get there late that afternoon. With a little luck, they would be in the main ranch valley the following day. Hopefully they could finish the branding in a week or so. Then start getting a herd of yearlings ready to ship.

Early afternoon they came around the last corner and were at the holding pens. After all the cattle were in the pens, it was suppertime. Rene, with Logan's help, had supper nearly done as the wranglers started walking toward the campfire. Rene looked at them and said," Sit." They all found a place to sit immediately.

Logan started laughing, saying, "Wow, she's got you, guys, all trained." This brought laughter from everyone.

Then Rene looked at Logan and said, "Hey, that means you too."

Logan dropped where he stood. That brought roars of laugher from the guys. Someone called out, "Hey, Logan, I haven't seen you move that fast since the cliff." That brought more laughter. They started to calm down.

Logan looked at Rene and said, "Honey, we really need to have that talk." That started it all over again.

Rene walk around, handing out dinner plates. Grabbing the last two, she sat next to Logan. One of the hands said, "Hey, boss, last again."

Logan just smiled as he looked at Rene. This time he looked just long enough for Rene to look back. She asked, "Is something wrong?"

Logan smiled and said, "Nope, just looking." Rene looked at him questioningly. Logan just smiled and started to eat.

Once again everything was cleaned up, put away, and bedrolls rolled out. Logan put Rene's next to him again. She walked over, kissed him gently, and lay down next to him. They talked quietly for a few minutes. Then she reached out and kissed him again.

Logan whispered in her ear, "Don't start something we can't finish."

One of the guys yelled, "Oh, for god's sake, take her for a walk."

The camp exploded with laughter. Logan smiled at her as he pulled her close, he closed his eyes and fell asleep.

Rene lay there feeling Logan next to her. *What am I doing?* she thought. *Can I live this life? All my friends are back east.* She knew that she as in love with him. She knew that he could never leave this ranch. It was his life. He lived and loved this wild country. Taking him to a city would be like putting him in a cage.

She felt the strength in his arms. She thought of him slipping on the edge of the cliff trying to save that cow. A cold feeling went through her. *Yes,* she thought, *I do love him. I will stay here as long as he wants me to. I would rather have what time he'll give me than another life time without him.* That thought settled her, and she fell asleep wrapped in the arms of the man she loved.

Rene woke slowly. She reached for Logan with a start; she jerked wide awake. Logan was gone. She sat up and saw him sitting by the fire drinking coffee. She lay there just looking at him. Slowly she started to stand up and walked to the fire. Logan poured her a cup as she sat down next to him. She took the cup from Logan and said, "Good morning."

He put his arm around her, giving her a squeeze, answering, "Good morning, you." They sat there quietly drinking their coffee. They watched the sky change colors from purple to orange and finally red as the sun slowly climbed over the eastern mountains.

Rene sat in total amazement, admiring this beauty of this wild country. She thought of the large cities. The people in a hurry, never stopping to just look. Most of them would never get the chance to see this. She thought of the settlers 150 years ago. What did they think of this area? She slowly turned to look at Logan. She was surprised that he was looking at her. He bent down and kissed her gently. All she could think of was, *How can such a man like this be so gently? A man that can live in this wild and rough country yet pick wildflowers and hand them to me.*

The rest of the guys started to wake up. There morning quiet time was over. She felt like there was more. Like Logan wanted to say something. The spell was broken, and the day was about to start as she stood up to make breakfast for ten hardworking cowboys. Bacon, eggs, and panfried potatoes along with a couple of gallons of coffee.

Breakfast was over, and everything was cleaned up, packed up, and the cattle were moving. Yes, the day was underway. She hoped her and Logan could find a few minutes to talk later that day or maybe later tonight. With the exception of a few cows trying to break away, the day went smooth. Just before dark, the last of the cattle were in the main valley. It had been a long day.

Rene removed the saddle from Star and put her in a stall at Logan's ranch just as Logan came in with CJ. They talked as Logan removed the saddle and bridle and put CJ in a stall. Together they walk toward the ranch house. Logan reached for Rene's hand. As Rene took his hand, she felt a tingle traveling through her. Her mind went to work immediately. *I've had other boyfriends*, she thought, *never has a man made me feel this way. What kind of power does he have over me? Is this real? Will it work? Will it last?*

It was late, and she didn't know if she was going home or staying there.

Logan gave Rene a tour around the ranch house, showing her the living room, kitchen, bathroom, office, and den. Then walking together, they walked upstairs. This area was off limits to the hired hands. It was Logan's private domain. Three more bedrooms along with a bathroom for each. When he showed her the master bedroom, Rene's mouth fell open; she just stood there. She absolutely could not believe what she saw.

A huge four-poster bed stood in the center but against one wall of the room. A huge split rock fireplace took up the entire wall in front of the bed. The ceiling was vaulted with elk, mule deer, big horn sheep, and mountain goat mounted on the walls. Two large walk-in closets. A large flat screen TV was mounted on the wall between the closets. A couple of reclining chairs. One corner next to the bed had a rolltop desk.

There was a sliding glass door that opened onto a private deck overlooking the backyard. The most beautiful scene Rene had ever seen. The majestic Rocky Mountains reached for the sky. Rene opened the door and walked into the deck. Logan watched as she stood there looking at the mountains. Slowly he walked up behind her. Putting his arms around her, she turned and looked into his eyes. Logan reached down and tenderly kissed her.

Together they walked back inside. Rene continued to look around. Looking through the other two bedrooms, she said, "This is fantastic."

Next Rene opened the door to the master bath. It was just as beautiful with a large jetted bathtub. A glass-enclosed shower and two sinks. Opening another door revealed a private room including the toilet. Rene turned to find Logan standing behind her.

Logan put his arms around her and asked, "Do you think you can live here with me?"

Rene replied, "Oh absolutely." Pausing, she then said, "Although I need a day to let this all sink in. I know I love you, but this all happened way too fast. Can I have a day, say until tomorrow, to think it over?"

Logan looked crushed although he knew it was a big decision and Rene needed a day. *Okay*, he thought, *let her have the day or even two.*

Rene looked into Logan's eyes and asked, "Do you want me to stay with you tonight?"

Logan replied, "Only if you actually want to."

Rene smiled as she put her arms around him and kissed him. Quietly, she whispered, "I want to stay tonight and every night for the rest of my life. I don't need to think about it, I saw my answer in your eyes."

Logan said, "Rene, I'll love you for the rest of our lives and beyond." Kissing her again, he scooped her up and continued kissing her as he carried her to bed.

Joe and Kay

A rriving home from Montana, Joe needed time to heal. His arm was doing great after breaking it, falling from a rock outcropping trying to find the horses that had been spooked by a mountain lion. The antibiotics were working at controlling the infection in the gash in his thigh. He had gotten while crossing a river as they tried to find their way out of the Bob Marshal Wilderness Area.

Joe spent a couple of days going over the gear that they had taken to Montana, trying to fix what he could and making a list of what needed to be replaced. With the list completed, he spent the rest of the day walking around, sporting goods stores.

As he drove into the driveway, Kay met him, and the two carefully carried all the new gear into the garage where they would repack it.

Making packing for the next job so much easier. As they were about finished Kay said, "I'll go start supper, see you inside shortly." Looking over her shoulder as she walked away, she continued, "Please, don't stay out here all night, you still need to relax."

Joe walked in, grabbed a couple of bottles of beer, and sat on the couch as he watched the fire. Kay walked in, sat next to him, and said, "Dinner is nearly ready."

Smiling at her, he quietly thought, *How did I get this lucky? Beautiful, great cook, and she actually loves me.*

Kay smiled as she asked, "How's the arm and leg doing?"

Joe replied, "A few more days I'll be as good as new. Although I may have overdone it a little today."

Looking over at her husband, Kay asked, "How much walking did you do today?"

Joe replied, "Maybe just a bit too much. My leg is a little sore."

Kay looked at him and said, "Stand up and slide your pants down." Joe started smiling as he stood up looking at his wife.

Kay snickered, saying, "That's why I love you. You'll never grow up. Now drop your pants and let me look at that cut."

Joe started laughing and replied "Aww, bummer" as he dropped his pants.

Kay carefully removed the wrap and packing that was covering the large gash in Joe's leg that he gotten in Montana while trying to cross a flooded river. They were nearly across the river when a log hit Joe, pushing him under the water and ripping a large gash in his thigh. Kay had put stitches in it, but the leg had become infected and she had to cut it open again. They went to visit a doctor after getting safely out of the mountains. That was about three weeks ago, and the leg was finally starting to heal.

Kay looked up at Joe and said, "It's bleeding again, you reopened it some. I need to clean this and recover it. Come on, Mr. Mountain Man, I'll do it before dinner."

After cleaning and putting a fresh dressing on, Joe limped to the dining room for dinner and then helped cleaning up after. Joe disappeared shortly before the kitchen was clean.

As Kay walked into their bedroom, she called out, "Joe, are you in here?"

Joe had lit a few candles around a hot bath he had run for Kay, smiling and giving her a kiss and handing her the book that she had gotten earlier that day. Looking at the cover, he said, "I read a few pages. It's really good. Is that the author you follow online?"

Kay replied, "Yes, he's a trucker, poet, and now he's writing fiction."

He asked, "Can I read it when you're done?"

Kay replied "Sure. I have all four of his poetry books. Plus his first and second book of stories" as she watched him walked out of the bedroom.

Joe headed back to the living room and put a few more pieces of wood on the fire; grabbing a beer, he eased onto the couch and enjoyed the fire.

About an hour later, Kay walked into the living room in a very sexy robe. Joe could see the beauty in the woman he loved. The way she walked, dressed, and acted in public was nothing short of elegance. Although it was the way she looked at him when they were alone that Joe really loved. It was the glistening in her eyes that told the story. She loved him past the point of no return. As far as Joe was concerned, there wasn't another woman on earth that could ever replace her in his life or heart.

Sitting down next to him, Joe quietly got up and got two more beers. He opened them, handing one to Kay. Then walking to the fireplace, he put more wood on the fire. As he turned to walk back to the couch, he froze. Standing there, he just watched as Kay slowly crossed her legs and took a sip of her beer. Smiling, he walked up and gently kissed her; sitting down, he put an arm around her. The two sat quietly, watching the fire and drinking their beer.

Kay looked into Joe's eyes as she put her bottle down. She reached up and kissed him as she slowly and carefully rearranged herself to sit on his lap, facing him. Softly, she kissed him again, moaning softly as their tongues started the romantic dance. She could feel the reaction in Joe as he responded to the kiss. She quietly whispered in his ear, "How's your leg?"

Joe softly whispered "What leg" as he put his arms under her and stood up.

Kay looked at him, saying, "Honey, I can walk."

Joe just continued to kiss her as he carried her to their bedroom.

*****

As Kay's eyes started to open, she reached for Joe, finding an empty spot where he should be. She felt his side of the bed and found it was cold. Quietly she slid out of bed and found her robe laying on the floor where Joe had dropped it the night before. Walking into the living room, she saw Joe as he turned away from the fireplace and walked toward the couch. A craft of coffee and an extra cup was sitting on the coffee table.

Sitting down, she asked, "Have you been up long?"

Joe replied, "Long enough to shower, make coffee, and start that fire." He handed her a cup.

Taking the cup, she sat back against the couch, closing her eyes and took a sip. Breathing in the rich aroma, Kay asked, "How's the leg this morning?"

Joe, laughing, replied, "Hurts like hell although after last night, it's so worth the pain." He reached over and kissed her.

Kay laughed as she replied, "Don't start that again. I'm not going to be the reason you end up on crutches."

Joe reached and hugged his wife, whispering, "I still think it would be so worth it."

Kay hugged Joe a little tighter and said, "Pour me a little more coffee and I'll make you breakfast."

Joe reached for the coffee, saying, "How can I refuse that kind of deal."

As Kay cooked breakfast, Joe made another pot of coffee and toast. They sat at the table when Kay said, "Joe, I think I want to retire and travel with you."

Joe looked up, saying, "Can we afford that?"

Kay replied, "Yes, I think we can. I looked at it last week then talked to our financial advisor. He said that with everything we have paid for and the money you make, what we draw out of our retirement will be minimal. In fact if we are just a little careful, we won't need to draw anything at all. Also part of my retirement package is my health insurance which is paid for me. So we'll only have to pay yours, and I can sit that up to come out twice a year."

Joe looked at Kay, saying, "I would absolutely love to have you come with me. Although what I do is dangerous. There may be times you'll have to stay in camp or a motel."

Kay started to pout as Joe looked at her. She started laughing and said, "Oh bummer, I'm not sure I could handle laying by the pool or going to the spa." Putting his arms around her, they stood in the kitchen and slowly danced to a song that only played in their minds.

Breaking away, Kay said, "Time to get this day going. I'm going to have a talk with my boss and tell him I'm done in a month or so. Although I'll stay until they find a replacement and help him or her get settled into their new position. I'm sure he can find someone in that amount of time." Adding, "I think he knows it's going to happen with the amount of time I've been taking off to be with you."

Joe smiled as he watched her walk away. *Wow*, he thought, *she has so many great assets.* Still smiling, she walked into their bedroom and out of sight.

*****

Kay walked into the office, put her belongings down, and headed for her boss's office. Steve looked up as she knocked on the molding next to the door.

Steve said, "You don't needed to knock. What's up?"

Kay sat down and said, "I'm thinking about retiring and going with Joe full time."

Steve replied, "That's great for you but bad for us. Although I knew this would happen the day of your wedding." Kay looked at him questioningly as Steve said, "I could see it in both of you. You two are made for each other." Looking around, he added, "The mountain man and the lady. What a movie that would make." Looking directly at Kay and smiling, he added, "What an idea, you are a writer turned editor. Do you think you could write articles for the magazine from your trips?"

Kay looked at the ceiling and said, "I would have to ask Joe to make sure it's okay with him."

Steve replied, "Put your retirement in writing and get it to me. I'll handle everything for you. I'll also get it set up so you can do some freelance writing. I'm sure the magazine will pay good for those kind of articles."

Kay smiled as she stood up, saying, "I'll see you this afternoon with my retirement resignation."

Steve replied, "I'll have your replacement in a few days. How long are you going to stay?"

Kay said as she turned to leave, "I'll stay and help my replacement get used to their new position plus a few day. Say about a month."

Steve answered as she walked away, "That's great and congratulations. I'm sure you two will have a blast traveling together."

Kay arrived home to find Joe in the garage going over more equipment. Kay asked, "How does everything look?"

Joe replied, "I think we are going to need a new two-person tent plus two sleeping bags. That wolverine really messed these up. I've taken them in to be washed three times, and you can still smell that stinky pest. I'm also going to get two new backpacks." Continuing, he added, "That trip out of the mountains was just too hard on them."

Kay asked, "What else do we need?"

Joe replied, "I have a small list." Continuing, he added, "I got most everything else yesterday. I'm just trying to make sure we are ready when someone calls."

Kay started to walk toward the door that lead into the main part of the house and said, "I'm going to start supper. Oh, and I talked to Steve about retiring."

Joe looked up and asked, "Oh, what did he have to say?"

Looking back, she replied, "He said he saw it coming." Smiling, she continued, "The day we got married. Oh, and he also said have fun."

Joe turned back to what he was doing and thought, *Wow, smart man.* Looking at the closing door as Kay disappeared, he thought, *How can a man from the woods in Pennsylvania find such an amazing lady?* Putting the last of the supplies away and putting the list in his shirt pocket, Joe walked into the house to help Kay with supper.

Joe walked into the living room and got the fire going again, few small pieces of wood adding larger pieces as they caught. In a few minutes he threw a few large pieces on and closed the doors. Kay walked in with two bottles of beer and sat on the couch. Joe walked back to the couch and sat down; he picked up one of the bottles and sat next to her. She handed him the other for him to open as she snuggled up against him. Smiling, she reached up and kissed him. Joe smiled and pulled her a little closer. They sat in silence, just enjoying the closeness and the fire.

Joe turned looking into Kay's eyes as she turned away from the fire. The light flickered and danced in her dark eyes, and Joe found himself mesmerized. He could not look away, she was the total package. Beauty and elegance, looked fantastic in an evening dress or old faded blue jeans and a T-shirt. Again Joe thought as he sat next to her how lucky he was.

Kay had one hand running up and down Joe's chest, and every so often she would run her hand softly down his thigh. She could feel the muscles in his chest and legs. She never knew just how strong he was until he carried her out the Alaskan wilderness the year before. How he had climbed nearly ten thousand vertical feet to reach her and then descend the same distance to get her to medical help she so desperately needed.

While she was going through physical therapy, one of the doctors told her what condition he was in when he carried her into the hospital that day in late September. How he walked in and put her on a hospital cart before collapsing to the floor. How he slept for nearly six hours and then tore out his IVs and electrical monitoring wires to get to her side where he then refused to leave.

That few hours without Joe standing there, she found out what kind of man she had married. The doctors had said that Joe had done what many called impossible, and he had no idea what had kept him going. Kay knew why and what had kept him going. A little word with the most powerful of all meanings. "Love." That the entire time she was in a coma, he never left her side. He gave her all the sponge bathes and talked to her nonstop. At night he slept in a recliner until they finally gave up and brought in another bed.

Then one doctor said, "That man loves you more than he loves himself." Kay sat there thinking about all of this, and she knew that she had a man that truly was "one in a million."

Joe slowly stood up; walking to the fire, he threw in another piece of wood. Turning, he walked into the kitchen just as Kay took two more beers out of the fridge. Handing them to Joe, he opened both, handing her back one. Taking her by the hand, he led her back to the couch. Again Kay snuggled up tight against his side and under his arm. This was where she want to be. Right here, right now and for the rest of her life. Married to this amazing man.

Joe couldn't help but sneak a peek into Kay's eyes; the way the firelight flickered and danced was captivating, and Joe knew he was captured and he loved every second of it. Nothing on earth made him happier than the time he got to spend with her, and now that time was going to exceed every expectation he had ever dreamed. Again he looked into her amazing eyes. Taking the last swallow of beer, he stood up, walked over, and closed the fireplace doors. Walking back to the couch, he offered his hand. Kay took his hand, and they slowly danced to a song playing softly. As the song ended, quietly they walked to the bedroom.

Kay could smell something fantastic as she slowly started waking up. Joe had just sat down on the edge of the bed. As Kay started waking up again, she could smell the rich aroma of fresh brewed coffee. As she slowly opened her eyes, Joe's smiling face came into focus. He handed her a cup of coffee. Kay shifted, trying to raise up on an elbow. As she did she took the coffee and took the first sip. "Mmm," she said as she took another sip.

Joe stood up and got her robe. Kay started getting up, being careful not to spill as Joe slipped the robe over her shoulders. Taking her coffee, he turned and walked backward out of the bedroom. Laughing, Kay made a silly face, watching her coffee go with him.

Kay followed Joe and her coffee into the kitchen. He had already started making breakfast. Between the aroma of coffee and the fantastic smell of bacon frying, Kay sat down, and picking up the coffee, she slowly sipped her coffee as Joe walked over and placed a plate of bacon and eggs in front of her along with pancakes and orange juice. Taking her cup, he then filled it and sat down across from her. Kay looked over, smiling.

Joe smiled and said, "Thank you."

Kay looked questioningly at Joe who just smiled. Turning, he started to eat. Kay asked, "Thank you?"

Joe smiled and replied, "Yes, thank you."

Again Kay looked at Joe and asked, "For what?"

Joe smiled and said, "For marrying me, for being the fantastic lady you are. But mostly for loving me."

Tears started to form in Kay's eyes as she said, "Joe, you don't have to thank me for that. How could I not love you? I fell in love with you the very first time we met." Looking into his eyes, she added, "I'll love you for the rest of my life. No one could ever take your place in my life."

Joe looked at Kay and smiled. No more words were needed or said as the two sat quietly eating their breakfast. Everything passed between them in eye contact. Quick glances that only showed love and admiration. The mutual respect two people form as they fall deeper and deeper in love.

With only a few day left until Kay retires, the magazine was planning a retirement party. Everyone from the magazine was going to be there. With all the plans made, Kay and Joe walked into the private party and applause started. Kay was dressed in a skirt and Joe in a suit, the two made quite the couple. As Kay's boss called it, the mountain man and the lady.

Dinner dancing and a few drinks, everyone was having a great time. Steve got up and said a little speech, thanking Kay for twenty-four years of service to the magazine. Then he presented her with a beautiful plaque that showed her accomplishments.

Kay had tears in her eyes as she took the plaque from Steve. As she tried to dab the tears from her eyes, she managed to say thank you to the magazine and all her coworkers for the last twenty-four years. Then she looked at Joe and said, "I'm the luckiest woman in the world because I get to spend the rest of my life traveling to fantastic places with the only man I could ever love." With that Kay put down the microphone as she headed back to sit down, Joe met her. He wrapped his arms around her, and they stood there.

Steve picked up the mic and said, "When these two got married, I knew someday he would steal her away from us and the magazine. I wish them both the very best in the coming years. Thank you, Kay, for your years of service, and to you, Joe, please, take care of that fantastic lady you have. Then laughingly, he said, "I've always thought of these two as the mountain man and the lady."

With that everyone started whistling and applauding. Someone started the music playing. Joe took Kay into his arms as the two slowly danced their way to the dance floor and opened that part of the party. Joe and Kay danced and talked. Talked and danced.

Finally the party was winding down, everyone started saying goodbye to Kay and wishing her luck and happiness in the future. The two of them stood there shaking hands, smiling as Kay hugged and kissed most everyone. Joe stood at her side, handing her tissues as she continued to cry. She knew how much she would miss everyone although she was looking forward to spending more time with Joe.

With the party finally over, Joe and Kay walked out the door with Steve and his wife. Steve stopped and gave Kay another hug and wished her happiness in her travels with Joe. Turning to Joe, he said, "I knew the day would come that she would leave to spend time more with you. Be good to her, she really loves you."

Joe looked at Kay and said, "You'll never have to worry about that." Shaking hands, they headed for their cars and home.

As they pulled into the driveway, Kay said, "Oh, do I ever need to get out of these clothes?" Joe looked at her and just smiled. Kay started laughing and replied, "You'll never change. Maybe that's why I love you the way I do. You just never know what you'll say or do next." Joe reached over and gave her a kiss. They got out of the car and headed inside.

Joe helped Kay with her coat and hung it up. Walking into the bedroom, he asked, "Hey, honey, is there anything else you need help removing?"

Kay started laughing and said, "Go make us some tea and start a fire."

Joe walked out snickering and said," That's what I'm trying to do. Well the fire anyway."

Kay walked into the living room to find a fire burning and two cups of tea on the coffee table. Smiling, she sat down next to Joe. Slowly she crossed her legs as her robe slid open, revealing her very shapely legs. Joe let out a low groan as Kay looked at him with a very devilish grin. As they talked and sipped their tea, Kay would uncross and recross her legs. Each time she did this, her robe would open just a bit more.

Joe kept glancing at Kay's legs until he couldn't take it anymore. Slowly he kissed her, lifting her chin slightly. As she responded to the kiss, Joe slowly ran his hand up and down her leg. Now it was Kay's turn to let out a long, low moan.

Joe stopped kissing her and closed the fireplace doors. Kay picked up both empty cups, and Joe picked her up. She smiled, went from devilish to seductive as she put her arms around his neck.

*****

Joe slowly started to wake up. He could hear something although the fog was still a little too thick. As his eyes opened, he could smell also. A fantastic aroma of bacon and something else. Sitting up it started to come to him. Coffee. Kay was up and tormenting him. Coffee and bacon, now he was totally awake and looking for his clothes. Kay had moved them. He opened his dresser drawer. *No sweats*, he thought. Where were his sweats?

Okay, he thought. Looking around, he saw Kay's robe. "No," he said out loud, "I'm not putting that on." Opening his closet, he noticed that his pants were all missing. Looking around a little more, he swore under his breath as he put on Kay's robe. Walking into the kitchen, Kay started laughing.

Joe said, "Honey where are my clothes?"

Kay replied, "Packed."

Joe looked at her and said, "Packed?"

Kay replied, "Yes, packed. Look at the clock. It's nearly eleven in the morning. I let you sleep. Oh, and we got a call. There's a number by the phone. You need to return a call. Looks like we are going to Mexico."

Joe cocked his head and asked, "Mexico?"

Kay looked at him as she sat a cup of coffee in front of him, saying, "Yes, Mexico. Although I think you may want to find something else to put on. You look great in my robe but?"

Joe looked down and started laughing. The robe was open nearly to his waist where he managed to tie it closed.

Kay said, "You have clothes in the dryer. I washed and started packing. I'm sure after you talk to him we will be leaving later today or in the morning."

Joe walked to the dryer and grabbed a pair of pants and a T-shirt. After getting dressed, he picked up the number that Kay had left by the phone. Looking at her, he said, "Hector Ortiz?"

Kay smiled and replied, "Yes, that's what he said."

He placed the call, asking for Hector Ortiz. A man answered in Spanish. Joe asked, "Can you speak English?"

"Yes, sir, this is Diego. Can I help you?"

Joe replied, "Yes, Diego, can I, please, speak to Hector Ortiz?"

Diego answered, "Yes, sir, just a minute, please."

Joe heard as the phone made a few clicks, and soon a man answered and said, "This is Hector, can I help you?"

"Yes, Hector, this is Joe. I believe you spoke to my wife earlier today," said Joe.

"Yes, Joe," Hector replied, "did Kay tell you what's going on here?"

Joe replied, "Yes, she did. You have a problem with a mountain lion?"

"Yes, sir," replied Hector.

Taking notes, he looked at Kay and said, "Okay, you agree to the price. Here's my banking information. Please, wire half now and the rest is due the day we catch the cats. We'll take them at least a hundred miles away and turn them loose. Yes, yes, I'll have pictures and will document everything so you know we got them."

Listening he replied, "Yes, yes, we'll stay in the area for an additional week to make sure we caught the troublemakers. You say there are two mountain lions killing livestock and scarring the farmers in the area? Okay, I'll wait for your call, and we can leave as soon as you do."

Disconnecting the call, he looked at Kay and said, "You're absolutely correct, we are going to Mexico today."

Kay smiled, thinking, *Sweet a month in the sun and out of Chicago's winter and snow.* Joe poured another cup of coffee while Kay finished cooking breakfast.

After eating, Kay said, "I'll clean up here and finish packing."

Joe replied, "Okay, I'll hook up the trailer and start getting the rest of our gear together."

Walking into the office, he grabbed two checklists, one titled deserts and one titled mountain lions. Kissing Kay, he walked outside to start getting everything they would need. Grabbing two medium-sized live traps and the their side by side UTV, he loaded it into the back of their toy hauler travel trailer. Next was rope and camping supplies like a small tent sleeping bags.

Joe continued putting gear in the trailer and the back of his pickup, checking the list and making notes. Last he walked to the fridge in the shop. Removing a small box marked TRANQUILIZER and then over to a cabinet where he took out a tranquilizer gun. *Just in case*, he thought as he looked down the list again, double-checking everything he had marked.

As he looked, his phone beeped. Looking at the caller ID, he smiled and said, "Mexico." After a short call, he called the bank, confirming the transfer. Walking into the house, he looked at the stack of suitcases Kay had put in the entryway.

Smiling, he thought, *Four times as many as when I left alone for the same amount of time.* Laughing, he started hauling them to the camper part of the toy hauler. As he walked out, he met Kay. She had two hard gun cases.

Joe asked, "What did you bring?"

Kay replied as she handed them to him, "Your AR-15 (AR stands for "ArmaLite rifle," not "assault rifle" as many believed) and my .22-250 and mini-14."

Joe smiled as he carefully put them in the storage area under the bed. Walking back, he met her again with four ammo boxes. Joe said, "Here give me those and grab two 9mm plus holsters and a ammo box for them." Thinking, he changed his mind and said, "Two ammo boxes." After all the gun and ammo was safely put away, Joe went down the checklist again.

Handing them to Kay, he asked, "Can you think of anything not on these two lists?"

Kay read the list through several times. Looking at Joe, she said, "What about our passports?"

"Oh wow," Joe replied.

Kay reached in her pocket and showed them to Joe; walking to the truck, she put them both in the glove box. They both walked to the house, double-checking if everything was closed up and locked. Adjusting the air conditioner and setting the alarm, Joe looked at Kay and said, "Are you ready?"

Kay replied, "I've been ready and waiting for this day for nearly three months." Adding, "When you went on the short trip to Wyoming last month, I thought I would die before you got home." Joe reached over, kissing her. Putting his arm around her, together they walked to the pickup and the adventure that lay ahead in Mexico.

It was shortly after one in the afternoon, and Chicago traffic was moving at a good rate. Within an hour, they were on I-80 and headed for I-55 that would take them to St. Louis, Missouri.

Just west of St. Louis, Joe asked, "Hey, honey, should we find a place and call it a day?"

Kay replied, "How far are we from Oklahoma?"

Joe answered, "A little over two hundred miles or say three and a half to four hours."

"Wow, really?" Kay said. Adding, "Do you know a place we can stop for the night?"

Smiling, Joe answered, "Yep, there's a rest area just west of Rolla, Missouri." Continuing, he added, "When we get there, we'll about halfway across Missouri."

About an hour later, Joe flipped on the signal as he exited the intestate, pulling into the rest area. Making a wide turn, he pulled the one ton Chevy Dooley pickup and the 47-foot toy hauler in the parking spot.

*****

Joe woke early as was his custom when traveling to or from a job, sitting at the table drinking coffee and enjoying a beautiful fall morning. Kay walked into the kitchen area of the camper in a very seductive nightie. Smiling, Joe pointed outside where there were other campers plus a few trucks parked. Kay turned to look out the window. Looking down, she started to laugh as she hurried back to put a few more clothes on. Quickly she was dressed, jeans and T-shirt would be the attire for the day. Glancing in the mirror, she turned and walked back and stood next to Joe.

He handed her a travel mug. Taking her by the hand, the two of them walked through the rest area. Kay saw a path that led into the woods. Nodding that way, they followed the path to the shore of a small lake. As they walked into the opening that included a small beach and a picnic area, Joe spotted a bench where they could enjoy the peace and quiet of the beautiful fall morning. They looked across the lake as the sun started to shine over the trees and slowly burning off the morning fog.

Soon the travel mugs where empty, and it was time to get going. Kay went into the trailer, filling the travel mugs and threw a couple of breakfast sandwiches into the microwave as Joe did a quick walk around, making sure everything was ready. Kay did a quick double-check of the kitchen area of the trailer. Closing and locking the door, she walked to the pickup, opening the door and handing Joe a sandwich and full travel mug as she climbed in. Joe put the pickup in gear and headed in a southwest direction toward Joplin, Missouri, and then Oklahoma.

Joe asked, "Hey, what way do you want to go? Through Oklahoma and the North Texas or down toward Dallas and across to El Paso?"

Kay replied, "I've never been in the Dallas area. What's it like?"

Joe answered, "Wow, really? What's it like?" Laughing, he answered, "Too damn many people. Although if that's the way you want to go." As they left the rest area, Joe said, "I think we will stop in Big Cabin, Oklahoma. There's a nice truck stop there. I'll fill with fuel, buy you a meal. You don't have to cook, and you can look around the gift shop."

Kay replied, smiling, "Gift shop?"

Joe answered, "Yep, absolutely, in fact remember that big dream catcher I got you? I got it there coming home a few years ago."

Looking at Joe, Kay smiled and said, "Yes, and I absolutely love it."

Joe reached over and gave Kay a quick kiss as they slowed to pay the toll. Joe said, "Next exit is ours."

Kay replied, "Well that's a rip-off!"

Joe answered, "We will get money back at the exit. You pay to Tulsa but get a rebate if you exit early. Just give them the ticket and they refund your toll."

Kay replied, "Isn't that a lot of paperwork?"

Joe answered, "It's the way it's setup. Yeah, it's stupid but whatever, I guess."

Exiting the toll road, they pulled into the truck stop for fuel food and a short shopping trip before heading toward Dallas and then west to El Paso and Arizona.

Kay said "I'll see you inside" as she got out of the truck and headed for the gift shop.

Joe filled the pickup and the extra tank in the box, giving them enough fuel for about eight hundred miles before needing to fill again. Paying the bill, he found Kay with her arms full. Shaking his head, he took a few of what she wanted and help get to the cashier. Then storing the purchase away in the camper, they headed for the restaurant.

As they ate, Kay asked, "What lays ahead about the roads and area like?"

Joe simply said, "Watch for rattlesnakes. This time of year they are a little slow in the morning but back to their normal grouchy attitude by afternoon noon." He told her about the way people lived in the small villages and towns in the desert. They talked about the white sands area of New Mexico and made plans to spend a day playing there.

Joe handed the waitress his card for their meal, and leaving a tip, they headed for the pickup and Dallas. Kay was used to heavy traffic and relaxed as they passed through the Dallas area and headed west on I-20.

Kay asked, "Hey, honey, where are we stopping for the night?"

Joe replied, "We can stop most anytime or anyplace you want. These cats are not hurting people, just livestock, so it's not a time sensitive type job."

Kay said, "Great." Looking at the map, she asked, "How about Abilene?"

Joe replied, "That is still about two hundred miles. I think I'll make it that far tonight, and we can spend some time there tomorrow."

They kept talking about Mexico and what would happen after they got there, what the plan was, and how they would catch the two cats causing all the trouble.

Joe said, "I believe it's probably an old female with only one cub. Chances are she's too old to hunt her natural prey like deer and desert big horn sheep, and the domestic sheep and goats in the area are a second choice. If this is true, I'll contact the government and ask what they want done. More than likely they donate them to a zoo. Although if the cub is old enough to be on its own, I'll take it a hundred or so miles away and turn it loose."

Kay started smiling and said, "Do you turn most of the animals you catch free?"

Joe replied, "Absolutely, whenever I can. I would much rather see these beautiful animals back in the wild." Continuing, Joe said, "I'm hired to live capture and release whenever possible. I only kill when it's the absolute last choice. Like the bear in Alaska. He was hunting us, and I had no other choice."

Joe saw a rest area sign. Pointing, he said, "Looks like a great place to stay tonight."

Looking up, Kay said, "Oh thank God, I'm all in."

They exited the interstate into the rest area. Joe got the pickup and camper parked. Kay and himself walk into the building looking around. Kay found a map and asked, "Where are we now and does this show where we are going?"

Joe replied, "Sorry, honey, this just shows to El Paso. We will be going west from there and then south into Mexico. I'm thinking we will cross at Douglas, Arizona." With that they headed for camper and bed.

As the eastern sky was just starting to turn red, Joe woke up. Quietly he slid out of bed, making sure Kay was still covered. He made coffee and sat watching the morning come to life. Quietly he got a cup and walked outside. Sitting in the picnic area, he watched as the desert life changed. He watched a coyote chased a rabbit across the rest area. Joe watched as the sky turned from red to pink as the morning light raced across the desert. Soon the morning doves took flight, landing in a nearby water puddle.

Soon he heard the camper door open as Kay looked out. Carefully she walked to Joe still in her nightgown and robe. Smiling, she sat down and leaned her head against his shoulder, sipping their coffee as they just sat there watching the morning come to life. Kay heard voices as she jumped up and walked quickly back to the camper. Joe shook his headed and started laughing as he walked slowly behind her. As Kay was getting dressed, Joe started making breakfast, and she walked out into the kitchen area. Joe went to get ready, and Kay finished making breakfast. Soon they had finished eating; everything was packed away, and they were headed in a westerly direction to El Paso and on to New Mexico.

Late that evening they arrived in the Superstition Mountains of southeast Arizona. Joe figured that they would spend a couple days there before going across the border. Setting up the camper and a camp for a couple of days was quick and easy. Everything was in the toy hauler and in an hour or so. Joe and Kay were relaxing, drinking a beer, sitting by the fire.

Joe started talking about the Lost Dutchman Mine and the legend of Apache gold. Both were supposedly in the Superstition Mountains of southeast Arizona. Kay asked questions, and Joe did his best to answer although he admitted that he knew very little about the possible locations of either. As they talked, they decided that they would take their side by side and go exploring.

Kay looked at Joe and said, "It just doesn't get any better than this." Taking a sip of her beer and while looking at the fire, she said, "The first time I saw you at the party, I fell in love with you. I never dreamed there was a man out there like you, and after getting to know you, I now know why I love you."

Joe took a sip and, looking at Kay, replied, "I saw you that night across the room. I knew I had to meet you and walked over to where you were standing." Laughing a little, he continued, "I didn't know those others standing there, so I just introduced myself and talked to you for a few minutes and wrote that note and left the party, praying you would call me."

Kay started laughing and said, "You never told me you didn't know them."

Joe replied, "Nope, to tell you the truth, I never thought about it again. Will not after we met anyway."

Kay looked at Joe and said, "I'm most certainly happy you had the confidence to do that."

"Confidence," Joe said. "I was scared to death. It was like a do or die, and thank God it turned out do. Or I would still be dating that idiot."

Kay sprayed her beer everywhere and started laughing. Looking at Joe, she said, "I love you. Now come on and take me to bed."

Joe stood up and threw a couple of shovels of sand on the fire, taking Kay's hand; they walked to the camper, turn out the lights.

Morning broke cool and clear in the Arizona desert. Joe was still in bed but could smell something. *What is that?* he thought. *Bacon and coffee.* His eyes snapped open. Getting out of bed, he walked up behind Kay and put one hand on her hip. The other he moved her hair and kissed her neck.

Kay turned around in his arms and said, "Keep that up and I'll burn the bacon. Besides didn't you get enough last night?"

Joe kissed her and said, "I can never get enough of you."

Kay reached back and handed Joe a cup of coffee and said, "Go take a shower. I'll have breakfast done by the time you get back here."

Joe patted her on the rump and walked toward the shower, saying, "Nice, really nice."

After breakfast Kay headed for the shower as Joe cleaned up the dishes. He was outside getting their Arctic Cat Wildcat side by side ready to go as Kay came walking out carrying two soft sided coolers. Joe looked at Kay, and without him saying a word, she answered, "Water and a few bottles of beer," then looking at the other cooler she said, "Lunch and a few snacks."

Joe took the coolers and strapped them into place and check the extra cans of gas as Kay got in and started to strap herself in. Joe buckled his safety belts and set the GPS (Global Positioning System). A GPS uses satellites to show your exact position and is accurate to within a few feet. Joe punched in the location of where they were camped. That way he could easily find his way back. Starting the engine slowly, they left the camping area and headed into the mountains.

Joe followed the Salt River for a while before turning into the mountains; the Wildcat is narrow, and he had no problem maneuvering around rocks and cactus. Finding a trail, he turned and headed uphill around a few more large rocks and over a bank. As they dropped, Kay said "Stop" as she pointed at a small opening that looked to be a cave or maybe a natural tunnel. Joe quickly backup a few feet and turned toward the cavern. Stopping, he looked around as he unbuckled himself. Checking that his Smith and Wesson 9mm was secure, he walked into the cave and out of sight. About fifteen minutes later, he walked back and said to Kay, "Come on, you are not going to believe what's through that tunnel."

Joe and Kay walked into the tunnel and came out in a beautiful mountain valley about two hundred yards wide and a half mile long. In the bottom, about a hundred feet below them, was a small pond. Together they walked to the water's edge. Joe put his hand in the water, and it was cool and fresh. Looking around, he saw a small waterfall feeding into the northeast corner. Pointing at the falls, he said, "Look over there." He reached for Kay's hand to guide her over the rocks and around the cactus.

As the got closer to the falls, Kay saw a small sand beach and pointed. They changed direction, and Joe started watching the ground, pointing out animal tracks to Kay. Deer, desert big horn sheep, and coyote tracks mostly. Kay asked, "What are these tracks?"

Joe glanced and replied, "Mountain lion."

Kay nervously touched the 9mm Smith on her belt as they walked down the beach. Joe looked up at the surrounding mountains and said, "There are no human tracks here." Looking around, he continued, "Only ours." Joe took Kay's hand again as they walked toward a couple of rocks in the shade and said, "Let's go skinny dipping?"

Kay replied, "Joe what if somebody sees us?"

Joe answered, "From where? You can't see this pond until you are in here, and there are absolutely no human tracks. There hasn't been a person in here since the last rain, and that was probably last spring."

Joe started removing his shirt. Kay looked around and started removing her clothing also as the two of them jumped into the pond. The water felt fantastic cool and clear. Kay reached for Joe and pushed him underwater; as he came up, she was trying to get to shore. Joe reached her before she got there and started pulling her toward the deeper water as Kay laughed and tried to get free.

As she thrashed and tried to get loose, she said "Don't you dare. Joe, I mean it, don't you dunk me. Joe, Joe, I mean it" as he picked her up and slowly walked deeper and deeper with her kicking and laughing. They were in nearly six feet of water, Kay's five-foot-three; as Joe let her go, she didn't feel the bottom as she sank. Grabbing onto Joe, she put her arms and legs around him.

Joe started laughing and said, "Really, now. A few minutes ago you were scared someone might see us." And looking down, he said, "Honey, really." Kay let her eyes talk as she reached up and kissed him. Slowly while still kissing her, he walked with Kay wrapped around him.

Kay felt everything and care about nothing but what Joe was doing. His slow moments brought the woman in her fully to life as a wave started to build, and with a loud cry it crashed. Building and crashing again and again. Joe slowly kept the sensation going with his movements. Kay felt wave after wave building higher and higher before the body-shuddering crash came as Joe slowly moved, and with one slow steady push, Kay cried out again as she wrapped her legs around him and pulled him in tight.

Joe's movements were what she craved, and he knew what she craved. Kay cried out, feeling the sensation build again and then crash as Joe released at the same time. Kay continued to hold Joe tight as the sweat glistened on their bodies in the warm desert sun. Joe continued to kiss her neck and move slowly as Kay held tight, enjoying the sensation only Joe could give her.

Slowly the world came back into focus as they stood up and walked back into the pool. Kay looked at Joe and started laughing as he fell over backward into the pond. Joe came back to the surface and swam to where Kay was standing; he put his arms around, and the two of them stood there totally alone in the pond, somewhere in the middle of Superstition Mountains. No one else mattered at that moment. As they walked back and started getting dressed, Joe said, "It's still early, let's go look around a little more." Kay agreed, and they headed back to their UTV.

Getting all strapped in, they were off headed deeper into the mountains. As they drove along trying to avoid the rocks and cactus, they both looked up into the mountains for anything that caught their attention. The land was barren and dry with a few exceptions like the little valley and pond that they found. Joe turned off on to a narrow trail that went up the side of the mountain they had been going around. The trail made a sharp turn and leveled off.

Stopping, he said "I'm hungry" as he undid his safety belt and got out. Grabbing the coolers, they walked into the shade of the mountain and enjoyed a quick lunch and a beer.

Kay started looking around and saw a narrow trail going up the mountain. Pointing at the trail, she said, "I wonder where that leads to."

Snickering, Joe replied, "Hopefully somewhere as fun as the last place."

Kay replied, "Oh, really."

Joe looked at her smiling and said, "Oh absolutely."

They quickly put the coolers and trash back into their UTV and headed up the trail. Nearing the top, the trail divided. Joe looked carefully at the tracks; looking around, he made a mark on a small tree and took the trail less traveled. Kay asked him about the mark on the small tree.

Joe replied, "Just a safety precaution when we come out. This country all looks the same, and I don't want to miss a turn. I have no intention of sleeping out here tonight when we have a comfortable bed in that camper."

They kept following the trail, and it came out to a sheer rock wall. Joe walked to the edge, looked over, and said, "Wow, now that's a climb."

Kay looked over the edge, and stepping back, she asked, "How far down do you think it is?"

Joe replied, "It must be two thousand feet. I'm really happy we don't have to climb down that. Although it would be fun to repel."

Kay replied, "Oh no, not for me. Not a chance."

Joe looked around and saw another trail leading off. Taking some medium-sized rocks, he made an arrow going down. Kay looked at him, smiled, and up the hill they went.

About halfway Joe heard a stiletto buzzing sound. Stopping, he told Kay to freeze and not take another step. Looking around quickly, he found a long stick. Using the stick, he pick up the four-foot rattlesnake and carefully removed it from the trail, putting it down below the bushes on the side and watched as it moved deeper into the brush.

Kay let out her breath and asked, "Was it close enough to bite me?"

Joe replied, "Yes, but I don't think it wanted to fight. It just wanted to warn us it was there."

Kay asked, "What would you have done if you couldn't find a stick?"

Joe simply said, "Tell you to step back and hope it didn't strike at you or maybe shoot it. Every situation is different, and I try to find a peaceful ending. Although I'll never let anything or anyone hurt you. Not as long as I'm alive. That was a promise I made to you before we got married." Kay looked at Joe through eyes of pure love as she reached for the only man she could ever love.

Joe looked at the sun and said, "It's time to head back. I'm sure it will be dark about the time we get to camp."

Turning, they headed downhill when Kay said, "I've been with you in the woods quite a bit. I've watched you, but until today, I never asked any questions. Let me lead as we go back. See if I can find all your trail markers to get back the Wildcat. You'll be here to make sure I'm right."

Joe replied, "That's a great idea."

They headed back down the hill; Kay was careful to check every trail to make sure she didn't miss a turn. Just as the sun was starting to get close to the mountain tops in the western sky, they arrived where they were parked.

Joe gave her a kiss as they climbed in and headed back to camp. About an hour later, they had made a large circle, and Joe drove around a rock outcropping and into their camp. Kay looked around, kind of surprised that they had left one direction and arrived back at the camp from another.

Looking around, she asked, "Didn't we leave headed that way?"

Joe replied as he opened a map, "Yes, we did. Look here, I'll show you pretty close where we were today." Joe pointed at a place on the map and said, "That valley we found is right about here. Although it isn't marked on this map. It's way too small. The steep cliff is right here. It is marked probably because it's so tall. We left there and went around this mountain." He pointed to the northwest. Continuing, he said, "Then we came back through this canyon. I want to do part of this trip again tomorrow through the canyon at off to the north."

Looking at the map, Kay replied, "That sounds like fun. I'll start supper if you want to start a fire."

Joe said, "That sounds fair. I'll be in to help shortly." He turned and walked toward the firepit.

Kay had everything nearly ready as Joe walked in. She could see the light from the fire as he opened the door. Kay handed him a couple of steaks to cook over the fire, saying, "Here's your part."

Joe smiled as he turned around and walked back to the fire. Kay joined him a few minutes later with two beers as the steaks sizzled on the grill over the fire that was burning, mostly dried mesquite.

It wasn't long and both steaks were ready. Kay went and got two plates with everything else dished up as Joe placed a perfectly grilled medium steak on her plate. They sat by the fire and enjoyed their meal and talked about where they would be doing and going the following day.

After they got everything cleaned up and put away, Joe grabbed a few more beers, and walking up to Kay, he handed one to her. She saw that the cap was still on and looked at him. Joe had always opened her bottles. He simply smiled and said, "It'll cost you a kiss." Laughing, Kay kissed him as he opened her beer. Sitting back down by the fire, Kay asked a few more questions about the following day trip into the desert.

Joe said, "I saw something on the map, and I want to go see. It looked like maybe another canyon except larger."

Kay started to smile and said, "Do you think there will be people there?"

Joe started laughing and said, "Probably not." Then with a big smile, he asked, "Why?"

Kay hit him on the shoulder and said, "Joe, that's not what I was thinking about."

Laughing, Joe replied "Yeah, sure" as he continued to rub his shoulder. Joe asked Kay if she wanted another beer.

She replied, "No, hon, I think I want a nice, soft bed."

Joe got up and threw a couple shovels of sand on the fire, turning around he said, "Now that's the best offer I've had since noon."

Kay started laughing and said, "It had be the only offer you've had since noon."

With a smirk on his face, Joe put his arm around her, pulled her close, kissed her, and said, "It's the only offer I'll ever want or need." Kay smiled and snuggled up a little closer as they walk to the camper.

Morning broke with beautiful red sky as Joe and Kay sat outside, enjoying the sunrise and the peace and tranquility of a beautiful desert sunrise. Everything was ready from the night before, and as soon as they were done eating breakfast, together they walk toward the UTV. Joe patted Kay's backside as she got into the passenger seat. Looking up, she smiled and said, "You like that, don't you?"

Joe simply nodded his head as he started to buckle himself in. Then he pushed the button, and with a roar from the 1000cc motor, they headed for the mountains on a northwest heading.

It was a little after ten when Joe stopped at the top of a large hill. Looking at the map, he nodded as he pointed to the northeast and said, "I believe it's over that way."

Turning the wheel slightly, he headed down a steep bank and across a flat plateau toward a large pile of broken boulders. Driving around the large mound of jagged broken rocks, Kay asked, "How would something like that happen?"

Looking at the rocks, Joe replied, "Earthquake, landslide. This area was once covered by a large inland sea. All that's left now is the Great Salt Lake in Utah."

Kay looked at the pile of rocks as Joe dropped over a bank and headed downhill again. Then she yelled, "Joe, stop. Stop!"

As Joe slowed and stopped, Kay was pointing at an opening in the cliff wall behind them and off to the left. Joe hit the gas, and with a spinning of tires and spraying of rocks and gravel, they headed for the bank.

Stopping at the cave entrance, Joe looked around as he climbed out of the Wildcat. Walking into the cave, he was back in a few minutes. Looking at Kay, he said, "It's a cave, and it goes back a long way. What are you wearing for boots?"

Kay pulled up her pant leg, and Joe said, "Oh, good. There may be snakes in there. You have good, heavy leather boots on." Opening a tool box, he grabbed two maglites and several reels of heavy braided line, something close to the fishing line although it was much stronger. Tying the loose end to the Wildcat, they walked into the cavern. Joe let the reel of line unroll as they walked.

Kay stopped and was looking around when she grabbed Joe's arms and nervously said, "Joe, Joe what is the red line, it seems to be following us."

Joe replied, "It's a safety line that glows in the dark. Just in case these lights go dead, we can still find our way out."

They kept walking forward, finding tunnels that branch of and ended or branched again. Joe would shine a light or whistle and listen for the echo return. As they moved through the underground maze, suddenly he stopped. Standing still for a minute, he lit a match and watched as air movement flickered the flame. "This way," he said as he slowly and carefully started forward again.

Stopping every time, he came to a split of a tunnel that branched off. He would light a match and watch the flame movement. Carefully he kept moving into the slight breeze. After several matches were lit, he could see sliver of light ahead. Stopping, he said "Honey, turn off your light" as he switched his off. It went totally black other than a very faint light ahead. Switching his light on, he asked, "Did you see that?"

Kay replied, "Yes, Joe, I did. Does that mean there's light in front of us? Could it be some kind of an exit?"

Joe looked back at Kay and said, "There is definitely a light ahead, and, yes, hopefully a way out." Looking at the reel of string that he had been letting out, he said, "This reel is nearly empty, and it the last one I have. I think we have come about three miles underground. The florescent part of this stuff last for a few hours. I'm sure it will be dead before we get headed back although we can still follow it back if we have to." Together they started moving forward again.

Stopping, Joe said, "Okay, now we have a problem. We just ran out of string. We either turn around now and follow this out, or we go forward and hope there's a way out. I think I can find this spot again." Joe turned, and shining his light on the back trail, the string started to glow. "Look," he said. "It's glowing. If I hang this here around this rock, I think it will glow if we hit it with the lights."

Kay asked, "What about your GPS?"

Joe replied, "We are underground, it needs to pick up a satellite to work." Again he turned forward and switched off his light. Kay immediately did the same. Switching on the light, he asked Kay, "Honey, do you trust me?"

Kay replied, "Oh absolutely."

Joe said, "No, honey, do you trust me with your life? If I'm wrong and we don't find that string, we could very possibly die in here."

Kay looked into the eyes of the man she loved and said, "I know we could, but I also know you have saved my life more than once. As long as you are alive, I know I'll be okay. So, yes, Joe I do."

Smiling, Joe kissed her and said, "Okay, let's go." He started forward, switching his light off every couple of minutes to make sure that there was still a light up ahead. As the light got brighter, Joe turned off his light and put it in his pack; they came around a corner and both stopped dead still. They were standing in a huge underground cavern. There was a large lake along with trees and grass growing.

Joe walked to the water's edge and dipped his hand. Putting a small amount in his mouth, he said, "It's a little warm, but it's fresh."

Kay stood there just looking around. There was a large crack in the ceiling that let in water, light, and seeds. Joe walked over toward the wall and looked up. He said, "It's probably a three maybe four hundred foot climb, and I don't think you could free climb that. Maybe I should say I won't let you free climb this. Let's walk around in here and see if something looks like a way out." Joe picked up rocks, sticks, everything he could find to make a marker right in front of the tunnel they came through, making sure that he could find it again.

Kay found a log to sit on and rest. Joe walked over and sat down next to her. Looking at him she asked, "If I wasn't with you, would you climb out of here?" She turned and looked at the rock wall leading to the crack where the light was coming in.

Joe looked at it again and said, "I would think about it. Although I would look for the best and safest route. If I wasn't absolutely sure, I wouldn't take the chance. If I fall alone, no one would ever find me here. It would be a very painful way to die if I didn't die instantly."

Looking around again, Kay asked, "Are you sure you can get us out of here?"

Joe replied, "Yes, I've marked the tunnel that leads back to our safety line and that will lead us out of here. That safety line has a breaking strength of one hundred pounds."

Looking around, Kay said, "So are we going to look around this subterranean wonderland?"

Joe reached for her hand as he stood up. Looking around, he saw a few things that he can use to get back to this area, and they start walking down toward the underground lake. With stunted trees and grass growing, it truly is a wonderland. The moisture has formed calcium deposits and brought out the colors of the minerals. Red, orange, and blue streaks run down or along the rocks, and that water has a blueish green tint.

Joe turned and walked up to a place in the cliff, faced and ran his hand across the rock wall. Turning to Kay, he said, "If I'm not mistaken, this is gold," looking to his right, "and I think that's silver."

Kay replied, "Gold, are you sure?"

Joe looked again, taking out his knife, he answered with a smile, "Oh absolutely, and this is a rich vain."

Kay looked at him and said, "Rich! Really? Like how rich?"

Joe looked around a little more and replied, "Really rich, and I'm sure this is public land. I think after we do the job in Mexico, we should come back here and check if we can file a claim." Looking at the ground, he shone his light, and the gold sparkled back at him. "Kay," he said, "Kay, look. OMG, Kay, honey, look. There could be thousands here." Looking around again, he said, "I think we can come back in through that crack in the ceiling."

Joe reached down and scooped up some of the dirt on the ground containing the gold specs. Walking down to the water, he carefully moved his hand as the dust and dirt were washed away. Standing and turning at the same time, he said, "Kay, could you pick out the larger rocks?"

Kay carefully picked out the rocks, and Joe put his hands back in the water and started to move them, watching as the light sand washed away, leaving some black sand and several specs of gold dust.

Looking at Kay, he said, "I probably lost most of what I had in my hand, but there is a lot of gold here. Let's get out of here and file a claim if we can."

With that Joe careful poured the contents of what was in his hand into a plastic bag that he had in his backpack. Together they walked to another log and ate another sandwich and drank a bottle of water. Kay placed the empty bags and bottles in her backpack as Joe looked around. Again he looked at the cliff that reached the opening in the ceiling.

Standing up, he walked a short distance and, looking again, he said, "There's a shelf up there. If we can get to that, I think we can walk out."

Kay looked at the cliff and said, "Joe, let's go through the tunnel back. After that trip into the Bob Marshal area in Montana, I really don't want to climb out of here."

Joe turned and looked at his wife. He could see in her wilting and how scared she was. Reaching out, he gently pulled her against his chest and held her for a minute, saying, "I promise you I would never let anything hurt you. Remember when I said that before we were married."

Kay slowly nodded her head as she held on to Joe. Standing together for another couple of minutes, they slowly turned at the same time and headed for the tunnel that would lead them back to the surface and sunshine. About twenty minutes into the tunnel, Joe knew something was wrong. He had not found their lifeline yet. He knew they were in the correct tunnel; stopping, he shut off his light and looked around. No red line that lead to the outside. Trying not to look worried and turned to look at Kay, he said, "I haven't seen any of the red line. Have you?"

Kay replied, "No, I haven't."

Turning, Joe continued down the tunnel until he came to the first place where the tunnels split. He knew that if he made a mistake they would be lost forever in this maze, and it would only be a miracle if they found their way out.

Standing there, Joe turned to Kay and said, "Honey, I think we have a problem. I know we are in the correct tunnel, but I haven't found our lifeline yet. I don't think I can find our way out of here. I figured that we would just follow that line out. I think we had better turn back and go to the lake and think this over."

Kay replied, "I'll follow you wherever you go and do what you ask or say." With that they were soon back in the large cavern containing the lake.

Joe kept looking at the wall and said, "Help me find firewood. I think we are going to spend the night here and figure out how to get out of here tomorrow."

As they gathered dry wood, Kay asked, "How does this wood get in here? There are not enough trees in here to produce this much."

Joe replied, "More than likely during the spring and fall rains. It comes in with the flood waters that formed that lake. As they evaporates, the wood is left behind. I haven't seen one human print in here. With all the turns, a twist, and branch tunnels, only a very experienced in tunnel rat would come in here. There is a very strong possibility that no one has ever seen this cavern."

Soon they had enough firewood to keep a small fire going all night. Joe got a fire going and soon was going through both backpacks. Anything that was not needed or empty was placed in a pile to be burned later.

They had a light dinner and soon were relaxing against a log watching the fire. Kay asked, "Are you nervous about getting out of here?"

Joe replied, "No not at all. I know I can climb that." He pointed at the cliff. Continuing, he said, "I just don't want you to. In the morning we will look for another way out before we climb out."

They sat there listening to the sounds of the night. They could hear the yips of a coyote and other desert night life. Joe took the two space blankets and placing one on the ground. Then he placed their backpacks for pillows and covered up with the other space blanket and were soon sleeping.

Joe woke before it was light out. He took his canteen, put a coupe scoops of coffee in it, and placed it on the fire. Kay woke up as she felt Joe slide back in next to her. He handed her a cup of camp coffee, and they watched as the light slowly started down the western side of the cavern.

As the light was slowly traveling through the cavern, Joe saw something that excited him. It looked like a better way out. Pointing, he said, "That looks like it goes to the opening in the roof. I think we had better look at that before we try to climb out." Kay sat and looked, trying to see what Joe thought he saw. She sipped her coffee as she watched the transformation of this amazing underground world change.

They had a very small breakfast, eating the last of their food they had packed for a day trip. Joe threw all the waste that would burn into the fire and made sure it was totally gone. He turn slightly and looked at Kay. He could see the worry in her eyes. He had promised to always protect her, and where they were now would test that promise.

She saw Joe looking at her, and a large smile came to her instantly. Joe stood up and walked over to her and said, "We are in a bad spot. But I promise you, I'll figure a way out of here."

She held him just a little tighter and placed her head against his chest. There she could hear the heartbeat of a man that loved her more than his own life. Looking up, she went up on her tiptoes and kissed him, long and tender. The kind of kiss that could have put them back on the blanket.

Joe leaned back and looked at Kay. The look in her eyes had change to one of trust and love. Taking her hand, they headed to the area where he thought there could be an easier way out. As they started to climb, in just a few minutes, Joe could tell that Kay would never make those last part, but he thought, *Maybe we should get to the top to make sure there wasn't something else.*

As they reach the point that he knew he would never let Kay climb, he looked around. The last forty feet was impossible. To free climb, that would be suicidal. It was past vertical, and there was one point where you would be hanging from your hand holds. He wasn't sure if he would even try that with climbing gear. Still looking around, he saw absolutely nothing else. *Well*, he thought, *I guess it's a climb on that damn cliff.* As he walked around a rock outcropping, he saw a narrow ledge going up and out of sight.

Looking at Kay, he said, "Honey, I'm going to check this out. Hopefully we can go through there. Wait here and I'll be right back." Joe turned and disappeared up the narrow ledge. Kay found a place to sit down and wait. Looking around, she heard Joe as he walked around the corner.

Walking up to her with a smile, he said, "I think we can get out that way. It's really tight, and I'm sure you're going to squeeze your boobs, but the choice is to either squeeze boobs or to climb that rock cliff."

Kay turned and looked across the cavern at the cliff, turning with a huge smile and said, "I hope you'll kiss all my sore spots. Come on let's go I wanna shower."

Joe took both backpacks. Taking the gold sample out, he put it in his pocket. Then he tied them to his belt with enough rope so he could still move and drag them behind. They headed up the ledge and started into the crack. Kay looked up and could see light ahead.

Joe said, "You go first so I don't kick things loose. The last thing we need to have something fall on you. Also I'm dragging these backpacks, but if they get stuck, I'll cut them loose that might cause you a problem. When you reach the top, stick your head out, but if you can safely get out, wait for me."

About halfway up Kay said, "You were absolutely right. I'm squishing my boobs, and they are sore."

Joe started laughing and said, "Good, I can't wait to kiss them and make you feel better."

About that time the backpacks got lodged. Joe pulled and kicked the rope, but they were stuck. Taking out his knife, with one quick movement, the packs were cut loose.

Joe caught up to Kay as she crawled out of the crack which was in a ravine coming down the side of a mountain. Joe was just seconds behind her as she stood up and looked around. It was very steep but looked like they could get down without too much trouble.

Joe made a pile of rocks that everyone could tell was man made. Then he took a picture. As they descended the side of the mountain, Joe kept look looking for something familiar. Soon he saw what he thought was the outcropping near where they had gone in. Changing direction, they kept moving.

Kay saw it first and said, "Hey, look over there. Isn't that our Wildcat?" Joe looked where Kay was pointing, and changing directions again, he slid down the side of the mountain until they reached a spot that they could stand up and walk.

As they approached the Wildcat, Joe could see the safety line trailing off and knew what had happened. A deer or possibly a goat came through and took it with them as it ran off. Thinking to himself that stupid mistake could have cost both of them their lives.

He looked around, he made another rock pile right next to the entry to the cave. He then took another picture. Turning, he took a deep breath as he slid in behind the wheel. He hit a few spots on the touch screen of the GPS, and looking at Kay, he said, "I think those two rock piles should be sufficient enough to file a mineral claim. I've lock our location in the GPS so we can get back here. Although we will have climbing equipment so we can get out of that nightmare easier."

Smiling at Kay, he flipped the switch and pushed the button. Slowly he looked at the GPS and touched the screen. The location of their camp turned green. Looking at Kay, he pressed down on the gas pedal, and slowly they headed for the camp. After they both got showers, Joe got a fire going while Kay made a quick dinner. As they ate, they talked about their trip into the underground cavern.

Joe said, "I made a major mistake that will never happen again from now on. If I ever go underground again, I'll map it as I go. I've used a lifeline like that before. This time it could have been fatal." As he talked, his eyes filled with tears; he wasn't scared for his life, he had put Kay's life in danger. The kind of danger that could have been fatal. That was something that could never happen again.

Kay got up and walked behind him. Wrapping her arms around, she held him as they talked. She told him that she never once doubted that he wouldn't get them out alive. That he was the best at what he did. She said, "There isn't another man on earth that could stay calm in the face of danger like you and always come up with a solution that would work." Then she started to slowly turn him in her arms and kissed him, not romantically but lovingly, and held on as they started again to sway in time to a song only in their minds.

Joe held on tight, slowly he looked at Kay. Smiling she kissed him again and said, "You are nothing short of amazing. You carried me off a mountain in Alaska that saved my life. Then a few months later, you brought me safely out of the wilderness with a broken arm and a huge gash cut in your leg. It was your knowledge of the outdoors that made that snow cave that kept us alive during that blizzard."

Kissing him again, she said, "And now it was your eyesight that saw that ledge and the fact you were smart enough not to try and find our way through that underground tunnel maze. I never once doubted the fact that you would get us out." Continuing, she said, "At first when Steve started calling you a mountain man, I was pissed, but as I thought about it, you are exactly that, and if you were living two hundred years ago, that's what you would be."

Joe smiled and kissed her; holding on to his wife, he thought, *She is amazing along with being beautiful. How can a mountain man end up with such a fantastic lady?*

Joe kissed her again and said, "Should we head for Mexico tomorrow?"

Kay replied, "I'll follow you where you go. That's all I want or will ever want."

Joe replied, "Before we leave, I think we should go into town and see about filing a mineral claim."

Kay looked at him and said, "Gold?"

Joe's face broke into a huge grin and said, "Yep, that's what it is!" Kissing him again, Kay took his hand and lead him to the toy hauler and bed.

Kay's hand started slowly sliding down Joe's stomach. Joe cupped Kay's chin as he kissed her. She whispered, "I thought you were going to kiss all my sore spots."

Joe carefully pulled her closer as he kissed her. Letting his hands start to wander. Kay's breathing started to change as he found her sore spots. Kay could feel as the wave started, peaked, and exploded with a feel of euphoria. Joe's hands and lips were everywhere at one time.

Kay reached and pulled him up as she started kissing him with all the passion she had. She loved him like she could never love anyone. Joe carefully cradled the back of her head as he kissed her. Kay felt another wave start; it broke with enough intensity for her to cry out. As soon as that wave broke, another started. She felt it as Joe's rhythm changed, and as the wave broke, she felt Joe release.

With her arms still wrapped around him, she kissed and held onto him, not letting him move. Whispering, she said, "I don't think you missed one sore spot, and I really do feel a lot better." Joe continued to kiss her neck and throat. Slowly he slid to the side, and the two fell asleep wrapped in each other's arms.

Morning came sooner than Kay wanted as she slowly started waking up. Turning slightly, she saw Joe staring out the window. She could smell the fantastic aroma of fresh brewed coffee. She sat up on one shoulder.

Joe heard her start to move. Looking, he picked up the extra cup he had gotten out a few minutes before, and filling it, he brought it to her. Kay reached for the cup, and she saw Joe's upper chest. Gasping she asked, "Did that happen in the cave?"

Looking down, Joe said, "Yes, on the crawl out. It was tighter than I thought."

Kay touched the black and blue marks on Joe's chest and asked, "Do they hurt?"

Joe smiled as he replied, "Only when I breathe." Standing up, he said, "I'll start breakfast while you get a shower."

Kay asked, "How about you? Do you want a shower?"

Joe turned and looked at her, saying, "I took one a couple of hours ago. I woke up early and couldn't get back to sleep."

Kay asked, "Are you that sore?"

Joe looked over his shoulder at her, saying, "No, hon, I just have a strange feeling. Don't ask me what, but there is something about to go wrong."

Kay walked out into the desert sun; looking around, she saw Joe packing everything away. Looking up he said, "I think we are nearly ready to go."

Kay walked up to him and said, "How's your chest?"

Joe looked at her, gave her a thumbs up, and said, "I'm good, honey. Really, don't worry. Walk around here with me and make sure we don't leave anything but tire tracks."

With everything cleaned up, Kay filled the travel mugs with coffee, and they headed for town to see about filing a mineral claim. After stopping at three places, they finally found the right office after providing pictures and the GPS location; all the paperwork was complete. Joe asked how long they had to produce a sample and how long that sample was good before they had to start working the claim.

Getting all the information he needed, he went back to the camper and brought in his small sample. The man looked and said, "This is sufficient enough to hold the claim for year." With that they signed the last of the paperwork.

As they walk to the pickup, Kay slid her hand into Joe's, looked at him, and said, "Do we really have a gold mine?"

Joe smiled as he replied, "Yes, we do, and where it's at a lot of work to get the," looking around he whispered, "gold out." Kissing her, he opened her door. Walking around, he climbed into the pickup. Smiling, he said, "You know, honey, I bet it will be a lot of fun to spend part of year in that cavern with you." He put the pickup in gear, and they headed for Mexico.

As they approached the border, they stopped at the US side. Joe and Kay talked to US immigration and customs, telling them what they were going to do. They also should customs all the paperwork they had from the Mexican government. They filled out and filed everything they needed to make coming back across easier.

With all the paperwork done and their copies in hand, they headed for the Mexican side. With all the paperwork they had from the Mexican government, crossing was a breeze, and in less than two hours from start to finish, Joe put the pickup in gear and they headed south into the Sonoran Desert of north central Mexico.

Looking at the directions they had, there was a paved highway that went south. They traveled south until they came to a fork in the road. Joe pushed the button and converted to kilometers, turning left onto a dirt road. He looked at Kay and said, "I hope these directions are correct or at least close."

Punching a few buttons on the GPS, they headed down the dirt road deeper into a beautiful desert landscape. Kay was thoroughly enjoying herself as she looked around and took pictures, rock formations, mountains, and canyons were spectacular.

As soon as they had traveled forty kilometers, Joe said, "Watch for a dirt road turning left and says here, it's hard to see but noticeable if you're going slow."

Joe saw the road about the same time Kay noticed a narrow two-lane track heading up into the hills. She pointed and said, "Could that be it?"

Joe slowed the pickup and stopped, looking at the directions again plus the map that Hector had sent with the other paperwork. Joe looked at Kay and said, "I'm not totally sure." Backing up a short distance, he said as he made a left turn onto the road, "If it's not, I hope we can find a place to turn around."

The road twisted and turned up then down for eighty kilometers or fifty miles; as they drove the scenery got better and better. The canyon lands of this desert were remarkable. Kay looked, tried to see everything at one time, and her phone flashed picture after picture as they drove.

Every time the road forked, Joe checked the directions and the map. Plus he put a waypoint in the GPS. This made sure that he could get back to the paved road. Finally early in the evening, they came to the village. As they stopped, people started gathering around.

Kay asked, "Is it always like this?"

Joe replied, "Usually, these small villages very seldom get visitors. And they have no idea what the outside world looks like." As he looked around, he added, "This is their life."

A man walked up and introduced himself. "Hi, I'm Father Tom," he said in perfect English, "I'm the priest here at the Catholic Church and mission."

Joe shook his hand and introduced Kay. As they talked, Joe found out that the cats had killed another goat the night before and scared the young man watching them. The dogs had scared the cats off or he may have been attacked.

Joe asked, "Where was the herd had been that night? Where they were now?"

After getting all the information he could, a plan had started forming. Joe was sure at this point that it was an old female with only one cub. Mountain lions generally have two or three cubs every year or two. Although there was a possibility that she had more and only one survived, the mortality rate is extremely high.

Joe told the priest what the plan was and that he would be live trapping the cats. His instructions were to live trap and take them out of the area and turn them loose.

Father Tom said, "Just, please, get them out of here." Then he said that the people here were extremely poor and it took all everything they had just to survive. Joe looked around and could tell that it was a very poor village.

Looking at Kay, he motioned toward the pickup, and they headed southeast toward the river that ran out of the mountains.

They found a place that offered a flat area plus shade from the overhanging cliffs where the river made a bend. After setting up the camper and unhooking the pickup and unloading some of the equipment he would need, he grabbed a pistol and a shovel and walked to the river. Digging a hole about ten feet from the water line, it soon started filling with fresh, clean water. Taking a small pump, he started filling two five gallon cans. Getting them back to camp, he set up a filter system that would clean all the sand and silt out of the water.

Then he got a propane fired burner to boil the water. As the water cooled, he transferred it to a large holding tank. Kay brought out a couple of beers, and they worked together, and in a few hours, they had a couple hundred gallons of fresh, clean, safe water. After they had finished getting everything set up for their stay, they walked back to the river to clean up.

Kay started supper as Joe walked around, picking up all the wood he could find. As he walked around a rock outcropping, he saw a huge pile of drift wood.

Breaking off all he could carry. he headed back to camp. Kay had supper done as Joe finished building a fire. He said, "There's a large pile of drift wood just around that corner. Tomorrow we should be able to get enough for several evening fires."

The following morning Joe was up early, wanting to get the wood before the sun got a chance to warm up the area. After cutting wood for a few hours, Joe was ready for a swim and some relaxing. As he started the fire, Kay brought him a beer. Joe sat back in a camp chair and slowly drank his beer, watching Kay as she walked to the river. Standing up, he followed her and sat on the bank as she walked in to rinse off, and cool down.

As the sun set, the evening was absolutely beautiful. The temps dropped and the fire was just right. They talked about the cats and what the plan was. Joe said, "I think I'll start scouting the area tomorrow and see if I can find where those two troublemakers are hanging out. Then I'll set up the traps the next day, and hopefully they would have the cats caught in the next day or so."

Kay asked, "Why does the government want them caught and relocated somewhere? Wouldn't it be cheaper to shoot them?"

Joe replied, "With the rise in trophy hunting and their opponents like the Sierra Club and Greenpeace, these cats and other animals are carefully monitored to try and keep both sides happy. It's always better to live trap and relocate than to kill the animals. The government makes big money off of licenses and trophy fees. Not to mention the money hunters spend hiring guides and outfitters. A cat hunt in Mexico cost between $4,000.00 for a desert hunt and upwards of $8,000.00 for a jungle hunt by the time everything is paid for." Continuing, he added, "That does not include transportation to or from the hunting area. Or hotels and food for the day before and after. After a successful hunt, there is a fee to ship your animal or animals plus the cost of mounting. So hunting pumps millions of dollars into the economy every year."

Joe paused for a minute, and Kay looked at him, saying, "You've hunted and been a guide most of your life. There are a few mounts in our home, but I'm sure you have shot a lot more than that."

Joe smiled as he replied, "Yes, I have, but I hunt mostly because I love the outdoors. The unbelievable beauty of the places I've been and things I've seen. When I'm hunting, I'm hunting for enjoyment or say for us. I spend more time exploring than actually hunting." Continuing, he said, "Like what we have found in Arizona last week. There are hundreds maybe thousands of places like that. Mother natural or Mother Earth is beautiful mistress, and once she has control of you, you'll spend all the time you can exploring her beauty."

Kay smiled as she watched Joe, he was absolutely right. The more he talked the more excited he get. She had only a few trips with him, yet she had had witnessed firsthand some of what he was talking about. Alaska, Montana, and Arizona were all beautiful in a different way. Alaska and Montana for the rugged beauty of the mountains. Then the picturesque beauty of meadows and glaciers plus other areas that the state offered.

Kay closed her eyes and pictured Alaska and Montana. Opening her eyes she looked the beauty that Mexico offered. *So much like Arizona*, she thought. Almost like a lunar-like landscape of the desert floor contrasted against the cliffs, rock formations, and riverbeds of the canyon lands of Mexico.

Sitting there, she started shaking slightly as she pictured the plane crashing into the side of the mountain. She heard herself scream as Joe reached for her and held her. Looking into his eyes, she reached up and kissed him, saying, "I'm sorry, I just started thinking about the plane crash in Alaska again."

Joe held her until the tears stopped and her breathing was back to normal. Looking up, Kay said, "I haven't thought about that in months. I guess all this talk about where and what you have seen and now what we have seen together."

Kay started calming down as the tears slowed and stopped. Joe took her hand and together they walked back to where the camp chairs were sitting. Then he walked to the camper and got them a couple bottles of beer. Handing one to Kay, he sat down. Looking into her eyes, he said, "I promise that as long as I'm breathing, you'll never go through anything like that again. I'll always protect you."

Kay took a sip and replied, "I know you'll protect me. That's one thing I've always know." Then Kay asked, "Do you ever run into those anti-hunting groups?"

Joe smiled and said, "Oh sure, a couple of times." Looking at the sky, he said, "I absolutely believe in a lot of what they say and stand for. That's why I always try and relocate when possible. Killing an animal is absolutely the last resort." Pausing he looked at the sky again then said, "If at all possible, I'll never let anyone that's with me be harmed or injured. That grizzly that I killed in Alaska, well it was either him or us, and in that case, well anyway if it's in my power, we will always walk away."

Kay sat there and thought about Alaska and what Joe had done. Many people said that he had done the impossible. When Joe would hear that, he would simply reply, "My wife was up there. Any man would do the same thing."

Kay finished her beer, and standing up, she walked toward the river. Joe watched her walk a few feet and got up and followed. Kay got to the water's edge and turned, looking at Joe, she asked, "Can we swim here?"

Joe smiled and said "Oh absolutely," as he removed his shirt and pants and walked into the river.

Kay was in her bra and panties just a few seconds later and followed him in. Joe gave her a hug as he slipped underwater and out of sight, coming back up a few feet away. Swimming back to Kay, he picked her up and carried her toward the shore. All of a sudden both him and Kay disappeared as Joe stepped into a hole.

Kay came up first and was trying to fight the current as Joe got to her. Calmly he said, "Kay, honey, I've got you. Look, Kay, look at me." Joe was standing up with the water only to his waist. Kay got her legs under her and stood up.

Laughing, she said, "Note to self, deep hole near swimming area." Joe started laughing as he took her hand, and together they walked to the camper.

*****

Kay woke up and reached for Joe. Feeling his side of the bed was cool, she looked around. Joe was sitting at the table in the dark drinking coffee. She slowly slid out of bed and walked up behind him. Putting her arms around him from behind, she asked, "Joe, what's wrong? You have been up early every morning."

Reaching up and touching her hands, he smiled, saying, "I just want to get this job done and head for home or at least back to Arizona."

Kay asked, "Is there something bothering you?"

Joe replied, "I don't know. I've had a strange feeling since we got here. Although everyone and everything seems to be fantastic."

Kay said, "You had been on edge since we got out of that cave."

Joe turned looking into her eyes and said, "That was a really dump mistake that could have killed both of us."

Kay kissed him and said, "Maybe, but it didn't, we got out and everything turned out great. Plus we have a gold claim."

Joe smiled, saying, "Yeah, yes, we do, and it looks to be a really rich one at that."

Getting up, Kay started breakfast while Joe stared into space. Turning slightly, he smiled as he watched Kay cooking in her night gown. *Wow*, he thought, *how does a guy from the Pennsylvania mountains meet someone like her?*

Standing up, Joe started getting everything he would be needing to find the cats and setting the live traps. As he packed he would sneak a peek at Kay who was sneaking a peek at him. Every now and then they would glance at each other at the same time. This would bring smiles as their eyes made contact.

Joe was laying what he took out of the hidden storage area on the bed. Pistol and rifle, ammunition, along with binoculars and a spotting scope.

Kay called "Hey, honey, breakfast is ready" as she sat bacon and eggs, panfried potatoes with green peppers and onions, along with another cup of coffee. They sat there eating and talking about the two cats and what the plan for the day was.

Joe put the rifle in the UTV and tightened the Velcro straps. Kay buckled in as Joe programed in the camp position and hit the starter. They headed south deeper into the desert and canyon lands of Mexico. After spending all morning looking for sign, Joe and Kay found a spot that offered them some shade.

Stopping, Kay grab a couple of sandwiches and two bottles of water. Relaxing against a rock, Joe said, "I really like this area. It's really pretty." Looking around, he continued, "Wish we were just playing and not looking for a couple of troublemakers."

Kay replied, "Well let's catch those two and spend a week exploring."

Joe winked at her as he got up and walked to the Wildcat. Looking around, he pointed and said, "Up there. Let's see if we can get up there?"

Kay looked up and said, "I hope you mean drive because I'm not climbing that."

Joe started laughing and replied, "Where's your exploring curiosity?"

Kay looked up again and said, "I think I left it in the camper."

Joe punched the starter, and they headed out trying to find a path or trail that would take them to the top of the cliff. A few hours later, they parked the UTV and looked out over the desert valley with a green ribbon twisting through the center.

Kay said, "Oh, Joe, that has to be one the most beautiful sights I have ever seen."

Joe handed Kay the binoculars and said, "Look over there and tell me what do you see?"

Kay focused the binoculars and asked, "Where? What am I looking for?"

Joe replied, "About halfway up that hillside, there is a rock out-cropping. Look just to the right in the shade."

Kay kept looking and said, "It looks like a tan colored rock. OMG, it moved." Lowering the binoculars and turning to Joe, she asked, "Now tell me. How did you see that?"

Joe just smiled and said, "You can read through a manuscript and see what will sell and what won't. Me well, I can spend hours looking through binoculars looking for something that doesn't fit in the area. Once I see what I need to, then the work starts. Tomorrow I'll bring the traps here and try and catch those two troublemakers."

Kay asked, "Will that take long?"

Looking, Joe asked, "To set the traps? Or catch them?"

Kay replied, "Both, setting the traps and catching the cats."

They got up and started walking back toward the Wildcat. Joe said, "A couple of hours to set the traps and catching the cats. Well that depends on the cats. If they are smart or wise to traps, it could take weeks to catch them."

The ride back to camp was fun once they were off the mountain. Joe cut across the valley floor. That way they could see the mountains on both sides. Kay took pictures as they weaved back and forth through between and around cactus, rocks, and other vegetation. Arriving back at the camper, Kay started supper while Joe got the traps ready.

Joe talked about and described where and how he would set the traps the next morning. After everything was cleaned up, they walked back to the river and took a swim, rinsing off the dust from the day trip into the desert. Holding hands, they walked back to the camp and sat by the fire as they enjoyed a cold beer.

Kay got up and kissed Joe; turning, she headed for the camper and looked over her shoulder. "I think it's bedtime," she said with a very seductive smile. Joe threw some sand on the fire and followed her to the camper.

Morning broke to the sound and aroma of Kay making breakfast. Joe slowly got out of bed and quietly walked up behind her. Brushing her hair to the side, he kissed her neck and pulled her back against himself. Kay tipped her head to the side as Joe nibbled and kissed his way up and down her neck.

They started talking about where Joe would place the traps as they ate. While Kay was cleaning up, Joe went and started getting the equipment loaded for what he wanted to get done that day.

Kay walked out of the camper and asked, "Do you want me to come with you, or can I stay here and clean the camper?"

Joe said, "Stay here, I should only be gone a couple of hours." Taking the .22-250, he slid it into the travel boot, kissed Kay, and headed out.

As Joe left, Kay went into the camper and slipped into a pair of shorts and a tank top. She looked at the camper, trying to decide on where to start. Filling a bucket with water, she started in the kitchen area. A little while later with only the floor left, she looked at the water in the bucket. Then her arms and legs, she decided she needed clean water.

She poured out the water as she walked toward the river. Walking in up to her knees, she rinsed off her arms and legs, filled the bucket, turned, and headed back to the camper. She heard someone coming.

Thinking it was Joe, she sat down in the shade. A large man walked around the camper. Kay slowly stood up and politely said, "Hi, I'm Kay, my husband Joe is here to catch the two mountain lions that are scaring the people in that village over there." She pointed in the direction of the little town and mission.

The man just looked at Kay and smiled. Kay didn't like the way he was looking at her. She felt like she was suddenly on display. Turning, she slowly walked toward the camper. Just as another guy came walking around the corner, Kay made a break for the camper door. He reached out and grabbed her. He pinned her arms against her sides. Kay kicked and screamed as the man lifted her clear of the ground. As she thrashed around, four more guys showed up in two jeeps. Kay kicked out and caught the fat guy in the nuts. She was slapped and thrown to the ground for her effort while everyone was trying to help the fat man back to his feet.

Kay took that momentary distraction and again to tried to get into the camper. One of the guys saw her as she made a break for it. He caught her by the hair and yanked her backward. She landed hard as her top half had stopped and started going backward while the bottom half was still trying to go forward.

Kay looked up as the fat man reached down and pulled to her feet. He backhanded her a couple of times and let her go. Kay dropped to the ground, holding her cheek. Finally all six guys grabbed her, tying her hands her behind her back. They loaded her into one of the jeeps and headed southeast.

Joe had been headed back when he saw something was going on. Backing up quickly to get out of sight, he then climbed to the top of a small hill. He carefully crawled to a spot where he could watch the goings-on from about four hundred yards away and above the valley floor. As he watched through the scope, he saw the guy caught Kay by the hair. His finger tightened on the trigger and then backed off.

He knew at this range that he could kill three maybe four but not all six. The gun only held five shots, and Joe was sure that one of those animals would hurt or maybe even kill Kay. Joe continued to watch through the scope as the fat guy hit Kay, knocking her to the ground. The crosshairs of the scope were on his throat. It took everything Joe not to kill that asshole right there and then although he made a promise that man would die.

Looking at every guy there, he remembered their faces and swore that they would all pay. They would pay with their lives for what they had just done. Joe's finger tightened on the trigger several more times before Kay was tied up and they all left.

Joe slid backward from the cliff's edge where his worst nightmare had come true. This had to be the most terrifying sight he had ever seen. Looking at the Remington 700 BDL, he cussed; if he would have had his AR-15, all six of those guys would be dead or wounded. Joe quickly loaded up and was in camp fifteen minutes later. Looking at the tracks, he quickly ran inside.

They had found the extra guns they had brought but not the ammunition. Joe grabbed a couple of boxes of 9mm and all the .22-250 ammo and started following their tracks. About four hours later, Joe lay on top of another cliff. watching as Kay was roughly pushed into an old, wooden building. Watching carefully, Joe tried to figure out how many people were there. He guessed about thirty to maybe forty.

Joe sat there watching until dark. Slowly he backed away from the cliff and walked to where the UTV was parked. Joe punched a couple buttons on the GPS, checking his location while actually marking Kay's location.

He left the area as carefully and slowly as possible. Trying not to make any more noise than he had to, using the moonlight to see his way around, through, or over the rocks and cactus.

Finally he found what he was looking for. A small canyon he had seen in the map. It was a box canyon, meaning there's only one way in or out. No one could surprise him, but if discovered, it meant he would have to fight his way out. Although it would be easy to defend if he was discovered. No one could get behind him or above him because of the overhanging cliff walls.

Joe built a small fire that was sheltered from sight by all the rocks and the changing angles of the cliff wall directly behind him. Laying there, Joe kept trying to figure out a way to get Kay without a gun fight. He didn't want to kill anyone although he would kill every one of them if he had to. He knew he would do what he had to, to ensure that Kay was safe and alive.

He lay there thinking about Kay. Sleep just wouldn't come. Looking through his phone, he found Hector's number. He looked at his watch, *four in the morning*, he thought. *I need to get a few hours of sleep to keep thinking clear.* He kept seeing that fat guy that hit Kay. He had placed the crosshairs on his forehead and felt his finger tightening on the trigger. Joe swore under his breath. That man would die. He swore that if she is hurt in any way, they would all die.

Joe woke up with a jerk that the asshole had hit Kay again. Looking around, he took a deep breath. *Wow*, he thought, *I must have been dreaming.* He lay there thinking. *How can I get her out safe? Who can I get that can survive here and also do what they have to?* Reaching to his left, he felt the cold steel of his 9mm. The eastern sky was just starting to lighten. Joe looked at the cliff wall, he could see the Remington leaning against the rock where he had placed it the night before along with two boxes of ammo.

While lying there, he mentally made a list of who he could call. He knew he needed help. This was Mexico. Who besides Hector could he trust? Could he trust Hector? Joe sat there thinking as he waited for the coffee to finish. He could smell the aroma as it perked in the old-style coffee pot. He slid a few more pieces of wood into the fire below the old pot. Carefully he poured the first cup. He inhaled the aroma before taking the first sip.

Joe watched as the shadows raced across the canyon. Reaching over, he jacked a shell into the chamber of the Remington and slid one more into the magazine. Looking at his phone, he had service. Quickly he dialed the number for Hector. A lady answered. He quickly asked for Hector. She asked him to hold a few minutes. When she came back, he was informed that no one named Hector worked in that department.

Joe asked, "Are you sure? I'm looking Hector Ortiz. He gave me this number plus he called me from this number a few times."

The lady said, "I'm sorry, sir, but, yes, I am. If it's the Hector I'm thinking of, he's a wanted man."

He swore under his breath then asked, "Can I speak to the supervisor or whoever was in charge?"

A man came on, saying, "Hello, I'm Pedro. How can I help you?"

Joe explained who he was and what he was hired to do and where.

Pedro replied, "I'm sorry, sir, but we've had no reports of trouble in that area, and I'm the guy who would be hiring someone." Continuing, he added, "I know who you are, but again I didn't hire you." Pausing for a moment, he then said, "We caught one of the guys from Hector gang working here. He may be the connection between Hector and yourself."

Joe replied, "How long again did you catch him? I was hired and partially paid about a month ago. Plus Hector called me this from number. He also gave it to my wife for me to reach him."

Pedro replied, "This is secondary backup number. Plus we figured out who was passing on the information to Hector a few weeks ago. He's now awaiting trial and is still in jail."

They talked for a few more minutes before disconnecting.

Picking up his coffee again, Joe thought, *Okay, Hector doesn't work there. Plus he's wanted. There was a spy in that office, must have seen the complaint and headed it off.*

Joe sat there thinking and sipping his coffee. *So now what do I do? Can I get Kay safely? Alone? No! I need help but who?*

As he sat there staring at his coffee cup, only one name came to mind. "Logan! Yes!" Joe said out loud, "Logan!"

Joe slowly got up, looking around. Stretching, he opened his phone and found Logan's number. They had gotten together several times since the hunting trip, and Logan had traveled to Illinois for the wedding.

Pushing the button, he called. Logan answered on the first ring, saying, "Wow, hey, Joe I was talking about you yesterday."

They talked for a few minutes, then Joe said, "Hey, buddy, I'm in trouble." He started at the beginning, explaining what had happened after they arrived in Mexico, including what he had seen the day before, where he was then, and what he needed.

Logan never hesitated for a minute. He simply said, "We will load up now and be on the way today."

Joe said, "I'll go back to the camper and send you the directions I have and the map."

Logan replied, "I'll be watching for them. Hey, Joe, see you sometime late tomorrow or the following morning."

Joe answered, "I'll meet you in the village. I think we can trust the priest there. Oh, and hey, Logan, thanks, man. I didn't know what to do, and you are the only one I know that I would trust when it comes to Kay."

Logan swallowed hard and said, "That's what true friends do. They help at the darkest of times. So they can laugh in the best of times. See you soon, buddy. See you soon."

Joe replied, "Thanks again, Logan. You have no idea what this means to me."

They discontinued and Logan called to Rene.

Logan and Rene

Disconnecting, Logan gave Rene the short story and said, "I'm going to be gone for a few days. Maybe a few weeks."

Rene replied, "Kay is my best friend ever, and there is absolutely no way you are going without me."

Logan said, "This is going to be dangerous, and I don't want you there."

Rene spun on her heel and said, "You are not going without me. She may need a woman when you two are done killing people, and I'm going! There is no more discussion on this." She walked out the door to start packing.

Logan smiled, thinking *Wow, okay, I guess I lost this one. I just hope all four of us come home alive* as he followed her upstairs.

Rene turned, looked at Logan, and said, "Go load the horses and tell Jarred what's going on and what to do while we are gone. I'll pack and meet you down at the pickup in an hour."

Logan headed back down the stairs as Rene called out, "Hey, what guns do you want to bring? Oh, and I'll grab all the papers we need to bring the horses across the border."

Logan said, "Your 9mm and my .44, also plenty of ammo. Plus all four of the AR-15 and lots of ammo, everything we have. Oh, and also that Remington 700, the one in .308 with the long-range scope that I bought last year. We can stop and get more on our way out of town if needed." Continuing, "We are also going to need groceries. We can stop and get them at the same time."

In less than an hour, Logan, Rene, CJ, and Star were ready to go. Logan had grab two extra horses the best he had on the ranch plus the tack he would need. Logan walked into the storage shed, and looking around, he grabbed a medium-sized box and a small box marked EXPLOSIVES. Taking them to the trailer, he carefully put them in a special hidden storage compartment; latching the door, he placed everything back where it should be.

Logan pulled the pickup and trailer up by the house. Rene started to carry the luggage out and handed him the two pistols and rifles. Within a few more minutes, they headed south to Mexico and the coming fight to hopefully save Kay from a fate worse than death.

Logan slid the .44 between his seat and the center counsel in the pickup. He had put the rifles in a storage area under the bed in the camper part of the trailer. Looking at Rene, he said, "Please, stay home. From what Joe said, this could be dangerous or even deadly, and I don't want anything to happen to you."

Rene looked at him and replied, "Kay is my best friend, and there is no way I'm not going. Besides she might need a woman's touch. Although I promise to do what you or Joe say when we get there. But I'm warning you right now, try leave me somewhere, I'll follow you. I'm going to be there for Kay if she needs me, come hell or high water."

Logan smiled as he dropped onto the interstate and headed south. Glancing at Rene, he thought, *That's my girl. Hard headed and stubborn as a mule. As loyal as CJ and so very, very loving.* Reaching for her hand, he said, "It's going to be a long day. We have a long trip ahead, and I want to be there tomorrow."

Rene filled his coffee cup and as she handed it to him, she said, "Let me know if you want me to drive for a while. You can lay down and take a nap." Continuing, she said, "I would much rather drive during the daylight. This thing still makes me nervous at night."

Logan replied, "You can drive after we stop for fuel in Casper, from there south it's pretty open and just a few small hills."

Rene reached over and kissed him as she thought, *He would do absolutely anything for Joe. I hope we all come out of this alive. Logan said Joe sounded really scared, and he doesn't scare easily.*

Rene filled the thermos and grabbed twenty boxes of .223 and twenty boxes of .308 ammo, paying for everything plus the fuel; she walked back to the pickup. Logan walked to the passenger door and got in. Rene handed him the bag as she climbed in behind the wheel.

He looked at her and smiled, thinking, *She's absolutely unbelievable gorgeous and a fantastic memory. She remembered that my AR-15 was in .308.*

Rene flipped on the turn signal as she dropped onto I-25; stepping on the throttle, she headed south toward Denver and Mexico.

Logan reclined the passenger side seat and had fallen asleep listening to the easy rock station playing on the radio. They eased their way south, and Logan woke up as she started to slow down to get fuel just south of Cheyenne, Wyoming.

While Logan filled the tank, Rene filled the thermos. Walking back to the pickup, she said, "They don't sell ammo here, do you think we will need any more?"

Logan replied, "I'll look later tonight or tomorrow. We can get it in New Mexico or Arizona before we cross into Mexico."

Rene replied, "I'll dive to Denver then it's your turn. I don't really want to drive in that traffic." Logan smiled as he reclined his seat.

Just north of Denver, Rene started slowing down to exit for fuel. Logan woke as she pulled into a fuel stop. She looked over and said "Hi, honey, I think it's your turn" as she shut off the engine.

Logan asked, "Where are we?"

Rene replied, "Just north of Denver, sleepyhead."

"Wow," Logan said, "I slept four hours?"

"Yep," said Rene. "You most certainly did."

Logan filled the fuel tank as Rene filled the thermos and paid for everything. Climbing back into the pickup, she asked," Where do you want to eat?"

Logan looked around and said, "There's a truck stop in Denver. How about there?"

Rene smiled as she answered, "Sounds good." Adding, "I'm starving."

Logan started laughing. "Yeah, me too. I've been so busy I forget to feed you."

Laughing as she looked at him, Rene replied, "Yeah, sleeping." She reached over and kissed him.

Logan put his arm around Rene as they walk across the parking lot. They left the truck stop and dropped onto the interstate.

About halfway through Denver, Rene asked, "Where are we going to stop to feed and water the horses?"

Logan replied, "There's a rest area south of Colorado Springs, we can stop there."

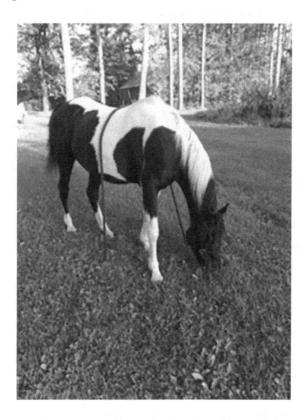

Rene smiled as she said, "About how long till we get there? They have been in that trailer for over ten hours." Logan said, "Oh, about another hour, maybe less."

Just under an hour later, they pulled into the rest area. Logan opened the trailer and brought out the two ranch horses—Buck, named for his buckskin color, and Lefty for his white sock on left front leg. He tied them to the trailer.

Rene lead CJ and Star out. Logan unsnapped the lead ropes and turned them loose. CJ pranced off tail and head high, followed closely by Star; stopping in the grass, they both started to graze.

Rene grabbed hay and grain for Buck and Lefty while Logan filled a couple of water buckets. Buck and Lefty drank their fill and went back to eating as CJ and Star returned to get water. After they finished drinking, CJ tipped over his bucket as Logan walked around the trailer.

Shaking his head, Logan called out, "Hey, you damn pest." This caused CJ to start his show as he pranced around, breaking into a gallop. There were people starting to watch as CJ put on his show then stopping to look at Logan.

Logan walked toward CJ and raised his hand, causing CJ to rear up on his hind legs and paw in the air. He came down and pranced away, stopping by a young girl who carefully reach out to pet him.

Logan walked over and asked "Would you like to ride him?" looking at her parents who nodded. This brought a huge smile as Logan picked her up and carefully set her on CJ's back. Logan looked at him and said, "Be good, no goofing around." CJ walked away, made a huge circle, and came back, stopping beside Logan.

There were a few other kids by now, and Rene whistled for Star, who came at a gallop, stopping at her side. Logan and Rene took turns lifting kids onto CJ and Star while talking to parents who took turns petting both horses.

One guy asked, "How long does it take to train a horse like that?"

Logan replied, "Depends on the horse. Horses are like people, some are naturally smart." He nodded at CJ. "He's about four. I got him, he was under a year. He's very smart and also a show-off. He absolutely loves attention and knows what buttons to push to get it."

CJ had wandered off. Logan whistled and called out, "Hey, get back here."

CJ walked over and put his nose under Logan's arm as Logan started to scratch his ears. Logan and Rene stood there talking to parents and asking CJ and Star questions. CJ and Star would either nod or shake their heads accordingly. About an hour later, it was time to load up and hit the road.

Logan snapped a lead rope into CJ then told CJ and Star to get in the trailer. Star reached over, took the lead rope in her teeth. The two horses walked across the parking lot and into the trailer. Rene led Buck and Lefty in and closed the back door.

As she walked around the trailer, Logan reached for her and gave her a hug. Rene went up on her toes to kiss him. Climbing into the pickup, she filled his coffee cup. As he reached for it, she pulled it away smiling. Logan laughed as he kissed her again. She handed him the cup and filled hers. Most everyone watched as they loaded the horses and got ready to go, waving as they drove past.

Logan looked at Rene and said, "That was fun. I think they enjoyed watching and riding."

Rene replied, "Oh absolutely, and I think the parents would have like to have ridden also."

Frowning, Logan stepped on the throttle and they headed for Mexico. Kay was in trouble and Joe needed help, and help was on the way.

Kay's Captivity

Kay sat with her back against the wall. She was tied with her hands behind her back, and her legs were tired in such a way that allowed her to walk in very short steps. She was allowed to move around the room she was in but not outside. Kay continuously looked at the mountains that surrounded the small camp. She sat there looking out the window.

Suddenly she heard something. Was someone coming? *Yes*, she thought. Looking around, she quickly lay down to fake sleep. It had worked once before.

The man walked in and kicked her, saying, "Hey, up the boss wants to see you."

Kay started trying to get up, slipping once she fell down. The guard reached down and grabbed her by the hair, helping her to her feet. Taking out a knife, he walked around her, looking her up and down in such a way that made her very nervous. Kay tried to smile and started backing away. The man grabbed her arm and cut the ropes tying her hands.

Then he said "Follow me, and if you try and run, you'll regret it in a hurry" as he looked at her chest.

Kay wanted to cover herself better, but she stood perfectly still, hopping the act of bravery would fool the guy. He grabbed her by the arm and led her out the door and down the row of ramshackle buildings that looked like they would all cave in most any minute.

Stopping, he opened a door and shoved her inside. With her legs still tied, Kay lost her balance and fell hard. He reached down and roughly helped her back up and pushed her forward again. Kay saw a large tub full of water as the guy removed the ropes tying her legs.

He looked at her and said, "Clean yourself up. Hector wants you clean." Kay walked over to the tub and started slowly washing her arms and hands. The man said, "I mean take a bath!"

Slowly Kay turned and looked at him, saying, "Not with you in here, I'm not."

The man smiled and said, "I've been nice to you, the others won't be." He turned and walked away.

Kay looked around, trying to find a way out. Not so much as a window. She also wanted to clean up, but she wasn't about to remove her clothing with all these asses a round. So she stepped onto the tub, clothes and all. A few minutes later, a girl came in with clean clothes for her to put on. The girl was young and pretty. But she had a faraway look in her eyes.

She handed Kay the clean clothes and said, "Put these on, and if you know what's good for you, don't make any trouble."

Kay looked at her. Slowly she reached and turned her arm. Kay replied, "OMG, what did they do to you?"

The girl replied, "Heroin and that, that is the nice things they do."

Then turning, she walked out. Kay looked around and put the dress on over her wet clothes and followed her. Three men were standing just outside as she walked through the door.

One looked at Kay and said, "Hello, Kay, I'm Hector Ortiz." Kay stopped in her tracks. He continued, saying, "Yes, that was me that contacted you. Now listen very carefully because I'm not going to say this again. We are going to have a lot of fun, you and I, if your husband doesn't do exactly what I say." Slowly he looked Kay up and down several times and said, "I hope he doesn't."

Kay's eyes went to the young lady standing off to the side. The same young lady that had given her the clothing a few minutes before.

Hector walked forward with a syringe in his hand. Reaching for her arm, the girl jerked it away. Hector backhanded her hard and roughly, pushed the needle into her arm. Kay watched in horror as the girl's eyes unfocused, and she sat down on the bed. She slowly started removing her clothing. Then slowly she lay down.

Kay stood there in terror, waiting to see what would happen next. Suddenly the door opened, and one of the guys she had seen outside walked in. He walked to Hector as he looked at Kay, saying, "What one?"

Hector replied, "Her, over there." He pointed toward the girl on the bed. The man walked to the bed, and looking at her, he said, "I would rather buy the one standing by you." He looked at Kay.

Hector answered, "She's not for sale yet." Smiling, he looked at Kay. "Although when she is, I'll let you know. She's going to be in high demand. I'm sure she'll go quite high at the auction."

Kay watched as the guy started removing his clothing and said, "I'm sure Joe will do whatever you say." The man crawled into the bed next to the girl and lay down.

Hector looked at Kay with the syringe in his hand and said, "I have one for you also. So we are going to make a video, and you are going to be the star." Taking her by the arm, he led her into another room where there was another bed.

Telling her to sit down, he said, "There is a paper next to you. I've written what I want you to say. Read it a few times." Making sure she would get it right the first time, he put a syringe down on the table and picked up his phone and placed it in a holder. Kay picked up the paper and started to read out loud.

Kay read the message several times, and just before he turned on the video, he slapped her hard enough to cause her lip to bleed and tore her dress so it looked like she may have been raped.

Kay started to talk, saying, "Joe, they have me, and this is what you have to do. They said if you want me back and not a heroin junky sold into the sex trade, then follow these instructions to the letter. Get $500,000.00 in US and go south of town. Ten miles you'll come to a river crossing. From there you'll cross the river on foot, and they will see you. They will be watching. You have five days to comply to this message. If you are not there on the morning of the sixth day, I will be on my way to another country addicted to heroin." Kay looked at the camera again and said, "Hector said he was quite sure there will be a lot of guys very happy to meet me. You have five days. They will be watching for you the morning of the sixth from today."

Kay made the video perfectly. She was done talking and telling Joe what he had to do. Then with the phone still recording, Hector stepped into the picture and gave Kay a shot. Kay jerked her arm away and sat down on the bed, looking at the trickle of blood running down her arm and waiting for the drug to start working.

With tears running down her face, she looked up at the camera and said, "I'm so sorry, Joe. Please, hurry." As soon as they were done, Hector walked into the other room and filmed the young lady and the man for a few seconds.

Walking back to Kay, he asked, "What's Joe's cell number?"

Kay replied, "314-555-1212."

Hector entered the number and pushed send. Looking at Kay, he said, "That was just saline solution. If Joe don't comply or if he tries anything else, the next one will be enough to get you hooked, and you'll do anything we ask to get it."

Kay jumped off the bed and punched Hector hard enough to cut his lip. Grabbing him by the hair, she kicked him several times as he tried to protect himself from a lady gone wild. Hector screamed as Kay dug her fingernails into his face, upper arms, and neck. She also landed blow after blow and several well-placed kicks.

The door flew open as three of the drug runners busted into the building. Going into the wrong room first gave Kaya few extra seconds. She continued to kick and punch and gouge Hector, tearing, punching and kicking continually. A few seconds later, two of the guys got a hold of her and pulled her away, kicking and screaming as she called him every rotten name she could lay her tongue to. She also managed to connect a few blows on the guys pulling her off Hector.

When they finally got her under control. Hector backhanded her hard, knocking to the floor. Kay lay there, faking unconsciousness as Hector wiped the blood from his mouth and nose.

He looked at her laying on the ground and kicked her, saying, "When she wakes up, bring her to me."

Two guys grabbed her by the arms and dragged her to the building she was being held in. Pulling her to the middle of the room, they dropped her, walking out and locking the door.

Kay lay there, rubbing her cheek where Hector had hit her. Looking at her fingernails she saw chunks of skin and blood. Smiling, she thought, *He may have won, but he definitely knows I was there.*

A few hours later, two guys came and got Kay. As she stood in front of Hector, she could see the damage she had done. Hector's face and arms had scratches, huge gouge marks where she had scratched and tore at his face and arms.

Hector stared at Kay, saying, "If you try something like that again, I'll torture you to the point you'll pray to die. Then it'll get worse. There are five hundred thousand reasons you are still alive. And those are the only reason. Try that again and all the money in the world won't matter."

Kay stood there listening to Hector when she saw a reflection on the top of the hill. She knew what that was. Someone was up there watching. Trying not to smile, she looked away. *Joe,* she thought. She knew it was him. She had watched him trail a wounded animal with no more than a few blades of bent grass. She knew he could trail her and them to this place. Carefully she looked around, trying to notice if anyone else saw the flash. It seemed that everyone was watching and listening to Hector and never noticed. Kay decided that she had better stop causing trouble and give Joe a day or so to make a plan come together.

Hector looked at Kay again and said, "You have six days, and now I'm hoping he does something stupid just so I can have you before I sell you to someone in Asia."

Kay swallowed several times. Now she was scared; she had heard about sex trafficking and thought that would be worse than death. Looking at the top of the hill again, she prayed that Joe was watching, and as she stood there, she was hoping to hear the angry sound of a bullet while praying she wouldn't.

Finally Hector said, "Lock the stupid bitch up, we have work to do."

One guy grabbed her by the arm and took her back to the same building again. Pushing her inside, he locked the door and returned to where everyone else was waiting.

Joe's Plan

Joe looked at his phone after talking to Logan. He knew Logan would be there sometime late tomorrow or the following morning. He also knew that Logan would show up with a small armory. Thinking of what he needed to do, he headed back to the camper to move back to the village. Joe just threw everything in the trailer and loaded the Wildcat; in about twenty minutes, he was on the move.

Arriving at the village, the priest was the first one there. Joe told him what had happened and that his contact didn't work for the government anymore and that it sounded like he never did.

The priest said, "I'm sorry to say this, but you probably can't trust anyone. Please, don't say anything to anyone in the village." Then he looked at Joe and said, "I hate to say this, my son, but the men that took your wife are probably drug runners, and they will sell her to a human trafficker." Joe swore under his breath as the priest said, "I will pray for her safe return and for your safety also."

Joe looked at the priest and replied, "Father, you had better pray for them also because I will get Kay back." He turned and walked out the door.

Sleep was a long time coming for Joe as he lay there and started planning what and how he would get Kay back. He was sure that Logan would come heavily armed and those men would pay for this, and if she was hurt or harmed in any way, they would pay dearly.

Joe was up and gone early. The first thing was to check the traps. He brought the tranquilizer gun, also hoping that he would need it. Stopping a few hundred yards away, he looked through the

114

binoculars to see if the trap was still set. One looked like that the door was down. As he approached, he heard a low snarling coming from the trap. Looking inside, he saw a fairly good size mountain lion. Smiling, he said, "Good morning, beautiful, you are going to take a nap and be really pissed when you wake up."

Joe filled a dart and shot the cat in the right hind leg muscle. The big cat was out in a few minutes, and Joe carefully loaded the trap onto the trailer and headed back to the village.

Talking to the priest, he asked, "Where can I keep her until I catch the other one? She needs to be in a dark area with fresh air. Oh, and tell everyone to stay away."

The priest replied, "I have just the spot. Let's put her in the back of the church. We can go through the back door, and no one ever goes back there."

After the cat was safely inside the church, Joe said, "Father, please, stay away. If she gets a chance, she will bite or attack you. Mostly because she's just as scared as you are." Continuing, he said, "I'll feed and take care of her until I catch the other one. Oh, and one more thing, Father, where can I find some rattlesnakes?"

The priest looked at Joe with a puzzled look and said, "I don't think I want to know what you are up to but snakes over by the corn storage. There are always some in that area. They hunt the mice."

Joe smiled and shook the priest's hand and said, "It's probably better you don't know." He turned and walked out the door. Joe stopped by the camper; looking around, he said to no one, "I need a sack." Looking around, he found a small cooler and thought, *This will work.* He grabbed a steel hook he used to open and close the hitch on the pickup. Smiling, he got in the Wildcat and headed to the corn storage area.

A couple of hours later, he had three rattlesnakes. Getting back to the camper, he found a larger cooler and got some ice out of the freezer. Putting the snakes inside along with the ice, he closed the lid and said, "There, that will cool them down and make them just a little less mad."

Wrapping a strap around the cooler to secure the lid then opening the drain, he put it under the camper and went to check on the cat. The priest met him at the door and said, "Our guest in the cage is still sleeping, I think. I walked past and didn't hear a thing."

Joe replied, "Good, the longer she sleeps the better. I'll be back in a few hours. I'm going to check and see if my luck keeps up today."

Joe headed back into the mountains to see if the other trap had a new guest. He stopped a few hundred yards away and could see that the door was still up. Looking at his watch, he thought, *Maybe I should go see what's going on at the idiot camp.*

As he headed that way, he worked the action on the Remington and check his pistol. Parking the Wildcat about a mile away, he headed for the hill where he watched from the day before. Joe lay there for nearly an hour before he saw Kay. One of the guys had her by the arm and was moving her from one building to another. Joe zeroed the scope on the man's head and moved his finger away from the trigger. Watching, he swore, "If she's hurt or one of you guys touch her, you'll all die." Carefully he slid backward off the hill and headed back to the UTV.

Arriving back at the church, he saw the priest. Joe looked and could tell that the cat was awake just from the look on his face. Joe walked up as the priest said, "Your guest is awake and in a very bad mood."

Joe replied, "Yes, I'm sure she has a terrible headache. It's a side effect of being tranquilized." Walking into the church, he opened a small door and slid in a couple pieces of fresh meat. The cat snarled and stayed near the back side of the cage. Joe then slid in a pan of water and walked out.

Looking across the church, he headed to where the priest was working and said, "Thank you, Father, for your help today. I'll see you in the morning."

The priest said, "My name is Tom."

Joe smiled and stuck out his hand, saying, "Thank you, Father Tom."

Tom took the hand and said, "You are most welcome, my son."

Joe stood there for a few seconds looking at Father Tom. He could tell that there was more to this man than just the church. Smiling, he turned and headed for the camper.

*****

Morning came way too early as Joe spent most of the night thinking about Kay. He saw a message flashing and opened it to see Kay standing next to a bed. Tears started flowing down his face as the message played. When Hector stepped in and gave her the shot, Joe went beyond mad. A calm, cool feeling came over him as the plan to get Kay back came clear, he had five days.

Joe had seen the video and knew what he had to do. He lay on the hilltop. Carefully he watched everything that happened below. He had seen when Kay looked straight at him. He knew she had seen a flash of light off the barrel or scope lens. Carefully he took a handful of sand and let it trickle on the barrel and scope. Looking through the scope, he slowly started to squeeze the trigger then let it go. He swore that they would all die, some fast, but the fat guy would die slow and very painfully.

Joe zeroed to scope on the fat man's knee. He could picture in his mind as he slowly squeezed the trigger. The fat guy would drop to the ground, clutching his knee. It would be pain beyond pain. He thought about the 50-grain bullet as it tore through the knee, destroying bone and cartilage as it busted the kneecap and joint. He smiled, he knew that shot would come. Joe moved the scope to another guy as she grabbed Kay by the arm. Placing the scope on the guy's forehead, he watched as Kay was taken to the same building again.

Joe continued to watch what was going on in the camp. Making mental notes on where everything was and what parts he wanted to destroy if possible. He had figured out where everyone slept and ate also what building the drugs were stored. What day they came in from down south.

A few hours later, he carefully slid backward away from the hilltop and headed back to the Wildcat and the village.

Friends to the End

Late that evening Logan and Rene arrived at customs. With all the paperwork in hand, they were in and out in an hour. About noon the following day, they arrived in the little village. Father Tom walked out to meet them. Logan walked over and introduced himself and Rene.

Shaking Father Tom's hand, he asked, "I'm supposed to meet a friend here." Looking at Joe and Kay's camper, he said, "Have you seen either Joe and Kay?" Not knowing how much Joe had told him.

Father Tom replied, "Aww yes, Joe. He should be back anytime, he left about two hours ago to check a trap."

Logan pulled the pickup and trailer over by Joe's, and together they unloaded the horses so they could eat. Next they started setting up the camper part. Noticing that Joe's pickup was hooked up, Logan left the truck hook to the trailer and grabbed a bale of hay for the horses.

Rene started making dinner as Logan checked on the horses. Turning CJ loose, he played with the beautiful stallion. CJ absolutely loved to perform for Logan. It was a friendship bound that crossed all boundaries and limitations. CJ had proven his love for Logan the evening that the mountain lion had attacked. CJ had the herd stallion instinct, and Logan was part of his herd.

Logan would raise his hand, and CJ would rear up on his hind legs and paw at the air. Logan would wave his arm in a circle, and CJ would start canter around the same direction; if Logan changed directions, CJ would change. Logan would run up behind CJ and jump, placing his hands on CJ's rump and land on his back. If Logan pointed right, CJ would sidestep to the right. If he pointed left, CJ would sidestep left. If he walked at him with his arms out, CJ would walk backward. When Logan put one hand on his nose and the other on the top of his neck near his shoulders and push back gently, CJ would lay down.

Then Logan could lay down next to him or on his back, and CJ would stay there. If Logan said up, the stallion would get up even if Logan was on his back. As Logan worked with CJ, everyone that lived in the village started watching, and before long, there was an audience of about one hundred people. They would clap and cheer every time CJ did a trick. Some of the younger children had worked their way to the front of the crowd, and before long, Logan had also turned Star loose. Soon both horses were doing tricks. The *owws* and *awws* from the people that lived in the village.

Father Tom stood in the door of the church, also watching the show. He was the first to see Joe coming back and knew that the show was about to be over. Joe parked the Wildcat and walked to where Father Tom was standing. Looking at Father Tom, he asked, "How long have they been here?"

Father Tom replied, "A few hours. Looking at Joe, he asked, "Is there going to be trouble?"

Joe looked away and said, "Yes, I'm sure there will be." He handed the priest his phone.

Father Tom watched the video and looked at Joe, saying, "I'll pray she's okay and you get her back safe."

Joe looked away then he turned to the priest and said, "I think you had better pray for them because in a few days—" Joe stopped as he looked at Logan who had just seen him standing next to the priest. Joe said "Well anyway" as he walked toward Logan.

The two men shook hands and hugged each other. Father Tom saw the friendship bound between them and immediately understood what was about to happen.

Logan looked at Star and CJ and said, "Go to bed." Star took CJ's lead rope in her mouth and lead him toward the trailer. CJ looked back at Logan as he followed Star into the trailer.

Rene saw Joe and ran at him. Joe caught her as she jumped toward him, hugging him as she cried. Joe said, "Come on, you two, let's go for a walk."

As they got by the corn storage area, Joe saw three more rattlesnakes. He said, "Hey, watch them." He ran back to the trailer, getting his snake hook and a small cooler. In a few minutes, he had all three snakes in the cooler and kept looking for more as they walked and talked about what's was happening and what the plan was. Logan smiled as Joe laid out his idea for getting Kay back.

Getting back to the trailer, he put the three new snakes in with the six he had already caught along with more ice. Closing the lid on the cooler again, he put the strap around it and pushed it under the trailer.

Joe walked into the trailer and got three bottles of beer. Sitting down, he finished telling Logan and Rene what he had planned so far and then asked, "So what do you think?" Waiting for a couple of minutes, he asked, "Do either of you have any ideas?"

Joe looked at the weather forecast and saw that severe storms were forecasted for the following night and next day. Joe looked at Logan and said, "When the storms hit, we go and get everything set up. If everything goes just a little right, Kay will be leaving with us."

Logan got up and said, "I'll be right back."

A few minutes later he walked in with a case of dynamite and blasting caps. Putting it down on the table again, he walked away and came back with two AR-15 and several boxes of ammunition. Putting them down, he said, "I think we should all stay together if they know we are here or decide to try and get to us before we get to them. It would be better to be together."

Joe looked at Logan and then at Rene and said, "That sounds like a really great idea." With that the three of them settled in for the evening.

Morning came, and Joe wasn't the first one up although he could smell the rich aroma of fresh brewed coffee as he saw Rene sitting at the table. Joe slowly slid out of bed; getting dressed, he poured a cup and sat down with her. Rene said, "Logan's feeding the horses, and I'm just kind of keeping an eye on him."

Joe walked outside and told Logan that he was going to go check the trap. He really wanted that second lion. That would complete the plan he had. One mad lion was good while a lioness with a cub would be absolutely fantastic. She would be protective and aggressive. Continuing, he said, "I know she would do most anything to protect that cub."

Gabbing his pistol and the Remington, he headed for the Wildcat. Logan stopped him by handing him an AR-15 in .308 caliber. Joe looked at Logan and said, "Thanks, buddy. You have no idea how much I wanted one of these the day Kay was taken. At four hundred yards, all six of those guys would have died and Kay would still be here with me."

Logan slapped him on the back and said, "Your plan is perfect, and it's going to work. This time tomorrow, Kay will have her arms wrapped around you, and we will all be back in Arizona having a beer and talking about this nightmare."

It Begins

Together they walked back into the camper. They watched as Joe picked up his phone and checked the weather. Joe looked up smiling and said, "Looks like the storm is developing in the southwest. I'm sure tonight is a go." Turning he said, "I'm going to go check that last trap and bring it back here. After we get Kay, we are leaving, and I'll have all this stuff loaded so we can go."

Logan said, "I'll go with you."

Joe replied, "Absolutely not. That's how they got Kay. You stay here and protect Rene and the rest of our stuff. I'll be back in a few hours." Joe slid into the Wildcat and headed south out of town.

In about thirty minutes, he was looking at the trap. The door was down. Parking, he started walking toward the trap. He could hear the cat snarling inside as he approached. Looking through the vision hole, he saw the second lion. Joe loaded a dart, and in a few minutes, the cat was taking a nap. Loading everything, he headed back to camp.

As he came into camp, he saw Logan, and headed that way, he said, "I need your help. I need to figure out how much to give both these cats so they wake up tomorrow about five am, just in time to help if something goes wrong and we have to fight our way out. After that I want to see if we can find another snake or two. I think the more the merrier when it comes to them helping us."

Logan started laughing and said, "I totally agree."

Father Tom walked in as Joe and Logan started weighing the cub. Joe took the weight, looked at the chart, and subtracted the amount he had already injected. Looking at Logan, he smiled and said, "Let's have them wake up say around four in the morning, that way they should be totally awake and have a terrible headache so they are really grumpy if anything goes wrong and we need them."

Logan started laughing, saying, "I would hate to open a door and have two mad and scared mountain lions looking at me."

Joe chuckled as he replied, "Let's not forget our rattling friends. I think we should place four or five outside the doors of the two buildings where everyone sleeps. Better yet, if it's really bad out, I'll put a few inside the buildings."

Tom asked, "Is there anything I can do to help?"

Logan looked at Joe and said, "I think we might need someone to take both pickups and trailers back across the border. We can go cross-country on the horses to make it difficult for them to follow us."

Father Tom replied, "I think I can arrange that. There are a few people here I trust." Continuing, he said, "Do you have extra keys?"

Both Joe and Logan said, "Yes we do."

Then Father Tom replied, "Then please let me do that. I'll put them both the public parking area just north of customs."

Joe looked at Father Tom and said, "I've been watching you. The way you walk and act tells me you are a lot more than a priest."

Tom looked around and replied, "I was once. That was a long time ago."

Logan looked at Tom and said, "Okay, spill it, Father."

Tom just smiled and said, "Patience, my son, in time."

Joe looked at him and said, "You've had military training." It wasn't a question.

Tom smiled and said, "Yes, army special forces. So I'll get your campers out of here." Then he opened a map and said, "Take this with you. I'll show you a way out of here. It has all known streams or natural springs marked. I'm sure you four on horseback can go although it will be nearly impossible for anyone to follow you in a vehicle."

*****

He walked over to the cage where the second lion was and opened the vision door. Aiming the tranquilizer gun, he fired, hitting the lioness in the rear leg muscle again. She snarled and lunged at Joe. Stepping back, he said, "She must remember the headache she had last time. She's a little on the grumpy side already."

Weighing her, he did the math and gave her the second injection. Carefully they put both lions back into the cage. Joe looked at Logan and Father Tom and said, "Let's go snake hunting."

They walked along, talking about the plan to get Kay back as they looked for rattlers. Finally Father Tom stopped and looked around.

Joe said, "I have something I want you to see. There is a very good chance we will have to fight our way out after getting Kay tonight or tomorrow morning."

Handing Tom his phone, he pushed play. Father Tom watched the video; closing his eyes, he said, "Okay, listen, you two, and, please, don't repeat anything you are about to hear." Looking around, Father Tom said, "I've only been partially honest with you. I'm actually DEA, and we have been trying to catch Hector on the US side of the border. If you two kill him tomorrow, it will save US taxpayers the cost of feeding that slime ball, and I don't think anyone would care if he died. He is one very evil person. Besides transporting heroin, he also deals in human trafficking. There are warrants for him and most of his helpers although they are only good in the US. He's been able to get back here every time."

Joe looked at Logan then at Tom and said, "I'm sure he's going to die tomorrow. He injected Kay with something plus he's hit her several times. On that video, he also injected that young lady, so if I get a chance, I'll kill him."

Tom replied, "I'm sure no one in the US would give it a second thought."

Logan looked at Joe and then at Tom and said, "Say a prayer for us and consider Hector in the past tense."

As they talked, they managed to catch four more of their little rattling buddies. Logan said, "With these plus the eight we already have."

Joe said, "This should give those idiots another nice surprise."

Logan looked at Joe and said, "God, I hope you are never pissed at me. You, my friend, are a master at getting even."

Joe looked up smiling as he put the last snake back in the cooler along with a bag of ice. Leaving the lid open, he hooked the largest snake and placed it on the ground. Looking at his watch, he timed how long it took for the snake to start warming up to where it started to move on its own.

Looking at Logan, he said, "Okay, it takes about an hour in the sunlight, so I'm guessing about two hours tonight, maybe just a little longer." Hooking the snake, he dropped it back in the cooler and closed the lid. "That should be about perfect."

Joe checked the weather again and said, "Hey, Logan, tonight is a go. That storm should get here about eleven tonight. So we should leave here around two thirty so we can be leaving there about sunrise."

Logan said, "Let's get everything put together and then try a get a few hours' sleep. We need to be sharp if we have to fight our way out."

Joe smiled and said, "All I want is Kay, but I really hope that fat guy shows up. I've never wanted to hurt someone the way I want to hurt him, and a bullet is way too fast. That asshole gave Kay a shot of something and then hitting her. He needs to be taught a lesson. He's into human trafficking. He's going to die very slowly. So he knows what those girls he sold felt like. Also if that crap he put in Kay's arm was heroin, for that alone he will most certainly will die. Slowly!"

Logan looked at his friend's face; he could see the worry and hatred at the same time, he could see the love he had for Kay, and Logan knew that if Joe got a chance, he was going to kill that man.

Walking up to Joe, Logan said, "Come on, let's get ready." Putting his arm around his shoulder, he said, "Kay wants you to come get her. She wants to come home."

Joe smiled and gave Logan a hug and said, "Yes, she does. Let's go get her."

An hour later everything was loaded and ready to go. Joe said, "We are going tonight, storm or no storm. I want Kay home." With everything figured out, it was time to go. Buck did not like the idea of the two sleeping lions on his back, not to mention the snakes although he was a very well-trained horse and trusted Logan. Joe, Logan, and Rene left the camp at 11:00 p.m. to get Kay, to save her from a fate worse than death.

Just after one in the morning, they stopped on the back side of the hill that Joe had watched from several times. Rene stayed with the horses, making sure they were secure. Then she grabbed several clips plus a few extra boxes of shells and positioned herself where she could provide cover fire and try and make sure that Logan and Joe were protected as they went in after Kay.

Logan looked at Rene and said, "Remember this, it takes two guys to help a wounded guy to safety. No one to help a dead one although that decision can't be made until you're about to pull the trigger."

Joe and Logan led Buck around the hill and toward the drug camp. They stayed close to the cliff face as possible until they were at the back side of the building that held most of the firearms.

Carefully Joe unloaded the two lions and carried one at a time inside. Once inside, he removed the ropes that he had tied them with just in case they woke up early. Quietly he closed the door and headed back to where Logan was waiting.

Next Joe grabbed the cooler full of snakes. Logan walked over and got the case of dynamite. Carefully they headed back toward the camp. Joe put on a pair of heavy leather welding gloves and carefully removed the lid. Reaching in, he picked up two snakes and carefully opened the door and laying them on the floor. Then he took a few more and put them on the ground outside and headed for the next building.

While Joe was putting together a wake-up surprise for Hector and his crew of human slime, Logan was positioning dynamite every place he thought he or Rene could see from the hill, plus alongside the building that stored all the drugs that they were about to transport into the US. They did not have timer-style detonators, so they had to try and hit them with a bullet from about three hundred yards. A new shipment had come in the day before, and Joe was sure that they had not made a trip to the US yet.

Logan simply smiled as he positioned enough dynamite to blow the entire camp up, knowing that some of the drug runners would die in the pending explosions. As soon as everything was in position, Joe headed for the place he and Logan were to meet.

As Joe sat there waiting, he saw movement. Looking back to the direction that Logan should be coming from, he saw Logan walking very carefully as he slipped from shadow to shadow. Just as he got to Joe, they heard voices. Logan headed back the way they came to cover Joe and Kay as they made their escaped.

Joe started working his way to where he believed Kay was being held.

Opening the door just enough to slip in and close it again, he headed toward a form on the floor. Silently he worked his way across the room and knelt down, placing one hand over Kay's mouth and the other behind her head. In one quick moment, Kay jerked wide awake. There was a moment of terror in her eyes. Her first thought was to fight as Joe carefully placed his weight on her. It took just a few seconds for her to focus and see Joe's smiling face looking at her.

Kay went instant tears and grabbed onto Joe. He kissed her forehead, her eyes, and finally her lips. Then carefully he eased her back and asked, "Kay, are you okay? Have they hurt you in any way? Can you fight and run?"

Kay sat there with tears running down her face, nodding she said, "All I want is out of here and a chance to kill that bastard."

Then very carefully and silently, he whispered, "Logan and Rene are sitting on top of the hill where you saw me a few days ago. We have several nice surprises set up for Hector and his band of assholes."

Then he carefully cut away all the ropes. Handing her a 9mm and four extra clips, they turned and quickly headed for the door. They could hear voices outside. Looking at Kay, Joe said," Shoot to kill if possible and don't worry about anything else."

Slowly he opened the door, and they started working their way toward Logan and Rene and safety.

Just as they rounded the corner, a shot rang out. Joe spun around shouldering the AR-15, aimed, and fired. The man standing fifty feet away grabbed his shoulder and dropped to the ground.

Joe screamed "Run!" as the alarm went off.

Men started running everywhere. Someone screamed while others yelled and started jumping around as they opened the door to find a minefield of snakes. There were several more screams as some didn't see the snakes on time.

Joe heard the anger buzz of bullets going past, and then he heard the reports of the return fire from Logan and Rene as he pushed Kay behind a large rock. Joe popped up and sent several shots into the camp as the drug runners started shooting at them. Then there was terrible screaming as they opened the door to find two very mad mountain lions protecting their guns and ammo.

Grabbing Kay's hand, together they sprinted for the next rock. As they took cover, Joe started shooting back again, making the guys in the camp dive for cover. Carefully he looked at the camp and saw someone taking aim at the hilltop. Joe zeroed the scope on the guy's hand and squeezed the trigger. The gun went flying as the 150-grain .308 bullet smashed into the forearm of the gun that he was holding. Carefully Joe sighted again and squeezed off another round. This one found the guy's upper arm and spun him around and down onto the ground in front of one of the buildings.

Just then a massive explosion rocked the area as Logan hit one of the dynamite packs laying by the drug building. Logan started laughing as he watched the confusion in the camp.

Rene tossed a small rock at him with a what-the-hell-was-that look on her face. Logan quickly worked his way to her. Logan said, "Like that, do you?"

Rene replied, "What the hell was it?"

"Dynamite," laughed Logan as he watched the guys as they slowly came out of their hiding places. Continuing, he added, "There's another bundle on the other end of the building." He aimed and fired at a guy trying to work toward where Joe and Kay were.

Rene slid a few feet to her right and started looking. Rene found the other package, and what was left exploded, leaving nothing but small pieces falling and heroin dust everywhere.

Joe grabbed Kay's hand and said, "Try not to breath that dust." They headed for the next cover spot as the entire camp opened up. Joe could hear the buzz of bullets going past. Then he heard Logan and Rene opened, causing the guys in the camp to head for cover.

Joe sighted a guy running toward cover and squeezed the trigger. The guy grabbed his butt and dropped. Joe laughed, thinking how it would feel to have a bullet go through both of his butt cheeks.

Grabbing Kay, they headed for the next cover spot as they dove behind a yet another rock. Chips started flying from where Joe should have been.

This time Joe dropped to the ground and started shooting back. Kay was on the right side; aiming high, she sent a few rounds into the camp also. Joe smiled as he heard the 9mm report, knowing she had joined in. About that time Kay saw a jeep coming at them. She tapped Joe's shoulder as they took off at a run for higher ground. Just as they ducked behind a cliff, chips started flying everywhere as several of the guys had seen them and opened fire.

Kay heard someone yell her name. Looking up, Rene dropped an AR-15. Kay jumped, grabbing the gun as Rene dropped back behind the cliff. Working the action, she sighted on one of the guys and squeezed the trigger. The guy disappeared, and Kay looked for another target. Joe heard someone yell his name.

Looking up and seeing Logan pointing to the side, quickly he turned that way and saw three guys trying to get between them and the edge of the cliff that offered the best cover. Joe knew that if they got between them, it would be trouble. He grabbed Kay's hand and then he ran as hard as he could trying to beat them. Suddenly he heard shots coming from behind. Kay had stopped and started shooting with no cover. She was making herself a target so Joe could get to cover. Joe looked at Kay and thought, *I haven't spent the last few days worried sick about you so you could get shot trying to escape.* Stopping, he took aim and fired. One of the three dropped, causing the other two to stop and drop behind rocks.

Kay started running again, and together they made the cliff. Logan and Rene met them with all four horses. Joe and Kay quickly mounted, and the four of them headed north for the safety of the mountains.

Joe was leading the way on Lefty as they headed up a narrow mountain trail. Joe had been on the trail few days before and knew where it came out. They kept climbing until the trail forked. There he headed down and around into a narrow valley. About a mile up the valley, he took a left and followed it as it twisted and turned until it started to get wider and opened up into a lush green valley. Joe kept going until he found a spot that they could stay for the rest of the day and camp that night. After the trip, getting everything set up and grabbing Kay, then having to fight their way out, they needed a place to unwind and reload.

They knew that there was no way anyone could follow them unless they were on foot or horseback. Logan hobbled Lefty and Buck and then turned them loose; next he removed the saddles from CJ and Star, and all four horses started to graze on the rich green grass. Joe had a small fire going, and in a few minutes, Rene and Kay had supper cooking. Logan had pack survival kits in all the saddle-bags. Looking at what they had, Rene figured that there was enough food to last about a week to maybe ten days.

After they ate, Kay said, "I'll take the first watch."

Logan replied, "You won't need to. CJ will wake me if anyone or anything enters this valley."

Rene started laughing and said, "Yeah, that he will. He's woke you a couple of times when danger was near."

Kay looked at Joe, and walking over, she wrapped in a hug, saying, "Just to set your mind at ease, other than getting hit a few times, no one touched me, and that shot Hector gave me was just saline. After he told me, I attacked him and was beating the hell out of him until a couple of the others step in and stopped me. Then that asshole hit me and nearly knocked me out."

Joe looked her and said, "I hope he chases us. I really want to make him hurt before I put a bullet in him that ends everyone's pain."

Kay replied, "Only if I don't end the pain first. If I see him, he's a dead man. Not necessarily for what he did to me but for what he did to that poor girl. And probably many others."

Joe's head snapped up, and his eyes developed the only look Kay didn't like as he said, "What did he do to you? Kay, what did he do that you haven't told me?"

Kay replied "Oh, Joe" as she walked toward him. "I swear, absolutely nothing, Joe. Absolutely nothing." Reaching him, Joe wrapped his arms around her. Kay buried her face in his chest and started crying. She couldn't get close enough or hold him long enough. And Joe, well he just couldn't let go. Ever since they had fought their way out of the drug runners' camp, if Kay came close, Joe would stop what he was doing and hold her as long as she wanted.

Rene caught Kay's eye, and the two women got up and walked away.

Logan called softly, "Rene." She turned around, he held up a rifle. Rene and Kay both turned to show they were armed."

Joe looked at Logan and smiled as he picked up several boxes of ammo and started filling the empty clips for both .223 and .308. Logan picked up his .44 magnum and opened the cylinder, dumping the empties and sliding loaded carriages into the cylinder. He flipped it closed and slipped it back into the holster.

Joe asked him, "Hey, why such a heavy caliber?"

Logan simply said, "If I hit something with this, they just don't get up again. Besides you know where I live. Some of those animals are just a bit grouchy and cantankerous."

As the two ladies walked away, Rene asked, "Are you really all right?"

Kay replied, "Yes, really. They treated me terrible, but no one touched me."

They walked a short distance and started talking. Rene told Kay about her new job, about the relationship with Logan, about the buffalo and what Logan had done, how she was helping Logan train CJ and Star, but mostly about her moving to the Rocking L. Kay told Rene about retiring, about the party, about what they had found in Arizona, and about the gold claim. The two ladies played catch up for a couple of hours. It was just like old times when Rene would call after getting back from a trip somewhere and Kay would say "Great, see you tomorrow."

As they walked back, they kept talking and Rene said, "When we get out of here, why don't you and Joe come to the ranch for a couple of days or even a couple of weeks? I'm sure Logan would love having Joe around." Then she turned, and looking at Kay, Rene said, "Besides I miss you." As they walked into camp, Logan handed both of them their rifles and several full clips.

Logan got up and went to check on the horses as Rene and Kay double-checked the gear that they had left. Joe kept loading clips and checking the guns, making sure everything was clean, oiled, and in perfect working order.

Morning broke cool and clear. Logan and Joe were drinking coffee as Rene and Kay woke within minutes of each other. Logan poured two more cups as the desert started coming to life. The valley was a little piece of heaven on earth with green grass and water. A small spring-fed pool was on the east side hidden under some over-hanging rocks, but the horses could get water along with the other desert animals. Logan watched as a desert big horn cautiously looked around before heading for the pool. As the valley came to life, Joe and Logan started getting the horses ready while the girls made a quick breakfast.

As they ate, Joe and Logan looked at the map that Father Tom had given them. Joe said, "I've been over that area once before look-ing for the cats."

They planned out the route that they would be taking. Logan asked, "Do you think a jeep can get through there?"

Joe replied, "Yes, it would be rough going, but I got through with the Wildcat, so it's possible."

Kay, looking through binoculars, asked, "Is there another way out of here?" She pointed down the valley. Joe and Logan both stopped and stood up, turning their scopes to the highest setting.

"Damn," Joe said, "I didn't think they would actually try to get in here."

Logan replied, "At least they are on foot. They must have left their jeep in the other valley."

Watching, Joe said, "I think we can get around on the right and maybe they won't see us if we stay as close to the wall."

Logan replied, "Looks like they plan on staying on the higher side of the valley."

Still watching through his scope, Joe answered, "They are about 350 yards. I think if we lead the horses, we should stay out of sight. I don't want a fight if we don't have to."

Rene looked at Logan and said, "Looks like we are ready."

Kay, looking at the guys working their way toward them, said, "God, yes, let's get out of here."

Joe reached over, kissed Kay, and said, "Come on, let's go."

Logan picked up CJ's reins and led the way, staying close to the cliff.

With Rene and Kay in the middle, Joe brought up the tail and kept watching to see if the gang of drug runners spotted them or if he could see them.

About halfway to the valley entrance, Joe heard the angry buzz of a bullet go past as the shot rang out. Quickly Joe aimed and returned a few shots, hitting close enough to send all of them running for cover.

Quickly they all mounted and rode low. The race was on as they headed for a narrow gap that would lead them to the larger valley and momentary safety.

Logan entered the gap first and let CJ have his head. All four horses raced through the narrow-confined area. Stopping just before they entered the larger valley, Logan looked carefully around, trying to see if there was anyone or maybe the possibility of an ambush set up. Not seeing anything out of place, he bent low and let CJ go. The others followed. They busted into the open and headed for the northern end of the valley. Joe turned to follow as he looked back at the entrance and saw that the jeep was parked behind some brush.

Turning Lefty toward the jeep, he dismounted as the horse came to a sliding stop. With his knife in hand, he stabbed the radiator a couple of times. Remounting Lefty, he raced after the others just as the drug runners came out of the gap.

Seeing them first, Joe swings slightly to the northeast and pointing his rifle in the general direction, he pulls the trigger several times. Without aiming, the shots hit the rocks as they ricocheted off, sending rock chips everywhere, sending the drug runners diving for cover. Turning Lefty loose, he raced across the valley a couple hundred yards behind the others.

Logan slowed as they started approaching the northern end of the valley, looking for the trail that would lead them into the mountains and safety again. Something didn't feel right as he continued to scan the surrounding area. Turning slightly, he saw a jeep coming toward them. He points to the west and yelled, "This way!"

He spun CJ, and the horse exploded into a run headed east. Joe saw the others turning east and turned early, heading to intercept them. Looking to the west, he saw the jeep.

As he approached the group, Joes saw the trail. Cutting across their path, he headed north, and the others turned to follow. Logan pulled CJ back so he would be the last one to enter the steep uphill mountain trail.

A couple hundred yards up the side of the mountain, they turned back to the east and starting to slow. Logan and Joe dismounted, grabbing their rifles and handing the reins to Kay and Rene, saying, "Keep going, we will catch up."

Together they then ran down the hill, taking cover in the rocks. Logan called out, "Hey, try and put the jeep out of commission if they try and drive up here."

Looking over his shoulder, Joe saw where the girls took cover, just as they disappeared behind some large rocks. As a shot rang out and echoed through the mountains, Logan raised his rifle as one of the drug runners tried moving closer. Sighting carefully Logan squeezed the trigger, and the man grabbed his upper leg and dropped to the ground. Joe could see him trying to crawl away; as he sighted the scope, he slowly squeezed the trigger, hitting the guy coming to help him in the upper shoulder.

Moving slightly, he could see a part of the jeep behind some brush.

Turning the scope down, he saw what looked like a tire. Slowly he squeezed the trigger and watched the vehicle's left side go down. Moving to the right, he figured about where the radiator should be and put four shots through the brush. Looking at Logan, he called out, "I think the jeep needs an out-of-order sign." Then jumping up, he sprinted to the next rock.

Sighting down the trail, he waited to see if anyone tried to follow as Logan ran past him to another spot that offer cover. One guy popped up as Joe squeezed the trigger, catching the guy in the upper part of his shoulder, sending him backward and out of sight. Joe turned and quickly ran past Logan just as he sighted down the trail. As he ran past, he heard Logan's gun went off. Joe stopped as the path made a sharp turn and sighted down the trail.

Logan jumped up and ran toward him. About halfway to the turn in the trail, he grabbed his neck and dropped. Joe yelled for Kay and Rene to cover him as he bolted toward Logan.

Both women started shooting down the trail as Joe ran from rock to rock, trying to work his way to where Logan was laying. Looking at the wound, he tore off a piece of his shirt, placed it over the bullet burn, and tied it in place. Grabbing Logan by the arm, they run straight toward Kay and Rene as the two girls opened fire, keeping their pursuers pinned down.

As soon as they were in a safe place, Kay grabbed the first aid kit. Handing it to Rene, she joined Joe at making sure no one tried getting any closer.

Rene got Logan all bandaged up and yelled, "We are ready! Let's get out of here."

Kay got up and headed for the horses, but Joe waited just a minute longer as one of the guys chasing them started running up the trail. Joe, aiming carefully, put a bullet in his upper thigh, dropping him. Then he ran to Lefty; grabbing the saddle horn, he vaulted into the saddle as Lefty broke into a run and followed the others.

They followed the trail up into the mountains a few hours later. Joe called to Logan, saying, "I think there's a place not far ahead.

135

Look for a trail that looks like it continues to climb. There should be a rock overhang just as it starts. Follow it, and it actually goes down into a valley with a spring. Plenty of grass and water. We can stay there tonight and headed north again in the morning."

Logan saw the trail and the rock overhang. Just over an hour, they had a small fire going, and Kay was cooking supper as Rene looked at Logan's wound while Joe took care of the horses. CJ walked into the camp and refused to follow the others. He stayed close to Logan until Logan finally got up and walked him down into the meadow. As Logan walked back into camp, he saw Joe standing, looking at the entrance. Stopping, he asked, "See something or just checking?"

Joe looked at Logan and said, "Just worried. There are about forty people in that camp, and we have only seen a few. Something tells me we are heading into a trap."

Logan asked, "What makes you think that?"

Joe shook his head, saying, "It's just a feeling. Like the one I had just before Kay's plane crashed a few years ago." Continuing, he added, "Plus the fact we've only seen a handful of those people that were in the camp. Where are the rest?"

Logan stood there, rubbing his neck. Looking around, he asked, "Do you still have that map of the area?"

Joe replied, "Yes, it's in my saddlebags."

Walking back toward the fire, Logan and Joe talked about the possibility of turning more east then heading north again. They opened the map and saw what looked like the county getting a lot rougher and steeper to the east. Logan looked at Joe and said, "What do you think? Should we try that?" Adding, "Hopefully we don't get in to an area that gets too steep."

Joe looked carefully at the map as he replied, "Hey, Logan, look at this." He pointed at a narrow blue line.

Logan smiled as he looked at Joe, saying, "If we can get there, I think it'll be too steep for them to follow. It looks like there are quite a few water holes." He pointed to several points on the map.

Still studying the map, Joe replied, "I think you are right and to go around it. Hector and his band of human scum would have to come way back down and around here." He dragged his finger across the map, showing Logan what he meant.

Logan said, "Let's get out of here early tomorrow, and hopefully we can get enough of a head start to stay away from them."

Joe replied, "I think we should change directions a few times. Always working the right general direction." Continuing, he added, "If they are trying to get us into a certain area where they could set up an ambush, that would hopefully mess it up."

Logan looked at Joe, saying, "You really think something like that could be happening?"

Joe looked at Logan, shook his head, and answered, "No, I'm not sure. It's just a feeling, and it's bothering me. I asked you to come help, so besides worrying about Kay, I'm also scared something could happen to you or Rene, and today we came within a few inches of something happening to you."

Logan unconsciously reach up and touched his neck and answered, "Yeah, I guess you are right. Besides that you are the professional hunter here." Adding, "I know you're not used to being hunted. So what do you think we should do?"

Joe scratched his head and looked at the heavens, saying, "Nothing normal, I mean I would head for the roughest steepest area I could find."

Logan looked at Joe and replied, "Okay, tomorrow we follow you." Turning, he walked to where Rene had already lain down. Covering himself, he pulled her close and thought, *Joe knows what he is doing, he's hunting all over the world and has seen how hunted or wounded animals act. We are just another species of animals, and at the end we will do what it takes to survive.* He closed his eyes and drifted off to sleep.

Joe looked over the map then he got all the empty clips and reloaded everything. Reaching for his 9mm, he checked the clip and then Kay's gun and clips. Filling the empty one, he put it back in her saddlebag. He knew that Logan and Rene's guns were over by them, so he walked to where Kay had lain down. Settling down next to her, he pulled a blanket over his shoulders and took small catnaps.

He heard something or someone moving as he came awake. Looking, he watched as all four horses walked into the camp. The last was CJ like he was bringing the rest in so they could be ready soon. Looking at his watch, he got up and started making coffee. A few minutes later, Kay walked up and wrapped her arms around him, saying, "Did you sleep at all last night?"

Joe replied, "Yeah, some, but the horses woke me when CJ brought them all to camp this morning,"

Kay looked at him, saying, "CJ brought them?" Joe looked at her, nodding his head as he poured her the first cup. Kay took a sip and said, "What do you mean CJ brought them?"

Joe started to chuckle as he said, "All four came walking in just before sunrise with CJ bringing up the rear. It sure looked like he gathered them up and brought them here."

"Well," Kay replied, "if he's half as smart as Logan and Rene say, he probably did."

Logan slowly woke to the smell of fresh coffee and CJ's breath as the beautiful stallion started to nuzzle him. Pushing him away, Logan said, "Dammit, CJ. You, pest, get out of here." CJ lifted his head, snorted, and looked to the south as Logan came fully awake.

Grabbing his rifle, he called to Joe, saying, "I think we might have company." He reached for his binoculars and started scanning the area to the south. A few seconds later, Joe was standing next to him. Kay and Rene quickly put out the fire and started packing. Then grabbing the saddles, they also got the horses ready.

After everything was packed, they led the horses to where the guys were standing and said, "We are ready. Let's get out of here."

In just a few minutes, the four of them worked their way to the steep trail that led up and out of this valley and across the top toward the river some thirty miles away.

As they rode Joe reached into his saddlebags and grabbed the map, folding it in such a way so he could see the area they were in. Calling out to Logan, he said, "It looks like there's an intermittent streambed just ahead of us. Take that and follow it until we come to an old road. That should take us back to the canyon we looked at last night."

138

Logan replied, "I think this is it."

Joe answered, "I think you're right." They turned into the streambed and headed east.

They headed down the streambed; Joe kept looking at the surrounding hills. He had seen a reflection of something, and he was sure that he knew what that something was, light reflecting off a rifle barrel or possibly binoculars or worse yet a scope.

Kay had seen it also. She knew what it was, she had seen it just a few days before as Joe had watched from the top of the hill where she was being held. Riding up next to Joe, she asked, "Did you see that flash up on the hillside?"

Joe replied, "Yes, I did."

Kay asked, "Is it what I think it is?"

Joe replied, "If you think it a reflection off a barrel or scope, then yes." Continuing, he said, "I don't like it, not one bit. Plus I hate the idea of someone putting the crosshairs of a scope on one of us. I think we are being followed or maybe funneled into a trap. That's why I keep changing directions."

Kay asked, "If it comes to a fight, do you think we have a chance?"

Joe looked around and said, "Yes, I'm sure we do. Logan and I are both excellent shots and so are you and Rene. So far we have been wounding those guys on purpose. Although if we are forced into a fight, I'm done being nice, and I'm sure Logan feels the same. We both have more at stake than they do. I'm hoping if we have gotten serious and start shooting more for keeps, they'll give up the chase."

Joe saw the road and changed directions again. This time someone up on the hill didn't like it, and a shot rang out as a bullet hit the ground just in front of them. All four horses exploded into a run immediately as Joe led them straight ahead. More shots hit in front of them as Joe continued to go straight ahead.

He saw a trail leading uphill and took it. As they headed uphill, the bullets started getting closer and closer. Joe saw another trail that led into a very rocky area and changed directions again. As soon as they were in the rocks, the bullets stopped, and Joe pulled Lefty to a stop as he dismounted. Grabbing his rifle, he handed the reins to

Kay and started looking at the hillside that was now below them. Soon Logan joined him, and they both sighted through their scopes, looking for anything that moved.

Logan pointed and said, "The girls are in those rocks over there. It's kind of a hollow, and I'm sure they are safe."

Joe replied, "That's great." He squeezed the trigger and watched as one of the drug runners grabbed his chest and dropped.

Logan sighted and squeezed off a shot as another guy ran to his fallen buddy. Joe said, "It's time to end this cat-and-mouse game. I think they need to know we are serious about staying alive and taking our wives with us." He sighted on another guy and pulled the trigger, making rock chips fly next to his head. The guy dropped out of sight as Joe's second shot went whining off.

Logan sat looking through his scope as his finger slowly started to squeeze the trigger. A man screamed as the 150-grain .308 found his upper shoulder. Grabbing his shoulder, he dropped out of sight.

Joe watched as several guys ran from rock to rock. Just as he was about to shoot, he heard a shot behind him and watched the guy fall. Looking over his shoulder, he saw Kay and Rene sighting down from above.

Smiling he thought, *Okay, now it's four against them. Maybe they won't like the odds and give up.* Joe rolled off the rock just as a bullet hit the rocks above his head. Looking, he saw the guy aiming uphill. He watched as Logan touched off another shot and the guy tipped backward off the rock and didn't move.

Logan looked at Joe and said "Well that should either make them think or make them really mad" just as a hail of bullets hit all over.

Joe slid out from behind the rock and started running toward where Kay and Rene were. Stopping, he sighted from between two rocks. Taking a few shots, he saw one guy grabbing for his forearm as he sighted the second guy and fired and kept moving.

Kay and Rene had an excellent spot as they rained a storm of bullets down on Hector and his band of drug runners. Kay had seen two guys drop and not move as she picked target after target. Rene kept trying to place her shots in arms and legs although a few of her targets were also not moving. Logan had stopped trying to wound as he placed shot after shot into the upper part of everyone he shot at. All four were taking their time trying to make every shot count.

Joe had seen a few guys getting through and was trying to head them off. He had to run across an open area. Kay watched in horror as a guy stood up and fired. Looking through her scope, she could see that it was Hector. Sighting too fast, she jerked the trigger, and her shot went wide. It looked like slow motion as Joe's hand went to the side of his head. She watched in horror as he started falling sideways, out of sight. Kay screamed as she fired shot after shot in the direction that Hector had been.

Slamming in another clip, she watched as Hector worked his way toward where Joe had fallen. Carefully she slid off the rock and dropped to the ground. She had seen where Joe had fallen and headed that direction. With tears streaming down her face, she only knew that she had to get to him. Joe was down, and all that mattered was getting there. She heard bullets angrily buzzing past as she ran, stopping and sprinting to the next spot. She topped a small rise and saw Hector raising his rifle. She saw Joe trying to crawl to safety. Looking through her scope, she saw the evil smile as Hector sighted on Joe. She remembered what Joe had said over and over, "When you're scared, take a deep breath before shooting. Calm your nerves or you'll miss."

Everything went out the window as she aimed and fired. Hector screamed as the .223 round entered his thigh just to the left of his groin and exited on the lower part of his butt. Grabbing his crotch and screaming again, he dropped his rifle and fell to his knees. Slowly he started trying to reach his rifle.

Quickly he again started trying to sight on Joe. Kay took a deep breath and sighted carefully on Hector. Slowly she squeezed the trigger just as Hector moved. The first bullet hit Hector in his shoulder, causing Hector's shot to go wide. Her second shot caught Hector in the neck, just missing his jugular vein. Hector dropped his rifle and grabbed his neck as he fell over backward.

Kay sighted on the guy next to Hector as he lifted his rifle. Slowly she squeezed the trigger. The man dropped the rifle and grabbed his forearm and fell out of sight. Kay looked around and saw that Rene and Logan were sighting down on the group of guys. She looked at where Joe should be as she ran to that direction. Grabbing his arm, she half pulled half carried him to cover as Logan and Rene continued to rain fire down on the gang of would-be kidnappers.

With tears pouring down her face, Kay tried to find where Joe had been hit. With blood running down his face and arms, he was a terrible sight. Logan and Rene kept what was left of Hector's gang of drug runners and traffickers running for cover. Kay ran to where the horses were and grabbed Joe's first aid kit. Getting back to Joe, she dropped to her knees and again started looking for the source of the blood.

Joe slowly started coming to. Reaching for the side of his head, he said, "God, my head hurts."

Kay continued to wipe the blood away and clean the wound. Joe continued to moan as she worked. As the flow of blood slowed, Kay could see where the bullet had cut a long furrow on the side of Joe's skull. By the time she got Joe bandaged up, Hector's gang had had enough and had decided it was time to give up on the idea.

Logan and Rene ran to where Kay was sitting by Joe. Looking around, Logan saw a place that they could camp for the night. Carefully he helped Joe to his feet, and with Logan on one side and Kay on the other, they slowly walked to the shade of an overhanging cliff. In a few minutes, Logan had a fire going while Rene stood guard. Then Logan ran and got the horses. Rene started cooking supper while Logan stood watching to see if anyone thought that maybe this would be a good time to get even.

The night passed without any problems as Logan and Rene took turn standing guard. Kay continued to check on Joe, and by morning he was up, walking very slowly. He walked around the camp, looking at and checking their equipment. Finally he went and sat next to Kay, saying, "God, Kay, my head hurts. I have a terrible headache."

Kay looked at Joe and said, "Honey, I'm scared to give you anything for the pain. I'm not sure if you have a concussion."

Joe replied, "If Hector was a better shot, I wouldn't have a headache."

Logan spoke up, saying, "No, buddy, if it wasn't for Kay, we would be trying to figure out how to get your body out of here."

Joe looked at Kay and said, "What did she do?"

Kay said, "Nothing."

Logan replied, "It was her shot that caused Hector to miss you with his second and third shot. She shot him in the groin then in the neck. I think she hurried her first shot, but the second one was placed where she wanted it."

Kay looked at Joe while answering Logan, "That ass had just shot Joe. He wasn't going to get a second chance. Not as long as I was alive."

All four of them sat there talking about the fight as Rene and Kay cooked breakfast. Logan, sipping his coffee as he started looking at the map, asked Joe, "Where are we? I found the town where we met and I know we are south of it, but you are the one that has been routing us, and I'm not really sure where we are."

Joe looked over and pointed, saying, "I think we are about here, but the way my head feels, I'm not sure either, and it hurts way too much to think."

As they sat there, Logan kept looking at the map and the surrounding area. Pointing out a strange looking rock formation then looking at the map again, he said, "Hey, Joe, look at that and then the map. If I'm right, we should be right about here. That's means the village is about thirty miles northeast of us."

Joe looked at both and said, "Yeah, buddy, I think you are right." Then he pointed at a trail going toward the village and said, "If we follow that trail, we should get close enough to maybe see it from this area right here." He put his finger on the map and pointed to a ridgeline. Continuing, he added, "Or hopefully from another nearby hilltop."

Logan got up to check the horses; a few minutes later he came back smiling and said, "Hey, Rene, I think Star is going to have a baby. I've been watching her, and I think she is gaining weight. Just now I checked and she's starting to form a bag, so I'm sure she's pregnant."

Rene spun around and replied, "What? When? How did that happen?"

Joe and Kay both started laughing as Logan replied, "Well you see, honey, when a male and a female get together and they—"

"Yeah, yeah", Rene broke in. "I mean who's the dad?"

Laughing, Logan looked at Joe and said, "I don't think it was Joe or myself, so that just leaves CJ."

Rene started to laugh as she looked around and said, "He's so easygoing I forget he's a stud. All the stallions I've seen before moving to Montana where a little on the rambunctious side."

Logan started laughing and said, "Yeah, that's because they are kept in a stall and not allowed to be horses." Continuing, "A horse need to be outside with room to run. They are a herd animal. A horse want to be with other horses."

Logan looked at Joe and asked, "Do you think you can ride? If so we should get started."

Joe looked over at Lefty and said, "Yeah him and I get along great, and I'm sure he'll sense that I'm hurting and take it easy."

In less than an hour they were packed up. The horses were saddled. All four mounted up, and they were on their way to the village and hopefully home.

They were riding side by side with Logan and Rene in front with Joe and Kay right behind. Talking and joking as they headed for the village, Logan and Rene's wedding came into the conversation.

Rene said, "I want a western style wedding."

Logan asked, "What's a western style wedding?"

Turning, Rene looked at Kay and said, "You know like the ones we see in those magazines."

Kay replied, "You mean where the guys are dressed in blue jeans, western cut shirts, string ties?

"Yes," replied Rene. "Oh, and boots and new Stetsons. The really nice ones." Looking at Logan, she continued, "You know what I mean?"

Logan replied, "Yes, but that's like most weddings in Montana."

Rene started smiling and said, "You mean it's possible?"

Logan replied, "Absolutely, and I think you should show up at the wedding in a horse-drawn buggy. Oh, and let's have it at the ranch. I'm sure the hay shed should be about empty, and I think there would be more than enough room in the building we store the hay. For both the dinner and dance."

Rene started smiling, and with tears in her eyes, she dove off Star into Logan's waiting arms. He pulled her up into his lap as she started kissing him. Looking over Logan's shoulder, she said, "Kay, would you be my maid of honor?"

That was all it took. Now Kay was crying as she replied, "Oh absolutely, I would love to."

Logan half turned while holding on to Rene and said, "Joe, I need a best man. Want the job?"

Joe smiled as he replied, "It would be an honor."

Then Logan asked, "Can you drive a horse and buggy?"

Joe replied, "Nope, never have. Although there is this guy I know that I'm sure can teach me. Since it's going to be his future wife in that buggy with me."

Logan started laughing as he replied, "It's not hard, and you already get along with the horse that pulls the buggy I'm thinking about."

Joe reached down and patted Lefty's neck, saying, "Looks like you and I will be together again before long." Lefty decided to nod his head at that moment. That caused all four to start laughing.

It was getting late, and Joe told Kay that he was about done for the day. Logan saw a stand of trees ahead and said, "I think there should be water there." He pointed ahead, just to the right of where they were headed.

Nudging CJ into a canter, he rode to the trees and dismounted. Tasting the water, he quickly mounted CJ and galloped back. "Come on this way," he said as he spun CJ around and galloped back to the beautiful, little water hole.

Dismounting, Logan removed the saddles from the horses and hobbled Lefty and Buck. Then looking at CJ, he said "Okay, you take care of Star" as he turned and headed to help Joe. The two walked around and got enough wood to start a fire as Rene and Kay looked through their dwindling supplies to make something for supper.

Joe and Logan kept gathering wood and soon supper was ready as they all sat down to eat. As soon as they were done eating, Logan and Joe walked to the water hole and filled every container they had. Then Logan and Rene went to the pool and cleaned up the best they could.

As soon as they were done, Joe and Kay took their turn. The water was crystal clear and felt fantastic. Kay walked out to her knees and sat down. She could feel the nightmare slowly drifting away as she watched Joe. She could tell that he was still nervous as he glanced in all directions, always returning to look at her.

They sat around the fire for a couple more hours, talking about and making plans for a upcoming wedding. Kay said, "As soon as we are back in the US, let's go find you a wedding dress."

Rene couldn't be happier as she kept talking and making plans. Kay kept coming up with ideas about all parts of the wedding. Rene sat there listening and talking.

Logan had rolled out the bedrolls near the fire. Joe quietly got up, walked across the camp, and lay down. Logan sat up for a while before he asked, "Are you two going to talk all night? It's not bothering me although I want to know if I should go over there and sleep on that side of the fire." Rene reached for his hand as she said good night to Kay. Turning, she hugged and kissed Logan as she lay down next to him and pulled the blanket over her shoulders.

Morning broke to the smell of freshly brewed coffee as Logan, Rene, and Kay all started to wake up. Joe had gotten up an hour before and had a small fire going with coffee brewing. He sat watching the sun rise and sipping on his second cup as Kay walked over and sat down next to him. He poured her a cup and noticed the other two starting to move, pouring two more as he hand one to Kay. They silently watched the desert change from darkness and shadows to color-filled daylight.

Kay got up to help Rene try and figure out something for breakfast as they were about out of food. Logan walked over and sat next to

Joe. Looking down over the desert, he said, "This is absolutely beautiful in its own way although I'll stay with the mountains and snow."

Joe chuckled as he replied, "Yeah, it gets just a little too warm for me also." Looking over at Logan, he continued, "We haven't seen or had any trouble since the day Hector was shot."

Logan replied, "Yeah, I was thinking that same thing last night. We also didn't stand guard last night."

Joe looked over at him and said, "Yeah, we did. I was up most of the night." Taking a deep breath, he continued, "I hope it's over, but I won't feel safe until we are back in the states and a long way from here."

Followed

J ose sat looking at the map and asked, "Has anyone reported in?" Juan was very clear that he wanted both guys dead and those two women brought to him.

Pablo replied, "Sorry, Jose, I haven't heard a word from anyone yet." He walked over to where Jose was sitting. Just then a Pablo's cell buzzed. Looking at the caller ID, he said, "It's Carlos." Answering, he said, "Hey, Carlos, please, tell me something good. Juan is about to start killing people around here. He went about crazy when we told him Hector had lost the lady and then was shot trying to get her back."

Carlos replied, "Well, it's Carlos to the rescue again. I've been following them for two days. They are by El Diablo Canyon, and it looks like they are headed back toward the river and village where they were parked."

Looking at Jose, he replied, "Stay with them, but don't make contact until we talk to Juan. Yeah, *si, si*, okay, talk to you later."

Jose looked at Pablo and said, "You had better call Juan right now. He will be really pissed if we don't tell him immediately."

Pablo swallowed and replied, "I would rather someone else talks to him. I don't want to tell him this if it goes wrong."

Jose laughed and said, "*Si, si*, yeah, I don't blame you for that. He has a very short temper when it comes to getting what he wants." Laughing, he continued, "And he sure wants that America woman." Pablo found Juan's number and touched call.

Juan answered on the first ring, saying, "Someone had better tell me something good soon or else."

Pablo replied, "Yeah, *si*, Carlos has found them and is following them." Pausing, he closed his eyes and said, "He thinks they are headed toward the village where they were staying before."

Juan replied, "Tell him not to lose them and call a couple of times a day." Continuing, he said, "Now listen good, put a team together and be ready to go when we know where they are going to be staying for a few days. And don't underestimate them again. Hector did and he's dead."

Jose looked at Pablo and mouthed, "Hector's dead?"

Pablo stood there with a shocked look in his face and finally shrugged his shoulders and said, "No, it can't be."

Juan continued, "I want Joe and that idiot cowboy in the same condition soon, and I want Kay and the other one now." With that Juan disconnected.

Pablo looked at his phone then at Jose and said, "Man, he has a short fuse and a one-track mind. I sure hope they don't give Carlos the slip because if they do, Juan will kill us all."

Jose asked, "What else did Juan say?"

Pablo answered by saying, "He wants a team put together that can be ready to go in a moment's notice." Then taking another deep breath, he added, "And we had not underestimate them again. If we do, we will all end up like Hector."

Over the next few hours, Jose and Pablo started talking to the guys in the camp and making a list of who would be going after the Americans. They knew that Juan would probably be joining them, so they made the list of only the most loyal and best fighters they had.

This would also anchor their position in the drug trafficking trail to the US and hopefully also lift their position in the sex trade.

Pablo looked at Jose and said, "This looks like a good group of guys. I'm sure Juan will be happy with us."

Jose replied, "I hope so because if he's not, well I don't want to think about what he will do."

A few hours later, Carlos called in and reported them that the Americans were just about to the village and he would stay with them and report back everything that happened. Pablo and Jose started making plans to head for the village, getting everything in place before they called Juan, making sure that the plan was about foolproof.

They would put everything in motion, and after they had the two American women, they would personally bring them to Juan. Jose looked at Pablo and said, "You, my friend, are simply brilliant. Maybe just maybe Juan will give us some time with those two amazing American women also."

The next day was like boot camp as Pablo and Jose put their team through to the test, shooting both short and long range, plus handguns out to fifty yards. They read a map and went over everything they could think of. They knew that if they fail to kill Joe and the cowboy and catch the two girls, Juan would kill them both.

Carlos checked in everyday and stayed close to the group. With his knowledge of the desert plus knowing the area, he had no trouble staying close but out of sight. Over the next couple of days, it was clear that they were headed to the village.

Carlos called Pablo and reported that he was on the cliff overlooking the river just four hundred meters from the church and he was watching as all four stood there talking to the priest.

After the call Carlos moved to a new position where he could stay for a few days. It was only a hundred meters to the river although it was a very steep climb back up. He figured that he could sneak into the village at night and try and steal food and maybe get more information.

The following morning Jose woke to the sound of a very loud and obnoxious person yelling outside. It took a moment before he realized that it was Juan. Jumping to his feet, he scrambled outside to see what was going on. Juan stood in the middle of the path between the buildings where everyone slept, screaming at the top of his lungs for everyone to get outside now. As the guys started lining up, he continued to yell. Soon the entire camp was up and listening to him.

Juan looked at the men and asked who was going to be on the mission to go after the four Americans. As the team started stepping forward, he looked at Pablo and said, "I think we should all go." Then he looked at the men and said, "When Joe and that cowboy are dead, I'll give each of you $10,000.00."

Then he started walking; looking at each man there, he said, "Whoever brings me those two American women, I'll give that guy or guys $25,000.00. So now who wants to go?" The camp exploded into activity as they all started running to get ready.

Pablo and Jose walked to Juan and asked, "We thought you wanted a team?"

Juan spun around and said, "I want those two American men dead and those two women in my possession now. Do you understand? Now what has Carlos found out and where is he and where are they!"

Jose looked quickly at Pablo and said, "They are in a small village about forty-five kilometers north of here. There a priest there at the mission they have become friends with."

Juan broke in, saying," I don't care if they have become friends with Mary and Joseph, I want them both dead! Now when are we leaving to get them?"

Pablo swallowed and said, "We?"

Juan replied, "Yes, we! Do you think I would actually let you two idiots run this? Now tell me everything so I can figure out what we are going to do and when."

Together they walked into the small building used as a meeting area. Jose and Pablo started explaining where the village was and the different ways to get there.

Juan looked at the map and said, "What way is the fastest and what way offers the most cover? I don't want them to know we are coming."

Pablo traced his finger on the map as he explained, "This would be the fastest although there is very little cover." Then he showed Juan the route that he thought would be better. Looking at Jose then at Juan, he said, "If we go this way, there is a cliff about four hundred meters from the church and the village courtyard. That seems to be where the priest likes to take everyone to talk."

Juan jumped to his feet and started to walk around, looking back at Pablo, he said, "We cannot kill them in the church courtyard." Then he continued, "See why I'm leading this!"

Pablo replied, "It's not the church courtyard, it's the village courtyard."

Juan looked at Jose and asked, "Who's the best shot at that range?"

Jose stood there thinking for a few minutes, *If I say either Pablo or myself and we miss, Juan will shoot us on the spot. What one of the guys do I think could maybe hit at that range?*

Juan walked outside and looked off into the distance. "Get a couple of guys to place a target about four hundred meters away." Then looking around, he said "You and you" as pointed at a couple of the men. "Get that table and bring it here."

The guys ran and grabbed the table, placing it where Juan was standing. Then they just stood there. Juan shook his head and said, "Get the damn chairs also." Looking around, he mumbled, "Idiots. I'm surrounded by idiots." Then he asked, "Who want to shoot first? Whoever hits that target will get the first shot at either Joe or the cowboy."

Walking across to where his Land Rover was parked, he reached inside and grabbed a rifle with a scope on it. Walking back to the table, he handed it to the first guy in line.

The guy sat down and sighted on the target. *No wind*, he thought, so he held a little high and click.

Juan grabbed the gun and hit the guy hard saying, "You didn't even look to see if it was loaded." Looking around, he said, "You can't fix stupid, not even with a club." Shaking his head again, he worked the action and handed it back to the guy that was still rubbing his jaw and said, "Try again."

The man sighted again and pulled the trigger. The shot went high and wide. Juan looked at the group and asked, "Who really thinks they can hit that target?"

One of the guys asked, "Is that rifle sighted in for that distance?"

Juan said, "Go put a target out there about a hundred meters." They all looked at each other, knowing that very possible they would become the target.

Finally one guy grabbed a target and jogged out and stuck it in the sand. Turning, he jogged back and was handed the rifle. Sitting at the table, Pedro sighted on the hundred-meter target and squeezed the trigger. The shot was three inches high directly above the bull's-eye. Then he sighted just a little high on the four-hundred-meter target and squeezed the trigger. The shot hit just a little low and center.

Juan slapped him on the shoulder and said, "You, my friend, will get the first shot at either Joe or the cowboy and a chance to get $10,000.00."

Pedro smiled as he stood up and handed the rifle to Juan. After a few more guys hit the target, it was time to pack so they could leave as soon as Carlos called in with the rest of the information they needed.

Juan walked in and sat behind the desk that Jose used and put his feet up. Jose walked into the back to get a bottle of mescal and three glasses. He stayed back there a few extra minutes. He absolutely hated Juan. There was absolutely nothing about the guy that he liked. Juan was ruthless, and the only reason people went around him was he had money.

Jose dreamed of the day that he could kill him without getting caught. Putting on his best fake smile, he walked back into the front. He lifted the bottle and said "Shall we celebrate?" as he poured three shots of tequila. Raising his glass, he said, "To a fast and successful trip."

Juan tipped his glass and downed to shot. "Aww," he said as the feeling of alcohol slowly slid through his body.

Pablo put his glass down just as Juan said, "Fill it again." He placed his glass on the desk.

Jose poured three more shots as he looked at the man he hated and smiled. In his mind, he saw Juan on his knees begging for his life with tears running down his face as he continued to cry and beg Jose not to kill him. Jose shook his head to clear the daydream.

Juan lifted his glass and said, "To the Joe and the cowboy. May they die like cowards they are. Running from a fight on horses. I think they have watched too many Western movies."

Jose and Pablo tipped there glasses as they said, "*Si*, here, here."

Juan slammed his glass on the desk and said, "Fill it again."

Jose smiled as he filled all three glasses. Now he saw Juan in the crosshairs of a scope. *Aww what a fantastic dream*, he thought as he put the bottle down. Juan picked up his glass, saying, "To Kay and the other woman. May they spend hours in my bed before they bring me thousands in the sex trade in Africa or Asia."

Jose thought, *That ass is going to get them addicted and keep them for himself.* All three tipped their glasses. The alcohol slid through their bodies as Juan said, "Another, I want another."

Jose poured, and they drank shot after shot. Juan took out his pistol, and the red laser sight traced a trail across the room, stopping on different targets. Pablo saw it stop on Jose's chest and then move. He knew that Juan was pointing a loaded pistol at him. He thought, "That drunken fool."

Juan kept moving through the room when suddenly *bang* as the 230-grain bullet hit a lamp, causing glass to fly everywhere. Laughing, Juan got up and headed for the bathroom.

Jose looked at Pablo and quietly said, "I want to kill that ass like the snake he is." Pablo nodded as he got up to start cleaning up the shattered lamp.

Juan came out of the bathroom swearing, "I can't believe what pigs these guys are. Most can hit a target over four hundred meters yet miss a toilet at one foot."

Pablo said, "Well I know you can hit my lamp at ten feet. I hope you hit the toilet."

Juan glared at him, saying, "Yes, I hit the toilet and your lamp. Maybe next time I'll hit you." With that he turned, picked up the bottle, and walked out the door.

Jose said, "Pablo, be careful, he's not overly stable, and I'm sure it wouldn't bother him at all if he shot you."

Pablo looked around and said, "Maybe one of these guys will hit him soon." He dumped the remains of the lamp into the trash.

The Village

As the sun rose in the eastern sky, Joe and Logan finished saddling the horses. Mounting up, all four headed for the village. Just before noon, they rode in and stopped in front on the church. Father Tom had seen them coming and stood on the steps like a welcoming committee. Logan and Joe dismounted and handed the reins to Kay and Rene.

Logan said, "See if you can find a place in the shade with some grass for them."

Father Tom said, "Take them around to the back side of the church. There's a small courtyard there with grass and a natural spring. I'm sure they'll like it there in the shade." Then he looked from Joe to Logan and back and asked, "What do you need?"

Joe replied, "Supplies like food and any ammo you might have."

Tom got up and walked away, returning in a few minutes with two sets of saddlebags bulging with supplies and said, "It's only a day or so to the border. Although I put extra in there for you."

Both Joe and Logan said thanks as they continued to talk. Then Tom turned back to Logan and Joe, saying, "Now, please, tell me what happened in the desert."

Logan started walking toward a table sat up in the front courtyard. Tom and Joe followed along as they sat down. Joe started, "Well you know how it all started."

Tom broke in asking, "Did you kill anyone?"

Joe looked at Logan and said, "Sorry, Tom, but, yes, I'm sure we did. It was all in self-defense. Once we got Kay, they started shooting at us. So, of course, we return fire. At first we shot to just wound although after Logan got hit." Joe turned and looked at Logan as he pulled the bandage down on his neck, showing Tom where the bullet had burned him. Continuing, Joe said, "After that we started getting a little bit more aggressive."

Logan said, "Yes, but after Joe got shot, I started shooting to kill. They were playing for keeps and so was I."

Tom replied, "I need to call the authorities and report this. I'm sure they're going to want to talk to you." He got up and walked into the rear of the church.

Joe looked at Logan and said, "So what do we do now?"

Logan replied, "Do you still have that little movie Hector sent you?"

Joe looked around and said, "Sorry to say but, yes, I do."

Logan smiled and said, "Problem solved. As soon as the police see that along with what we tell them," he paused then continued, "I'm sure they won't press any charges or even say anything to us." Looking around, he then asked, "Where are the girls and the horses?"

Joe pointed and said, "Over there behind the church."

Logan looked and said, "I'm going to check on them." Walking away, he thought, *At least I hope they don't.*

Kay and Rene had hauled water and found a place with green grass for the horses. They sat talking about the upcoming wedding as Logan walked up. Looking up, Rene said, "Hi, honey." Kay sat there and watched as Rene got up and walked toward him.

Tom walked out the back door, saying, "Good you are here." Looking around, he asked, "Where is Joe?"

Joe replied "Right here" as he walked into the courtyard.

Tom looked, saying, "Good, the federal police will be here in a hour or so. They want to ask you some questions although I'm sure they won't hold you here."

Kay and Rene looked from Tom to Logan and finally to Joe and asked, "What kind of questions?"

Tom replied, "Just what happened and why. Maybe where did the fight take place." Looking at Joe and then at Logan, he continued, "They trust me, and I already reported it a few days ago. They know who and what I am. I filled them in, so it should go quickly.

Joe looked at Kay and said, "I still have the video. That should be all the answer they need."

Kay got up and walked to Joe. Putting her arms around him, Joe stood there holding her, saying, "It's all over now. Soon we will be in Arizona and headed north."

They stood there talking about the fight in the desert as several SUVs drove in. Tom lead the four of them out of the courtyard and to the front of the church. Stopping, he watched as ten men dressed in the uniform of the federal Mexican police got out and walked toward them.

Tom recognized one of the men and walked toward him, saying, "Pedro, these are the people I told you about." He introduced Joe, Kay, Rene, and finally Logan. After a few more introductions and handshakes, Tom started talking, telling, and explaining what had happened in the desert and what caused it.

Joe took out his phone, pressing play as he handed it to Pedro.

Pedro stood there watching the video. Looking up, he looked around and asked Kay, "Did they hurt you in anyway? Do you need a doctor for any reason?"

Kay shook her head, saying, "Believe me, they never touched me. Other than a few bruises, I'm fine."

Joe heard the angry buzz of a bullet as it flew past his head. Pedro looked at Tom as he grabbed his chest and dropped to the ground. Joe yelled, "Run!" He grabbed Kay and sprinted toward the church. Stopping just around the corner, Logan nearly ran over him as he turned the corner with Rene in tow.

Joe peeked around the corner as Tom grabbed Pedro and was dragging him to safety. Out of the other nine officers, three were laying in front of the church as the desert sand became saturated as the life drained out of them. The five remaining officers had made it to cover although they couldn't reach their rifles as Juan's gang of drug runners poured a deadly spray of lead into the area in front of the church.

Logan looked at Joe and said, "Our rifles are on the horses, and that Remington is in the back part of the church right where I left it."

Joe replied, "You get it. I'll get the rest of the horses." Turning, he said, "See you back here in a few minutes."

Joe sprinted across the courtyard, headed for where the horses were as Logan headed into the church.

A few minutes later, they met just to the side of the church as Joe handed guns to the others and picked up the .308, as he slung the Remington over his shoulder and picked up AR15. Looking at Logan, he said, "Pour some lead on the ridgeline while I try and get to Tom."

Logan looked at Rene and Kay, asking "Are you two ready?" as they worked the actions, making sure their rifles were ready.

Joe slipped in a new clip and worked the action. Looking around the corner, he quickly sighted on a round object on the ridgeline and slowly squeezed the trigger. All the round objects disappeared except one. Joe raised the crosshairs, sighted, and squeezed off three more shots as he ran toward Tom.

Logan ran to the steps, just getting down as the guys on the ridge started to again pour deadly fire into the area. Logan looked back as Kay and Rene opened fire. Kay was up high and Rene down low as they continued to send .223 bullet at supersonic speed toward the ridge. These lightweight, high-speed bullets caused more trouble than most would believe as they ricocheted all over, and the round objects again disappeared.

Joe made it to the picnic area and dropped under a table. He quickly set the bipod up, and working the action, he picked up a range finder. Getting the distance, he sighted on the ridge, waiting for someone to show themselves. Soon he saw what he was looking for as one of the drug runners poked his head up. Joe sighted and fired as the guy dropped from sight.

That shot brought more fire than the previous several times, and Joe quickly adjusted the scope, sighted, and fired. This time he saw the guy drop as the 154-grain .308 boattail bullet found its mark, and one of the drug runners was out of the fight forever.

The fire from the ridgeline kept getting heavier and heavier as Joe continued to find targets. By now the federal police were in the fight as they also started shooting at the ridgeline.

Pedro, although severely wounded, continued to give orders to his guys. Tom overheard one of the orders and slipped off to where Joe was tormenting the drug runners from.

Joe looked over and saw Tom trying to get to him. He quickly switched guns and sent twenty 154-grain bullets to the ridgeline, causing everyone to drop from sight.

Tom looked at Joe and said, "Pedro wants you four arrested and held pending an investigation. I think maybe you had better get to your horses and head north as fast as you can. I think they'll be busy for a while, giving you a good head start."

Joe asked, "Why would he want to arrest us? All we did was protect ourselves."

Tom looked around then answered, "He's wounded and not thinking clearly. I'm sure this will change after he heals, but I still think you had better get out of here."

Joe looked at Tom as he folded in the bipod and said, "Thanks, man." Looking around, he continued, "I think we owe you. You have our numbers. If you ever need anything, please, don't be afraid to call." Crawling out from under the table again, he looked around, shaking Tom's hand and said, "Thanks again. Keep your head down. I'm sure as soon as we leave, they'll follow us." Looking toward the church, he asked, "How far is it to the border going cross-country?"

Tom ducked as a bullet hit the tree just above his head. Joe quickly sighted on the ridgeline, and this time he sent an entire clip of supersonic 154-grain .308 bullets, causing everyone to find a place to hide as rock chips started flying. He knew it would be a complete accident if he hit anyone at that range. Smiling, he thought, *But accidents do happen.* He jumped to his feet and sprinted to the side of the church.

Logan, Kay, and Rene continued to pour lead in the direction of the drug runners. Joe dropped in next to Logan and said, "Pedro's been hit, and he wants us arrested and held. Tom said we had better get while the getting is good." Looking at the ridge, he again sent an entire clip, and everything on the ridge disappeared.

Logan looked at Joe and asked, "Are you up to a running fight across the desert? It's going to be a hard ride, and I'm sure a really hard fight." Pausing, he looked at the ridge and carefully sighted on a guy trying to sight on them.

Just before he squeezed the trigger, the guy grabbed his chest and dropped from sight. Logan looked and saw that one of the federal police officers was working the action on his rifle. Turning, he looked at Joe and said, "When we destroy their camp and their outgoing drugs all while stealing Kay back, well that really made them feel stupid."

Joe looked around and said, "Leave me your extra clips and take the girls and head for the horses. I'll keep those idiots pinned down and be right behind you."

Joe sighted on the ridge again, and as soon as he fired the first shot, Logan was up and running. Between Joe and the federal police, the drug runners couldn't get off a shot. As soon as he was out of ammunition, he jumped up and headed for the horses.

Ambushed

Juan screamed as the first shot missed Joe. Reaching over, he punched the guy, knocking him over. Grabbing his rifle, he sighted and started shooting.

As Juan fired, everyone else started shooting. As the bullets rained down on the area in front of the church tree, more officers fell. Juan yelled, "Kill Joe and that damn cowboy." He continued to sight and pull the trigger. Then he said, "I want those two guys dead, but make sure you don't hurt the two women. They must be alive." He continued shooting and yelling at everyone, "Make sure you don't hit the women. Kay and that other girl are way too valuable."

Juan looked at the guy next to him as Joe's bullet found its target. The man grabbed his neck. Looking at Juan, he tried to talk as the life left his eyes. He fell landing on top of Juan's back pinning him to the ground.

Juan screamed as the dead man landed on him. Kicking and pushing, he couldn't get the dead man off his back. Several of the men ran, trying to help, but with all the added men in a small area just made it worse.

Juan managed to crawl out from under the man and came up spitting mad as he yelled and threatened to shoot everyone.

Jose smiled as he looked at Pablo, saying, "Serves him right." Adding, "You can't be a total ass and not have something bad happened."

Pablo just smiled as he continued to shoot into the area in front of the church. Jose moved closer to Pablo and quit shooting. He instead just moved his scope from place to place trying to find the four Americans.

Pablo asked, "What are you doing? And why are you not shooting?"

Jose replied, "I'm trying to locate the Americans, maybe just maybe I can get a shot at Joe or the cowboy."

Pablo said, "If Juan sees you doing that, he'll shoot you. His orders were to get rid of the cops."

Jose looked down the line and said, "He's too busy being an ass to everyone." Laughing, he added, "I hope he insults one of these guys and they put him out of my misery."

Pablo looked at Juan as he walked around screaming orders and insulting everyone. He saw the looks on some of the guys. Looking back toward the church, he saw as Tom ran across and stopped just out of sight in the trees. Looking through his scope, he could see Tom's legs and raised the crosshairs to where he thought his body should be.

Pulling the trigger, he narrowly missed Tom. As soon as he had pulled the trigger, Juan had to duck and cover as Joe opened up, sending a hail of .308 bullets spraying the ridgeline, rock chips, bullet fragments, and sand flew everywhere.

Juan swore as a bullet fragment hit him in the arm. Grabbing his arm, he yelled for Jose, saying, "Get your ass over here and look at this! I don't want to bleed all over everything."

Jose looked at Pablo, saying, "Hey, he's trying. That hit him in the arm, hopefully the next is in the head." Looking to the heavens, he said "Please" as he made the sign of the cross and ran to help Juan.

Pablo worked his way to where Jose was bandaging Juan's arm and said, "I think the Americans left on the horses. I haven't seen them down there now for nearly an hour, and no one is shooting from where the two guys were."

Juan jumped up and started yelling, "Find the Americans now. I want those two guys dead and the women in my position now!"

Everyone started moving, trying to figure out where the Americans had gone. Juan had gone total nuts and was pointing his pistol at everyone, screaming, "Find them find them now or it's your asses!"

Pablo touched Carlos's arm and looked at Jose, saying, "One of these guys are going to shoot him if he keeps this up."

Jose replied, "I sure hope so and soon." He continued to look for the Americans.

Santiago stood up, pointing his gun at Juan, saying, "You were here also. Why didn't you see where they went? You can't blame us for everything that goes wrong."

Juan stopped and slowly turned around. Looking at Santiago, he said, "I was busy trying to get rid of the cops."

Santiago replied, "So were the rest of us. Just doing what you said. Okay, so now they are gone. We found them once, we can find them again."

Calmly he walked over to Juan's truck and grabbed the map. Opening the map on the hood, he said, "We are here. There is the border. I would believe that they would be trying to go north and get across before we can catch them." Pausing and looking at the map, he said, "They are on horses. I'm sure we can get ahead of them with the jeeps. If we set up lookouts across this area, we should know where they are later today."

Carlos walk over and pointed at a few spots, saying, "I know this area. If we do what Santiago says, along this line we will see them."

Juan glanced at Carlos then looked at the Santiago who still held his pistol in his hand and replied," Why are we still standing here? Come on, let's get going." Looking at everyone, he added, "Santiago and Carlos are in charge."

Santiago stopped and talked to Carlos as he watched Juan walked toward the Jeep. Carlos glanced at Juan as he walked away, saying, "Watch yourself. He'll back shoot you if he gets a chance."

Still watching Juan, Santiago replied, "Yeah he's the worst kind of a snake." Looking at Carlos, he continued, "A back shooting coward."

Juan walked back to the ridge. Looking into the valley, he saw as the four Americans left the courtyard. Turning around, he started yelling at everyone, "There they are! You idiots are letting them escape again! If they get to the border, they'll get away!"

He ran for his truck as everyone loaded in the vehicles to try and head them off. Juan screamed, "We have to get ahead of them. Now let's go." Looking at Carlos and Santiago, he said, "Find us a route that will get us in front of them. They are headed north on horses and we have trucks."

Run for the Border

Logan rounded the corner at a run. Grabbing CJ, he swung into the saddle, holding the reins to keep CJ from bolting. Looking at the girls, he asked," Are you ready?"

Kay asked, "Where is Joe?"

Logan replied, "He should be here any minute."

The gunshots continued. Joe came running around the corner. Kay tossed the reins for Lefty as he swung into the saddle. Together all four of them bolted out of the courtyard, out of rifle range of the drug runners and protected by the huge old church.

The four Americans headed across the desert of northern Mexico running for their lives, all anxious to get out of Mexico. They let the horses have their heads to weave their way through the rocks and cactus. Logan held CJ back, the young stallion had the instinct and speed to lead. Suddenly CJ jumped a rock pile, nearly unseating Logan as he landed next to Rene and Star. Logan cussed under his breath as he held on to the saddle horn, desperately trying to stay in the saddle.

Rene laughed at the look on Logan's face as CJ settled in next to her and Star, saying, "Nice landing."

Logan started to release his death grip. Star drifted to the right as CJ went left to avoid another rock pile.

Logan pulled CJ back again. He wanted to be last. This way hopefully he would see anyone or anything that could be possible trying to follow or catch them.

With Joe in the lead, they traveled as fast as possible. Star was getting bigger every day, and Logan knew that she would tire quickly.

Rene had asked several times if all the excitement could cause her to lose the foal she was carrying.

As they traveled farther into the desert, Logan carefully caught up with Joe and said, "Get to that mountain trail and slow down. Star can't take this strain for long."

Joe replied, "The trail is just another mile or so. From there I don't think they can follow us. It's just way too narrow and really steep."

Logan said, "Great we need to let her rest. Besides Rene would absolutely come apart if she lost that foal." Logan looked at Joe as he started to slow CJ. Smiling, he added, "I think I would too. It's CJ's first, and I'm curious if he throws color."

Joe turned to Logan with a puzzled look and asked, "Color? What do you mean? Color?"

Logan replied, "Yeah, color like him. His mom is a bay, and I'm sure his dad was a sneaky mustang I've seen a few times running with a herd in Wyoming."

Joe looked around and started laughing as he thought about what Logan had just said. Turning, he looked at Kay, thinking back about the first time they had met. How he had walked past and slipped a note into her hand as he and his date left the party and replied, "Yeah, I think I know what you mean."

Now Logan had the puzzled look and asked, "Okay, buddy, what do you mean?"

Joe started laughing as he talked about the first time he and Kay had met. How the look in their eyes had told each other what the other was thinking and feeling. About how fast they had fallen in love. The ski trip where he had sneaked off and bought her ring and then hidden it in a hot apple surprise and the look on her face when she found it.

Logan looked back at Rene and said, "I didn't know I was in love until I thought Rene was going to get trampled by a herd of buffalo and how I had put her life in front of my own and CJ's." Pausing for a minute, he continued talking about the race across the valley where he had picked her up just yards in front of a stampeding herd. Looking back at Rene, tears came to his eyes as he thought about that day and everything that had happened. Looking back at Joe, he said, "When I thought she was going to die," looking up into the heavens, he continued, "all I could think about was getting to her."

Just as they came to the cut in the mountains that lead to the trail, Logan saw a reflection. Still talking to Joe, he said, "I think we have company up there. Can you think of another trail in this area?"

Joe never looked up, he just kept riding past the cut and replied, "Yeah, there is another trail. But I had to turn around with the UTV, it was way too steep."

Logan looked at him and said, "How far is it?"

Joe looked back at their wives, saying, "About two miles on the right. From what I could tell, it went up then circles to the north. I have no idea after that."

Logan paused for a minute; looking back at the girls then up at the mountains, he said, "We have a couple of the best ladies ever with those idiots trying to kill us and living like this in the desert. Yet they say nothing other than to hold on a little tighter when they can. I guess Star is just going to have to hold on also." Pausing, he added, "And find her inner strength."

Joe looked at Logan then back at the girls. It seemed that they were deep in conversation also. Looking ahead, he said, "The country from here to the border is rough and steep before it levels out and becomes flat desert."

Finding the trail, Joe turned uphill and started into the mountains once again, followed closely by Kay, Rene, and Logan. Taking a deep breath and looking to the heavens, he silently prayed, "Please, let me lead my wife and friends to safety." As they climbed, the trail got narrower and narrower.

Joe looked at the place that he had turned around a week or so before, thinking that feels like a lifetime ago as his vision started to blur. Wiping his eyes, he glanced back and kept climbing. The going was rough, and it was starting to cloud up. Looking to the west, he could see storm clouds forming as they slowly moved north. As they went around yet another turn in the trail, he saw Logan also looking to the west also.

Logan pointed at the clouds and said, "That does not look good."

Joe looked again, nodded, and replied, "Yeah, although it will make following us very difficult. It should completely erase our trail while it's raining."

Rene and Kay both looked at the storm clouds and then at the trail and up the mountain. Rene asked, "Will we make the top before it gets here?"

"Yes," Logan said then added, "They are miles away still and moving in a direction that should intersect with us farther north."

Rene turned and looked at the valley below. Stopping, she pointed and asked, "Please, tell me that's not what I'm thinking it is."

As all four looked down into the valley, Logan swore under his breath as Joe swore out loud. Looking at the rest, he said, "Why won't they just give up? What the hell makes this fight worth so much?"

Kay replied, "Rene and I are worth thousands in the initial sale." With tears running down her face, she added, "Even more later in say China or some other terrible place addicted to heroin and doing icky things to get it."

Rene reached for her as Joe dropped off Lefty and walked back to her. Helping her down, he held his wife and whispered in her ear, "Over my dead body. I'll be dead before they take you again!"

Rene road up next to Logan where he pulled her from Star's back and into his arms; kissing her, he said, "Not in a million years. Never will they take you!"

Joe looked at Logan and said, "Run or stand and fight?"

Logan replied, "We are seriously outgunned. I think we had better run until we either get across the border and find help or we have to stand and fight." Pausing, he looked back into the valley and said, "We have been trying not to kill anyone. I think it's time to change that. Maybe if several of those guys die, they'll give up?"

Joe stood there looking into the valley and replied, "Kay killed Hector. I know I killed a couple more. I'm sure you killed a couple more along with Rene. That leave say maybe twenty or so. How many have to die before they give up?"

Rene looked at Logan and then Kay as she turned toward Joe and said, "Kay and I can join the fight and make it a four-man fighting team."

Logan and Joe answered at the same time and said, "No! Absolutely not. You two just continue doing what you are doing."

Logan continued, saying, "Joe and I both hunt. We have a better chance and staying alive."

Joe added, "We are also better shots." Looking at Logan, he added, "How many boxes of shells do you have for that .308?"

Rene opened her saddlebags and said, "I have three." Looking at Logan, she added, "I think we should stop and see what we have so we know if we can fight or not and for how long."

Moving to a place of safety, they went through everything to figure out how much ammunition they had left. Logan looked and said, "Four boxes of .308, six of 9mm, ten of .223, two .44. If we have to fight, it's going to make every shot count. We don't have enough rifle ammunition to outlast them."

Logan handed everyone boxes of shells for what they carried. Looking at the .308 shells, he handed all four to Joe, saying, "Give me your .223. I'll shoot that giving you all the long range area if it comes to a fight."

Joe started laughing and said, "Oh, thanks, that's so nice of you."

Logan replied, "I can still reach out that far, but I think you are a better shot than me after seeing you drop that elk at over four hundred yards."

Joe smiled, remembering that hunt, and replied, "Yeah, that was a very lucky shot. By rights that elk should have gotten away. We sure had a great time. Although what I remember the most was hiking up and down that mountain getting that guy out." *Wow*, he thought, *all the trips up that mountain.*

Logan just stood there smiling for a minute before he started laughing and said, "Rough and steep. Wow, what a day."

The girls sat there watching and listening as the guys talked about one of the hunts they had shared.

It was getting late as Logan said, "I think we had better get going and try to find a place to camp tonight. We should keep going, but traveling in these mountains after dark just isn't safe. We could miss the trail or wander off a cliff."

As they topped a hill, Kay looked back and said, "Oh my god, would you look at that."

The other three stopped and turned around. Slowly one at a time, they turned their horses around and stared at the sunset over the western desert.

As the sun set, the colors went from yellow to magenta, slowly turning pink and finally red. Rene reached over and took Logan's hand as Joe slid off his horse and held on to Kay.

Kay smiled and said, "Wow, miles from anywhere fighting and running for our lives yet we stop to enjoy this?" She continued to hold Joe.

Rene reached for Star's reins as Kay swung into the saddle and said, "Sounds good, let's get going?"

Logan looked at Joe as he reached for the saddle horn and climbed onto Lefty. Grabbing the saddle horn, Logan swung onto CJ's back. Looking at the girls, they again headed deeper into the mountains.

Joe looked to the north; he turned to Logan and said, "Somewhere that direction is the border and safety."

Logan replied, "I think that's a great place to be. So come on, by this time tomorrow hopefully we will be back in the states."

The four Americans rode north, following an old game trail. Logan and Joe kept laughing, looking to the sides and behind, absolutely sure that someone was following them.

Just before dark Joe turned into a narrow canyon and followed it to where it opened into a small valley. There was enough grass to feed the horses and a small spring that drain into the desert sand about a hundred yards away.

Looking around, Logan found a small opening that led into the center of a rock pile. Walking in, he returned in a few minutes, saying, "This is perfect cover for us plus a place we can build a fire. If someone walks in here, they'll have a hard time finding us. I don't want another fight. We are dangerously low on ammo."

Watched

A half a mile away sat Juan watching through a spotting scope. He had the scope set up in such a way that only at a perfect angle could sunlight reflect off the lens.

Juan had warned the entire group that he wanted the Americans, and they were very close to the border and safety. He also said that if someone messed this up, heads would roll.

Next he picked a small group of his most trusted men and said, "Now listen up. You six will be responsible to locate the horses after dark and make sure they couldn't return to camp in the morning."

Juan continued to watch, and just before dark, he saw what he was waiting for. The camping spot. Juan quickly showed the group where the camp was and said, "Now make sure those horses do not and cannot return in the morning. Although I want them also. So don't hurt them."

Juan watched as the men headed in the direction of where the prize was waiting. He had another plan that he hadn't told anyone. And it was about to come together. Walking back to where the rest of his group were waiting, he said, "Now gather around and listen carefully." He laid out their part and privately hoped that Joe and that damn cowboy killed every one of them. More for him after he had the two girls and the horses.

As the moon rose, Juan watched as everyone started leaving the camp and could feel the excitement as the plan fell into place. He was sure that the guys he just sent to try and draw Joe and Logan away from the girls would all die. *Oh well,* he thought as he headed off the other direction. While watching, he saw a way into the valley that would offer him cover and a place to wait until the two guys were gone. Then he could get to the women and, yes, enjoy one or maybe both.

Jose, Pablo, Carlos, and Santiago along with the other two located the horses. While two of the guys stayed and watch them, the other four started looking for a place to hold them. Just before daylight, Santiago found it. A small side canyon. Quietly all six worked until they had them in the small canyon and blocked the entrance. Then finally they could relax and catch a few hours of sleep.

Juan had worked his way around to where he was sure that he could get safely into the valley. Then taking out a pair of binoculars, he watched as Jose, Pablo, Carlos, and Santiago got the horses moved out of sight. Turning, he saw the rest of the guys working their way closer. Smiling, he sat just waiting for the gunfire to start.

Carefully Juan started down the cliff wall, and in less than thirty minutes, he was just a few hundred yards from where Kay and Rene were sleeping. He could feel it. They were close, and soon he would know how they truly felt. Closing his eyes, he started fantasizing of what was about to finally come true. Kay was going to be his.

Morning broke cool and clear. Logan walked out expecting to find CJ. After a few whistles and nothing, he started to get nervous. Turning, he said, "CJ's not here. I've whistled a couple of times and nothing."

Joe looked at him, saying, "I'm sure he will be here soon."

Logan replied, "No, something is wrong. He always comes when I call." Grabbing his pistol and a rifle, he continued, "I'm going to look for him and the others."

Joe reached for his rifle and said, "Hey, slow down and I'll come with."

Logan hesitated. Looking around, he replied, "Do you think you can climb up there?" He pointed to a cliff a few hundred feet away and watched to make sure that no one else is in this valley.

Joe looked and answered, "Absolutely, give me about twenty minutes. From there I can cover almost this entire canyon." Checking his pistol then slipping his head through the sling on the Remington, he headed for the cliff and a short climb to his vantage spot.

Logan smiled as he walked to Rene and said, "CJ and the others didn't come this morning. I'm going to go take a look. Joe's climbing that short cliff to cover me. Just making sure."

Rene replied, "Wait a few minutes and I'll come with you."

Logan shook his head and said, "No, I think you and Kay should stay here. You are well protected and hidden. I won't be gone long. If trouble starts, you can cover us as we work our way back."

Rene looked over at Kay and said, "I want out of here and I mean like now." Reaching for the guns, she checked to make sure that they are both fully loaded. Then picking up Kay's pistol, she checked it and handed it to Kay along with the holster and belt.

Kay replied as she buckled the belt, "Yeah, no kidding. I've had about all of this area I can handle. Nothing against Mexico but!"

Logan glanced at the cliff, and with Joe nearly in place, he kissed Rene, walked out of the hidden camp, and started down the valley.

A short distance away, Juan watched as Joe started his climb then waited quietly for Logan to leave. Knowing then it will be safe for him to put the rest of his plan in action. Carefully he started to work his way to the place he saw Joe and then Logan walk out of the rocks. Looking up, he could tell that Joe won't be able to see into the camp from where he's watching from. Smiling, he knows his time with Kay then the other girl was coming close.

Just before Juan stepped into the open, Rene walked out of the hidden camp. Dropping behind a large rock, he quietly watched and waited as she slowly walked down the path headed for the nearby spring.

Logan whistled for CJ again and again. Finally he heard CJ whinnied a reply. Heading that direction, he smiled that he's alive but wondered why he didn't come. Staying close to the cliffs and trying to stay undercover and out of the open, he started to wonder what's going on. CJ had always come to his whistle. Seeing a narrow cut in the cliff wall, he slowly started to enter.

Staying low nearly a crawl, he saw the brush and logs that were blocking the path out. Carefully he crawled to a point that he could see the rest of the horses. Logan looked at the brush and logs blocking the path out of the narrow cut and knew it's man-made.

Someone is keeping my horses here, he thinks. *Why?* He knew the answer. Carefully he started looking for either men or smoke from a fire or anything that doesn't look right. As he scanned the area, he saw the outline of a man leaning against a tree. Focusing his binoculars, Logan smiled and though, *That guy is sleeping. Not much of a lookout.* He found a camp and the rest of the guys all asleep.

Slowly he worked his way to the makeshift gate and started pulling the brush and logs out. As he worked, he kept looking back and could see that the guys were still sleeping. Then he looked to where the lookout should be. "Damn," he said. He dropped and started to crawl between a few large boulders.

The man was up and was walking around. As he approached the area where Logan had been taking the gate apart, he stopped. Logan stepped out and drove his fist into the man's throat. The guy grabbed his throat and tried to scream a warning. All he can do was gasp as he slowly sunk to the desert floor with a crushed larynx.

Logan went back to work trying to be quiet, but he knew that if these guys were here, there were more. Just as he got a hole made, he heard a gunshot. Grabbing his rifle, he looked at the camp. The guys were up and were trying to figure out who shot and where it came from.

Logan aimed and took a few quick shots. One guy dropped as the rest dove for cover. Whistling, he saw all four horses running his direction with CJ in the lead. Logan grabbed a handful of his main and jumped along with CJ. He swung onto CJ's back as they headed through the gap and for the rock camp.

Juan looked up at the cliff once again. Joe was nowhere in sight. Slowly he started working his way toward the opening in the rocks that led to Kay and his dream. Carefully he walked through the gap and saw Kay standing by a small fire with her back to him. In a few quick steps, he grabbed her. Spinning her around, he ripped her top open, exposing her bra.

Kay grabbed her top, closing the ripped over herself. Juan grabbed her one arm and pushed his pistol up under her chin. Kay stared into his eyes, and she could see his evil intent. Silently, she prayed that the gun went off before he could fulfill his fantasies.

Kay quickly tried to knee her attacker in the groin, but Juan was ready and blocked her knee and backhanded her, knocking her to the ground. Kay hit the ground and let go of her ripped top. Juan stopped his attack and stared at her.

Kay took the few seconds, and this time the kick connected solid. Juan grabbed his crotch, and dropping to his knees, he cried out in pain. Kay kicked out again, catching Juan on the chin and knocking him backward onto the small fire. Juan screamed as his shirt caught fire. He rolled out of the fire just as Kay got to her feet and started to run. Juan reached out and grabbed her ankle. Kay tried to make a skip like hopping but she landed hard on her stomach. Juan dove forward and landed on her back, he rolls her over. Grabbing both arms, he then pinned her to the ground. His weight was more than she can lift, and Juan took a few deep breaths as he slowly starts gaining control.

His intent was plain, and she was powerless to stop him. She continued to fight with everything she had and slowly she started to realizes. He's just to strong. With both hands pinned over her head, he reached down and started to undo her jeans. Kay continued to fight, but she was losing. She can feel as her jeans started to slide down. The look in Juan's eyes went from evil to wonder as his eyes rolled up and he fell forward.

Kay pushed him to the side. Looking up, she saw Rene standing over them with a baseball size rock in her hand. Sobbing she jumped to her feet crying. Kay hugged Rene, saying, "God I'm glad you came back. I started to think you went after Logan."

With tears in her eyes Rene, answered, "I wanted to, but something told me no. To stay here and wait. I started to sit on that little hill but didn't want to be alone. I thought I would just come back and get you to sit with me."

Juan slowly rolled over and started getting up. Suddenly he launched himself toward the girls. Kay jumped to the side and nearly got away. With both girls now in his control, Juan grabbed the wrist of both, jerking them to their feet. Motioning then pushing, he moved Kay and Rene across the rock in closure to a point where they can be seen as someone walked in.

Standing next to the opening, he waited as Joe walked through. Juan stepped forward and pushed the barrel of his rifle into Joe's back. Joe froze in place as Juan reached around, removing his pistol and rifle. Carelessly he threw Joe's pistol and rifle on the ground. Then he pushed Joe forward again.

Rene watched where the pistol landed and then looked at Joe. Kay let her torn shirt fall open as Juan stopped and looked toward Kay. Joe spun, pushing the rifle barrel away. His left hand flashed as he drove his clenched fist, catching Juan between the eyes. Rene dove and grabbed the pistol; rolling she came up and fired. Juan screamed and grabbed his shoulder, dropping to his knees. Joe grabbed his arm and threw two more connecting solid with his jaw both times. Juan's eyes rolled up as he slumped over, dropping to the ground.

Logan carefully walked into the rock camp looking around. He saw Rene helping Kay and Joe doing something on the ground. Putting his pistol back into the holster, he walked toward Joe. Joe heard the crunch of the gravel. He spun, grabbing his pistol as Logan jumped sideways, saying, "Hey! Wow! Calm down, calm down! Joe, it's me!"

Joe looked at the gun in his hand and said, "Wow, Logan, I'm sorry." Pointing at the ground, he said, "This idiot tried to kill us all, and I guess I'm a little nervous. Do you have the horses?"

Logan replied, "Yes, they are just outside."

Joe stepped over Juan as he followed Logan out to the horses, saying, "Let's get them saddled and get out of here before the rest get here."

Quickly Logan and Joe got the horses ready to go as Rene and Kay finished packing what little supplies they have left, and the four of them headed north for the border and safety, leaving a wounded Juan in the rock camp.

As they rode, Logan asked, "What happened back there?"

Rene and Kay told the story as they rode, and about an hour later, Logan stopped. Joe asked, "What's up? Why are you stopping?"

Logan replied, "I want to go back and finish this. That, that umm jerk should be dead. All these assholes should be."

Joe reached over, touching Logan's shoulder, saying, "I'm sure we have wounded many and killed a few. All four of us are still breathing. Let's just get back into the states."

Logan looked back and said, "Yeah, let's go." They rode in silence for a couple of hours, staying in the shadows or close to the cliffs, following dry riverbeds as much as they could but always moving north.

Late that afternoon they topped a hill, and the desert opened up in front of them. Squinting in the afternoon sun, Rene pointed and said, "What's that there about halfway to the hills?"

Kay lifted her binoculars and said, "It's a truck with several cars following it, and there's a few going the other direction. I think it's in southern Arizona."

With a couple of hoops and a holler or two, they headed off the hill in a northeastern direction, hoping to find Douglas and their trucks and trailers.

Safe

Logan asked, "Did Tom say if he got the trucks to Douglas?"

Joe replied, "Yes, he said they were in the parking lot just north of customs. He also contacted the DEA and told them what was going on and to make sure the trucks are watched so no one messes with them."

"Fantastic," Logan replied. "I can't wait to get headed north. I'll never complain about cold and snow again. I've had enough desert to last me a long time."

Rene looked at Kay and said, "Should we tell him now or wait."

Logan turned saying, "Tell me what?"

Rene looked from Kay to Joe then to Logan and said, "About a gold claim in the desert north of here."

Logan looked at Rene, then turning, he looked at Joe and said, "Gold? What gold claim?"

Joe started telling the story about finding the cave and tunnel that led to the large underground cavern where they had found the gold and how they had crawled out.

It was getting dark as they rode, and finally Joe said, "I think we need to find a place to camp again tonight. Hopefully tomorrow we can ask someone where the hell we are."

A few minutes later, Kay pointed and asked, "Is that a light over there?"

All three turned together, and Rene said, "It looks like one."

Logan said, "It's not far."

"Let's check that out. Hopefully someone that speaks English can tell us how lost we are."

Rene added, "Oh, please, let it be someone friendly. I'm so sick of running and being shot at."

They headed for the light in the distance. Suddenly CJ stopped; looking carefully, Logan noticed a small river or stream. He coaxed CJ ahead and into the stream.

The stream was shallow, and about halfway, CJ started prancing and pawing at the water. Joe watched as CJ continued to play and act up. Joe said, "I think this is the border, and if so we are back in the USA. I think CJ senses that fact."

About an hour later, they rode into the small farm yard. A man came walking out. Joe noticed the way he walked and the bulge under his shirt. *Gun*, he thought. Looking around, he asked, "Are we in the states or Mexico?"

The guy laughed and said, "The states by about a mile or so." Pointing south, he said, "Mexico is that away."

Joe replied, "Thanks. What way to Douglas?"

The man pointed west and replied, "That away about twenty miles by road but maybe five over that mountain."

They stood there and continued to talk about the desert horses and living this far away from everyone and everything.

Then Logan asked, "Is there a good place we can camp around here?"

The man replied, "Sure, you can stay in my barn. There is hay and water for the horses and water for you to clean up some. I'm sure my wife has dinner ready. I'll tell her there are four more. She'll be delighted. We don't get much company out here."

Joe said, "No, please don't. We don't want to cause any trouble, but staying in your barn would be fantastic."

The man stuck out his hand saying, "I'm Jeff, and it's no trouble. Kelly would absolutely love to have a couple of women to talk to."

Jeff pointed toward the barn. Logan and Joe took all four horses and walked to the barn, unsaddled, fed, and watered them as the girls started setting up there bedrolls. A few minutes later, Jeff and Kelly walked into the barn just as Rene walked to the large watering trough to clean up.

Kelly walked up to the two women and said, "Oh no, you need to come up to the house and do that." Turning, she looked at all four then at Jeff and said, "All of you, please, come up to house. You can get a shower and wash some clothes if you want."

Kay looked at Kelly then at Joe and said, "I would kill for a hot shower."

Rene added, "Wash clothes? Really you'll let us wash some clothes?"

Kelly looked at all of them smiling and replied, "Absolutely, and I have supper nearly ready."

Together all six walked into the house for showers and a real supper. Not cooked over a campfire.

Rene and Kay helped Kelly clean up after supper, and they all sat down as Jeff asked, "What are you doing out in the desert?"

Joe and Logan looked around and asked if they had a phone so they could contact the authorities. Jeff pointed to the phone and asked, "Are you in trouble?"

Logan replied, "No, but if we tell you what's been going on, you'll think we are all nuts."

Jeff said, "Try me." Then he stopped and looked at all four and asked, "By any chance did you run into some drug runners?" His hand started to move toward the lump under his shirt.

Logan spun and focused on Jeff as Joe's left hand flashed, catching Jeff under the chin and lifting him clear of the floor. Then quickly Joe's hand swept toward the pistol under his shirt.

Kelly made a movement trying to get to Jeff as Rene brought her forearm across her throat. She hooked the inside of her elbow and placed her other arm on the back of Kelly's head, applying just enough pressure to ensure that Kelly would stop and stay in place.

Jeff hit the floor hard. He swore as he lifted his hand, producing a badge and said, "Calm down! Damn! I'm DEA."

Slowly he moved his hand to try and rub his jaw as Joe continued to aim the 9mm and said, "I hope you have more proof than that! More than just that badge."

Jeff raised his one hand as he slowly started trying to get to his feet. Joe glanced at Logan as he continued to point the pistol and watched as Jeff struggled to keep his balance. Shaking his head, Jeff said, "Do you know or maybe met a priest named Father Tom?"

Joe glanced at Kay then the others before answering, "Yeah, we know a priest named Tom. And, yes, we had a run-in with a group of should we say degenerates."

Kelly raised both hands and said, "We are both border agents. I have all the paperwork we need to prove what we say. Oh, and Tom is also on our team. We have been trying to get enough information to stop Hector and Juan permanently."

Logan replied, "Well Kay shot Hector and Rene put a large hole in Juan. So that problem should be over. It seems that after Hector was shot, they kind of slowed down although after Rene ventilated Juan, it pretty much stopped."

Rene released Kelly but watched very closely as she walked away to get the rest of their credentials. After verifying everything, Joe put his pistol away, and between the four Americans, they started telling a story that not even Hollywood could have dreamed of. A story so bizarre that Jeff and Kelly had a hard time believing what they heard. A story of a desire to manipulate a person into a kidnapping situation and the strange way that person was rescued. Mountain lions, rattlesnakes, dynamite, gun fights, and a race across the desert.

Kelly looked at Jeff and said, "I think we had better report this and find out what the hell we are supposed to do now."

Jeff sat their staring at the wall and replied, "Yeah, I have no idea what to do let alone who to contact."

An hour later they had contacted everyone they could think of, and finally two captains in the border patrol decided to come out and listen to the story.

Joe and Kay along with Logan and Rene started all over a couple of hours later as they again told their wild story with the aid of the video and an email sent from Tom.

The US border patrol forwarded everything to the Mexican federal police. All charges were dropped in Mexico, and they were free to leave and head for home.

Montana Bound

By noon the following day, everything and everyone was loaded and ready to go. Logan and Rene pointed their pickup and trailer in a northerly direction, followed closely by Joe and Kay.

The trip back to Montana was going smoothly with absolutely no problems other than the fact that every time they let CJ and Star out of the trailer, they would put on a little show that would always draw a crowd.

Rene called her folks as soon as they had been released to leave and told them about the upcoming wedding, leaving out the part about getting shot at and chased out of Mexico by a gang of drug-running, human-trafficking degenerates.

Her parents were tickled and said that they would be there. Rene gave her dad directions to the town and then the ranch. After disconnecting, she said, "Dad's absolutely tickled I'm getting married and can't wait for the honor to give me away. Do you think he would be able to drive to the buggy with me?"

Logan looked over and said, "Oh yeah, not a problem I'm quite sure everything will be just fine. Lefty knows what's he's doing, and your dad won't have a problem." Rene smiled as she stretched across the cab to give Logan a kiss.

Later that night they stopped at a truck stop just as they crossed into Wyoming after topping their fuel tanks. Joe told Logan that they were hungry and want to stay there for the night. Logan smiled as he replied, "That sounds like a fantastic idea. I'm running on empty and could really use a complete night's sleep without having to worry about someone slipping in and shooting at us."

Early the next morning Joe and Logan were sitting and enjoying their morning coffee, talking about the adventure they had just ended. Joe had tears in his eyes as he talked about Kay's abduction. Looking at Logan, he said, "I wasn't sure I could get her back. I know I couldn't have done it without you and Rene."

Logan reached out and put his hand on Joe's shoulder and said, "Joe, I would do anything you need. And I know you would have done the same for me."

Joe turned and looked Logan in the eyes and said, "You know it. Anytime, anyplace, anywhere, all you have to do is ask."

Kay and Rene came walking out all dressed with a full pot of coffee. The four friends sat there talking about the trip to Montana and the upcoming wedding.

Kay looked at Joe and said, "Joe, after the wedding and everything calms down, let's talk seriously about moving to Montana or maybe Wyoming. I would love to live close to Rene again, and I'm sure you would be much happier in the mountains rather than the city. Besides with the plane, we are still only a few hours from my kids and grandkids and a few more from yours."

Logan reached, taking Rene's hand, followed closely by Joe and Kay and headed toward the cafe. Just as they finished eating, Joe looked at the radar and said, "It looks like a clear skies all the way to Montana. and the forecast is for clear and dry for the next couple of weeks."

Rene smiled; turning to Kay, she asked, "Want to help me plan a wedding?" Smiling as she then glanced at Logan, she continued, "Before he changes his mind."

Kay started to speak as Logan broke in and said, "There's not a chance I'll change my mind. You're the one I've been waiting for."

Rene reached over and kissed Logan as Kay replied, "Oh absolutely. I'm thinking we can plan it in a few days and mail out invites next week. Joe and I have nothing planned, so we can stay with you until after the wedding."

Rene asked, "Are you serious about moving to Montana?"

Kay smiled and glanced at Joe before saying, "I know Joe would love living there, and with the plane we can still get to family things easily."

Joe smiled and said, "Yeah, and I want Kay to learn to fly also. That will make it real easy."

Rene looked at Logan and asked, "Do you think we could help them find something around us?"

Logan replied, "Absolutely, I'm sure there is something for sale."

Joe broke in, saying, "I'm thinking we might just buy land and build something we want."

Logan reached out and grabbed the slip and said, "Montana isn't getting any closer, so let's get going. We will have to stop and feed and water the horses in a few hours. We can talk more about this then." Looking at Joe, he said, "I'll sell you whatever you need to build on."

Joe swallowed and replied, "Wow, thanks, Logan, that would be absolutely fantastic."

Logan answered, "I need a good hunting guide, and I know you are one of the best. We can make this a win-win for both of us."

Joe smiled and said, "Now that sounds like a fantastic plan, and, yes, a win-win for both of us." With that they all walk toward the pickups and headed north.

The miles flew by as Logan and Rene talked about the upcoming wedding. How the bridesmaid and groomsmen would arrive. Logan picked up his cell and called Jerrod. After a few minutes on the phone, all was set, and the ranch hands would start cleaning out the hay shed and get things started.

Rene couldn't believe it. She was having a western style wedding complete with all the extras that women only dreamed about—horse-drawn carriages for her and the bridesmaids plus the groomsmen in western attire and arriving on horseback. It was nothing short of a dream come true. With the best part, her dad driving the carriage that would deliver her to her future husband.

As they traveled north, Joe and Kay talked about the wedding, but they also talked about moving to Montana. Kay was more excited than Joe. She asked, "Do you think Logan would sell us enough land to have a few horses?"

Joe replied, "Oh, I'm quite sure he would. Plus he plans on offering guided hunts on his ranch. That's where I come in. His ranch but my hunting and guiding experience. We will set up drop camps in the mountains for the people that want a do-it-yourself hunt plus offer fully guided hunts. With that plus a few animal control jobs each year, we should be sitting pretty good."

Then he turned and looked at her and asked, "Are you sure about moving out here? It's a big change for you. City life to ranch and wilderness living."

Kay smiled as she replied, "My life is where you are, and I'll be happy in a log cabin as long as you are there."

Logan's turn signal came, and Joe followed him into a rest area, saying, "Looks like it's time to feed the horses."

They pulled into parking spots. Joe watched as Logan walked out with Buck and Lefty; tying them to the trailer, he grabbed two feedbox and a hay net. Then turning, he watched as Rene walked out, leading CJ and Star loose. CJ immediately started showing off, prancing around with his head and tail held high. This got everyone's attention, and soon there was a crowd gathered to watch as Logan made hand signals, and CJ put on a show by prancing, sidestepping, and rearing up and walking on his hind legs.

Logan walked back to the trailer and got a buggy whip. This was not used to disciplined CJ but to direct him. Logan held the whip's end in his hand. The only time he cracked the whip was to get CJs attention.

After Logan put CJ through his routine, he called the beautiful stallion to him. Logan turned and walked toward the crowd. Leaning the buggy whip against his pickup, he started answering questions.

CJ walked over, and picking up the whip in his mouth, he then chased Logan around the parking lot. The crowd of people absolutely roared with laughter as Logan zigzagged back and forth with CJ right behind him. Logan finally hid on the back side of a pickup. CJ then turned to the crowd, and bending one front leg, he bowed to the crowd. Turning, he then walked to Logan; stopping, he tucked his head under Logan's arm. Logan patted his neck and scratched behind his ears then point to the side. CJ walked about twenty feet away and then turned to face Logan. Logan lifted both arms, and CJ rose onto his hind legs, and pawing the air, he walked to Logan. Dropping down, he then bent one front leg and bowed.

CJ loved to perform. He was a natural show-off. Logan stood there scratching CJ when Star walked up. She had a lead rope in her mouth. Logan clipped the rope to CJ's halter and said, "Go to bed."

The two horses headed toward the trailer with Star leading CJ. After they had loaded themselves, Rene walked and closed the gates, separating them from Buck and Lefty.

Logan talked to Joe for a few more minutes before they both got into their pickups and once again headed for Montana.

Kay and Joe continued to talk about moving. Kay said, "The wife of one of the guys at the magazine is a realtor. Should I call him and get her phone number?"

Joe looked at Kay and asked, "Are you sure you want to do this?"

Kay replied by picking up her phone and called the magazine. When the receptionist answered, she said, "Hi, Darcey, this is Kay. Can I talk to Dave Swenson?"

Darcey replied, "Wow, hi, Kay, how's retirement?"

Kay answered, "Absolutely fantastic. I'm so busy I'm not sure how I did everything before." Leaving out the last month, she thought, *I'm sure that will hit the media soon enough.*

Darcey said, "I'm so glad you are enjoying yourself. I'll put you through to Dave now."

Dave answered the phone, "Hi, Kay, how's everything in the retirement world?"

Kay replied, "Absolutely great. I'm not sure how I had time to work." Thinking, *If you only knew.*

Dave answered, "That's great. I'm sure you'll make the best of it. So anyway, how can I help you?"

Kay said, "Is Betty still in real estate? Joe and I are thinking about moving to Montana."

Dave said, "Yes, she is, and, wow, really Montana?"

Kay smiled and replied, "Yes, Montana. Joe got a business offer, and it's too good to pass up. Anyway we need to sell our house."

Dave answered, "Betty will love that, and I hope the new adventure works out for you two."

Kay replied, "Thanks, Dave. Can I get her number?"

Dave gave Kay the number, saying, "Hey, good luck, and make sure you stop at the magazine before you move to Montana. We would all love to see you again."

Kay replied, "Yes, I will. We should be back sometime next month to start getting everything arranged."

Dave said, "Great, see you then."

Kay said, "Thanks, Dave, and, yes, we'll see you then."

Kay looked at Joe; taking a deep breath, she said, "Yes, honey, it's what I want." She dialed the number and waited.

Betty answered on the second ring, saying, "Great Lakes Reality."

Kay said, "Hi, Betty, this is Kay. Dave gave me your number. Joe and I were thinking about selling our home and moving to Montana."

Betty replied, "We will be sorry to see you go. Although I'm sure you'll love Montana the way you love the outdoors."

Kay replied, "Oh, I know I will, and Joe got a fantastic business offer."

Betty answered, "That's great. I have most everything I need for now. I'll list your place and put a sign in the front yard tomorrow morning."

Kay replied, "That sounds great. Joe and I should be back in Chicago in a couple of months."

Betty said, "I'm sure your place will sell faster than that. Should I wait to list it?"

Kay looked at Joe and told him. Joe said, "List it if need be. We can fly home, get everything in place to have the moving company start, and then fly back. Besides we need to bring the plane here anyway."

Kay said, "Okay." She then told Betty, "Go ahead and list it. Joe says that we can do what we have to."

The miles flew past as Joe chased Logan north on I-25 in Wyoming. Just north of Sheridan, they got off the interstate and headed northwest on secondary roads. Just before dark they pulled into the Rocking L and parked in front of the ranch house.

Several of the ranch hands walked out to welcome their boss home. Logan introduced Joe and Kay to most everyone. The word had gotten out that Logan was going to marry Rene and there were handshakes and congratulations going around also. Everyone was in high spirits.

Jesse helped unload the horses and put the tack away while Logan and Rene started unloading the camper. Rene showed Kay where her and Joe would be sleeping. It took nearly an hour to get everything unloaded and put away.

Joe backed his camper next to Logan's and unhooked it then parked the pickup in the driveway and followed Logan into the house. Together they walked up the stairs to Logan's private retreat.

Joe looked around at the upstairs area of the ranch house then walked to the room that he and Kay would be staying. Joe started a fire in their room and was just walking toward the couch as Kay walked in with two cups of tea. Handing one to Joe, they sat down. They talked about the big change in their lives as they sat there. Getting a notebook, they made a list of what needed to be done in the coming weeks after the wedding.

Kay got up, saying, "I'm absolutely exhausted." She walked toward the bed. Joe put another piece of wood on the fire. Crawling into bed, he wrapped his arms around her and together they drift off. Joe held the woman he loved. Kay felt safe in the arms of the man she loved.

*****

Logan had coffee made as Joe walked into the living room area. Sitting down, Logan handed him a cup as he looked at the snow-capped mountains that surrounded the ranch.

Joe stood there, caught up in the beauty of the area. Turning, he asked, "Are you sure about selling us a building site?"

Logan answered, "Oh absolutely, and also about the outfitting and guiding service. This ranch has a lot of really nice deer and elk."

Joe replied, "Yes, it sure does plus other animals also." He thought about the buffalo and that huge, old grizzly that Logan had talked about a few days earlier.

Logan and Joe talked about setting up drop camps for the guys that want a do-it-yourself hunt. They figured that they could get a thousand dollars per hunter. They could offer extras at these drop camps at an additional cost. Like a camp cook and horses plus a wrangler to take care of them.

As Logan and Joe talked, it kept getting better and better. Then Joe started talking about the full service and fully guided hunts. Joe said, "You need to check into an outfitters licensing. I'm already a licensed guide with Montana, and I think this is going to be a moneymaking idea, especially when we advertise a ranch the size of yours that has never been open to hunting."

Logan replied, "I never thought about that. Oh, also I think I have all the information, and I might have already filled it all out and sent it in. I'll have to look through my paperwork."

Joe said, "I can set up the drop camps and do most of the guiding although if we offer horses, we will need to put a wrangler with them. About half of the hunters won't be smart enough to take care of them, like feeding them, not to mention water. Oh, and saddling unsaddling. We can allow ATVs but restrict their usage. Remember we will be dealing with a lot of city folk that don't understand how fast they can get hurt or killed up there."

Logan replied, "Yes, that too. Maybe for the first couple of years, let's just offer drop camps. Let's set up say ten camps with four hunters per camp and maybe up to say ten more with six hunters per camp. We can spread them all over the ranch."

Joe said, "Now that sounds great. I'm sure I could set up the camps in a couple of weeks after we go in and find the locations for each. It will take four maybe five guys to clear and help get the basics done. After that I can do it alone or maybe just one guy helping."

Preparation

In the coming days, Logan, Joe and a couple of the ranch hands started setting up the ranch for the wedding. The conversion on the hay shed was started. All the walls where covered. An altar was built that could be rolled away, making room for a stage that could be rolled out for the band and dance floor.

Grabbing a tape measure, Jarred and Gary started laying out the area for tables after the wedding, trying to get a place for most everyone to sit. As they worked, Gary stopped and looked around, asking, "Where are you going to set up the buffet and bar?"

All the guys stopped and started talking when Darrel walked out the side door. Looking around, he said, "Get a huge tent. Set it up here off this side door. You can set up the buffet and bar in there. Everyone can get their food and beverage and find a great place to sit.

The next day Logan spent several hours on the phone; he reserved every room in the area, along with hiring a couple of buses to move people from the motels to the ranch and back. He also rented a large tent that would be set up adjacent to the building that hold the largest wedding in south central Montana. The tent would serve as a place for the buffet and bar. He also rented tables and chairs and hired a caterer.

Feeding this number of people, the caterer thought they should roast an entire beef on spit over an open fire that the guest would enjoy watching their dinner being cooked.

Logan contacted Dale, a friend that owned a welding shop in town, and asked if he could make a rotisserie big enough to do the job. It had to be in a tent or enclosed in such a way to keep nature out but so it was visible at the same time.

About an hour later, Dale called back and told Logan what they could do and what it would look like. Logan sat there, drawing a picture in his mind—four-glass sides with one on hinges that would open allowing easy access, an electric motor that would drive a gear-reduction spit that would rotate the beef 360 degrees a minute, with a firepit large enough for wood-fired roasting. There would also be an exhaust fan that should keep it clear inside and send the aroma throughout the area.

Logan smiled and said, "Build it. I'll stop and drop off a check the next time I'm in town."

Dale replied, "Sorry, buddy, but this will be a wedding gift. You are a fantastic friend and a good customer. It will be my pleasure to build this for you and Rene."

Logan asked, "Oh wow, are you sure? It sounds like it will be expensive."

Dale replied, "I have most everything I need right here in the shop. All I need to buy is the glass. I'm thinking I can build this in an afternoon and deliver it to you the following day. It will be totally mobile. That way you can move it and use it again like anniversary parties."

Logan laughed and said, "Thanks. You are the greatest."

The word spread like wildfire across south central Montana and northern Wyoming that Logan was about to get branded, that there was about to be a queen at the Rocking L.

Rene and Kay sent out over five hundred wedding invitations, made over three hundred phone calls confirming that people were coming. The big day was drawing closer, and both Logan and Rene were getting nervous. The four of them went over the checklist every night, checking and double-checking that everything was either ready or arranged.

Late the next afternoon, a truck showed up with the four beautiful, matching, red carriages that would deliver the bridesmaids plus the white one that Rene would arrive in.

The next day Jarred and Darrel started going through the horses that they thought would work to pull the carriages.

Darrel asked, "Who's going to bring the girls to the umm," looking around laughing, he said, "hay shed?"

Jarred started laughing as he replied, "Four of you guys. Rene's dad is going to bring her. Lefty will be pulling that carriage. He's been hook to a carriage before. I'm sure with a five-minute lesson, he'll do just fine."

Darrel nodded his head, saying, "Yeah, and he's about the most easygoing horse here. Good, ole, laid-back Lefty."

They worked, checking the tack and making sure that everything was in good shape and that nothing could break, causing a problem the day of the wedding. They talked about who would be the best to drive the carriages.

Jarred said, "Logan wants it like this. The wrangler that drives the carriage would also grab the groomsmen's horse at the church, tie it to the carriage, then be back as the wedding ends, giving the carriage to the groomsmen where he would then follow Logan and Rene to the area behind the ranch house where they would take a few pictures." Pointing, he continued, "Anyone that want to watch can simply walk over there. It's directly behind the ranch house."

Darrel glanced at the mountains behind the ranch house, saying, "That is most definitely a fantastic backdrop for the pictures."

Jarred replied without looking up, saying, "I think it's among the most beautiful scenery in Montana."

They finished looking over the tack, putting the horses name with each harness, and hanging it all up so they wouldn't have to look for anything the day of the wedding.

Walking back toward the converted hay shed, they saw Logan and said, "The tack that goes with the carriages is all sized and put away, just waiting for next week." Laughing, he produced a small fire ring that was propane fired and a branding iron that a few of the cowboys had made and said, "Where should we put this? I can't wait to watch Rene slap a brand on your umm." He started laughing and quickly walked away toward the bunkhouse.

Logan walked over and picked up the fire ring and branding irons and carried it to the side where he and Rene would actually brand a piece of wood that they would later hang somewhere near the house, showing their marriage and partnership as they started their lives together.

Rene and Kay sat drinking coffee as they went over the total wedding plans one more time. Everything was either done or nearly done. They check it off as they talked about every aspect of the wedding that was only a few days away.

Later the following day, Rene's parents, Mark and Dorris, drove slowly down the driveway. Looking around, Mark turned to Dorris and said, "I think our daughter found a home in paradise. Just look at the mountains. This area is absolutely gorgeous."

Rene heard a car door close. Glancing up from her list, she screamed and flew out the door.

Logan heard Rene yelling and ran around the corner to see what was going on. Rene yelled and waved to Logan to meet her folks. Logan walked across the ranch yard.

Dorris elbowed Mark as Logan walked toward them and whispered, "Oh my, I think he's a real cowboy?"

Mark replied, "I'm thinking you're right, but he can't be Logan, can he?"

Rene walked to Logan and put her arm around him and said, "Mom, Dad, this is Logan. My fiancé and owner of the Rocking L. Logan, my parents, Mark and Dorris."

Logan shook Mark's hand and hugged Dorris and said, "It's nice to finally meet you after all I've heard." Looking at Rene, he continued, "Oh, and co-owner of the Rocking L. I've found my life partner."

Rene looked and saw Kay standing on the porch. Calling Kay over, she introduced her. Looking around, she saw Joe leading Lefty toward the stable. Calling Joe, she then introduced him. They all stood there talking about the trip out.

Mark looked around and said, "This has to be that heaven on earth place I've heard about all my life."

Logan said, "Come on, I'll show you around some, and in the next few days, we can take the horses and ride up into the mountains if you would like."

Mark replied, "Oh absolutely, that would be fantastic."

Rene, grabbing her mom's hand, said, "Come on, I'll show you around the house and where you and dad will be sleeping." Together the three women walked into the house, followed closely by the three guys.

Nancy has the day off, so Rene started making supper as they talked. Soon Dorris and Kay were up and helping, and in just an hour, the six of them sat down and enjoyed a fantastic supper of steak and baked potatoes along with garden fresh green beans and a salad. Everything was raised or grown on the ranch.

After supper they all went upstairs and enjoyed the beauty of the sun slowly setting behind the mountains, west of the ranch house.

Logan got up and walked into the room that Mark and Dorris would be staying in. He started a fire in the fireplace and made sure that there was everything they would need in there bathroom. Then he started a fire in Joe and Kay's room and finally in his and Rene's room.

They spent the next hour talking and enjoying the Montana evening. Logan got up about every half hour or so and put more wood on the fires, making sure that when they finally went to their rooms, there would be a fire going.

About ten in the evening, Mark said, "What time is it? I'm about to fall asleep sitting here."

Logan said, "It's about ten."

Mark replied, "It's been a long day, but that's not that late. Why am I so tired?"

Rene laughed, saying, "That's Montana time. It's about eleven for you, Dad."

Mark replied, "Wow, I'm headed for bed."

Dorris said, "I'm with you. I'm about all in." Giving her daughter and Logan a hug, she said good night to Joe and Kay and followed her husband to the bedroom.

Walking into the room and seeing the fire along with the other things that Logan had put in their room, she turned and walked back into where Logan and Rene were still sitting, and with tears in her eyes, she hugged them both again and asked if they had started the fire.

Rene looked at Logan and said, "Not me, Mom. That's all Logan."

Dorris hugged her future son-in-law again and turned to see Mark standing there. He said, "Thanks, you made this a night something special, and we know you'll take care and protect our daughter." Mark then put his arm around Dorris and together they walked back to their room.

Morning broke cool and clear and looked to be a beautiful day. Logan and Rene were sitting on the deck drinking coffee as Mark and Dorris walked out. Logan poured them both coffee, saying, "Good morning. Did you enjoy your evening?"

Mark said, "Oh absolutely." Dorris turned a little red. Turning and walking a short distance, she looked at the mountains behind the ranch house.

CJ walked around the corner. Rene said, "Good morning, CJ." CJ nickered and nodded his head as Logan patted his neck and pushed him away.

Dorris asked, "Does he always come say good morning?"

Rene replied, "He would come in the house if we don't keep the door closed. He can open some doors and most of the gates around here although he hasn't figured out the doors coming into the house yet."

Mark looked at CJ and asked, "Is he a stallion?"

Rene replied, "Absolutely, but you won't find a better behaved horse anywhere, and he has the run of the ranch. He's so gentle that we have let children ride him."

They all watched as CJ continued to graze in the yard and watched everything that was going on. When Logan got up, he smiled at Rene and walked into the yard. CJ stopped grazing and followed Logan.

Rene said, "Mom, Dad, come on. You are about to see something you've never seen before."

Logan stopped at the gate and pointed. CJ walked up and opened the gate. Walking through, he turned and waited for Logan then he closed and relocked it. He followed Logan out into the middle of the coral and stopped facing him.

Logan lifted both arms, and CJ reared up on his hind legs and walked across the coral. Then he pranced around and sidestepped back into place, stopping in front of Logan again. Next he turned and stretched out one front leg and bowed.

Turning sideways, he lay down so Logan could easily get on his back and then stood up. Again he started to prance in a circle, stop, and sidestep back to the center. Bowing again, Logan slid down his neck over his head and walked away.

CJ walked over to the fence and picked up the buggy whip. Holding it in his mouth, he chased Logan around the coral. This brought laughter from everyone including several of the ranch hands who had stop to watch.

Wedding

The next couple of days flew by, and suddenly it was the big day. Guest started showing up the day before, and the area was buzzing with excitement. Logan, one of the most eligible bachelors, was about to get branded, and everyone wanted to meet the lady that had turned his head.

Everything was done at the ranch; all the hands where busy showing people around the ranch. They had moved a few hundred head of cattle plus a small herd of horses into the pasture that surrounded the ranch headquarters.

As the guest drove down the driveway, they saw cattle and horses grazing on the lush pastures that surrounded the ranch house and the beauty of the snowcapped mountains that lay just to the west of the ranch. Arriving at the ranch headquarters, they would see the well-maintained buildings and the large log house that was hidden from view unless you were standing in the ranch yard.

Logan and Rene were visiting with everyone as much as they could and enjoying that excitement that was spreading through the area like wildfire.

Rene was dressed in an off-white, knee-length dress that slit up the side along with a brand of boots that had a narrow two-and-a-half inch heel.

Logan was wearing a tan shirt with pearl snaps and a string tie, new blue jeans, a black leather vest, his new black Stetson, black boots, and polished silver spurs. The rest of the ranch hands where all dressed the same as Logan with one exception, they all wore red shirts and tan Stetsons.

The unplanned party lasted well into the evening with that ranch hands putting on a small rodeo for the people that came from back east or the larger cities, with calf roping and saddle bronc riding. As the rodeo ended, Logan and Rene along with CJ and Star put on a show that would have the people talking for weeks to come. They went through all their tricks and ended with Star and CJ chasing Logan and Rene out of the coral.

With all the excitement from the day before the morning of the wedding had an electrifying start. The wedding was going to be at two that afternoon.

Early that morning, the fire was started and beef was placed in the wood-fired roaster. It only took a few hours, and the aroma started drifting through the area.

The guest started showing up about noon, and by one thirty, over three hundred people had gathered, and the wedding was about to take place.

The four groomsmen rode to the church dressed in red-and-white checked shirts with pearl snaps, string ties, brown, western-style leather vests, blue jeans, new, black Stetsons, and boots along with polished spurs. Logan was last on CJ and wore a white western cut shirt, black vest, blue jeans, a white Stetson, black boots, and his polished spurs. He dismounted, turned CJ loose, and walked into the church. The bridesmaids all arrived in the horse-drawn buggies and were met by the groomsmen and walked into the church together. All the girls wore light pink, knee-length dresses with off-white ladies' cowboy boots.

Rene arrived with her father driving the buggy and go ole lay back Left just walking ever so calmly, stopping and standing perfectly still right in front of the church. Mark got out of the buggy and helped Rene down. Rene's dress was floor length and gathered at the waist. It's buttoned-up at the back with a button and loop with a shear cover all the way to the neckline and a veil went over her face but ran way down her back. Her white boots just showed at the bottom of the dress and held it about an inch off the ground.

With tears in her eyes, she smiled and kissed her dad and walked into the church on her father's arm.

Together they walked to the altar. Logan stepped forward and hugged Dorris, then stepping up, he shook Mark's hand and took Rene's hand and together they walked up to the altar.

As everyone sat down, the minister asked Logan and Rene to turn and face each other and to join hands. Logan and Rene looked at each other and the minister started. The guests all sat quietly as the minister went through the wedding preparations and marriage vows. Finally he ended by saying, "Logan, you may kiss your bride."

With that Logan carefully lifted the veil, and reaching down, he gently kissed Rene to the *oohs* and *awws* of the guests.

Suddenly everyone started to turn as Star walked into the church with a beautiful, newly born, black-and-white colt, followed closely by a very proud CJ.

All the guest pointed and started taking pictures as together Logan and Rene walked to the side, and holding hands, they walked out of the church with Star and the new colt on Rene's side and CJ on Logan's side.

Logan called Jessie and said, "Put these three away."

Jessie said, "I did twice, but I think CJ opened the gate and brought them to show you."

Logan reached over and patted CJ's neck as Rene hugged Star and scratched behind the ears of the colt.

Joe and Kay walked up as Joe said, "I guess he throws color. That colt looks just like his dad."

Logan smiled and replied, "Yes, he most certainly does." He reached over and started petting the colt.

There were a few changes in the pictures as they took a few that included CJ, Star, and the new colt.

They all stood around talking, and the new colt walked up and put his nose under Rene's arm. Jessie pointed it out as Dale said, "Oh no, another ranch pest." All the ranch hands laughed.

The caterer announced that the food was ready. Everyone started walking in to the church again. They couldn't believe what they saw. The altar was gone, and about fifty tables had been brought in. The food was in a smorgasbord style, and the guest got their food and found a place to sit.

With lighthearted laughter and joking, everyone was in high spirits. As the evening progressed, the food was moved off to the side. The caterer kept the food full although the selection started to dwindle. The band started to set up for an evening that promised to be nothing short of fantastic.

Logan and Rene led off the first dance with Mark and Dorris joining in, followed by Joe and Kay then the rest of the wedding party. The evening was absolutely perfect with a light breeze blowing and temperature near seventy. Logan and Rene danced nearly every dance with each other, Mark and Dorris, Joe and Kay, or another of the guests.

Joe was talking with Logan and watching as Kay danced with Mark. Taking a deep breath, he reached for another beer and walked outside. A few minutes later, Logan and Rene followed by Kay joined him. Shaking Logan's hand, he put his arm around Kay as he stared into the black of the Montana night.

A half a mile away and halfway up the side of a mountain, Hector stared into the face of the man he hated. Jerking his eye from the spotting scope, he stared back and said, "Someday, soon, those two bitches will be mine, and you, Mr. Joe and Mr. Logan, will be dead.

To be continued

About the Author

Lance is still trucking and writing both fiction and poetry. His trucking takes him to all areas of the United States and most of Canada. Many of the pictures he puts in his books, both inside plus the covers, were taken out the window of his truck.

After finishing his third book of fiction, he started writing poetry and has nearly enough for another book of poetry. He also has many ideas for upcoming stories. You'll be seeing more on Joe and Kay along with Jayden trying to survive without Lief. Patrick and Sofia along with Larry and Angelina will show up again. Chase and Lilly are enjoying their lives in Colorado and Chase's new job.

Lance still lives in Minnesota and his home time. He enjoys spending time with his son, Josh, and the lady in his life, Judy. He also enjoys driving his collector cars. He enjoys everything outdoors from hunting and fishing to snowmobiling and riding ATV.

CPSIA information can be obtained
at www.ICGtesting.com
Printed in the USA
JSHW020603160120
3620JS00001B/12